THIS BOOK
BELONGS TO:

_____

_____

JOAN OF ARC

CHILDREN'S CLASSICS

This unique series of Children's Classics™ features accessible and highly readable texts paired with the work of talented and brilliant illustrators of bygone days to create fine editions for today's parents and children to rediscover and treasure. Besides being a handsome addition to any home library, this series features genuine bonded-leather spines stamped in gold, full-color illustrations, and high-quality acid-free paper that will enable these books to be passed from one generation to the next.

Adventures of Huckleberry Finn
The Adventures of Tom Sawyer
Aesop's Fables
Alice's Adventures in Wonderland
Andersen's Fairy Tales
Anne of Avonlea
Anne of Green Gables
At the Back of the North Wind
Black Beauty
The Call of the Wild
A Child's Book of Country Stories
A Child's Book of Stories
A Child's Book of Stories from Many
   Lands
A Child's Christmas
A Christmas Carol and Other
   Christmas Stories
Cinderella and Other Classic Italian
   Fairy Tales
The Complete Mother Goose
Goldilocks and the Three Bears and
   Other Classic English Fairy Tales
Great Dog Stories
Grimm's Fairy Tales
Hans Brinker *or* The Silver Skates
Heidi
The Hound of the Baskervilles
Joan of Arc

The Jungle Book
Just So Stories
Kidnapped
King Arthur and His Knights
The Legend of Pocahontas
A Little Child's Book of Stories
Little Men
A Little Princess
Little Women
Peter Pan
Pollyanna
The Prince and the Pauper
Rebecca of Sunnybrook Farm
Robin Hood
Robinson Crusoe
The Secret Garden
The Sleeping Beauty and Other Classic
   French Fairy Tales
The Swiss Family Robinson
Tales from Shakespeare
Tales of Pirates and Buccaneers
Through the Looking Glass and What
   Alice Found There
Treasure Island
A Very Little Child's Book of Stories
The Wind in the Willows
The Wonderful Wizard of Oz

JOAN OF ARC

Originally titled *Joan of Arc—The Warrior Maid*

By Lucy Foster Madison
Retold by Christine Messina

With Illustrations & Decorations by
Frank Schoonover

CHILDREN'S CLASSICS

New York · Avenel

Originally titled *Joan of Arc—The Warrior Maid*

Text copyright © 1995 by Random House Value Publishing, Inc.
All rights reserved.

This edition is published by Children's Classics, an imprint
and trademark of Random House Value Publishing, Inc.,
40 Engelhard Avenue, Avenel, New Jersey 07001.

Printed and bound in the United States of America

A CIP catalog record for this book is available from the
Library of Congress

Cover design by Mary Helen Fink
Production supervision by Roméo Enriquez
Editorial supervision by Claire Booss

ISBN 0-517-12203-0

10 9 8 7 6 5 4 3 2 1

COLOR ILLUSTRATIONS

Following
Page

One at a time, the children knelt by the Gooseberry Spring and
drank deeply of the transparent water 48

The saints visited her nearly every day. Often they appeared in
the little garden 49

"I have traveled many miles, all the way from Rome," said the
monk 80

There was no smile on his face this time. Robert de
Beaudricourt looked gravely at Jeanne 81

Far into the night they rode 112

An inspired young woman had been sent from God to lead
France to victory against the enemy 113

"Courage! The hour is at hand!" 144

"Forward! They are ours!" 145

PREFACE TO THIS ILLUSTRATED EDITION

The beauty and richness of the paintings and drawings of Joan of Arc in this book are a perfect representation of her beauty of soul and strength of character. They were done by Frank Schoonover (1877–1972), an outstanding painter of the Golden Age of American Illustration, a period lasting roughly from 1880 to 1920.

Schoonover was a student of Howard Pyle, the legendary Brandywine art teacher. Pyle inspired Schoonover to follow in his footsteps as a book illustrator. Indeed, Schoonover illustrated scores of classics for young people, including *Kidnapped, Tales from Shakespeare, Robinson Crusoe, King Arthur*, and *Ivanhoe*. His paintings and drawings greatly enhanced those tales and increased the pleasure of many generations of readers.

As a result of Frank Schoonover's fascination with history he also illustrated stories of the great men and women of the past; *Joan of Arc* is a superb example. The art in this book will certainly enable readers, young and old, to appreciate the full dimensions of this young woman's short, but extraordinary life.

CLAIRE BOOSS
Series Editor

1995

Editorial Note

The French name of Joan of Arc, is Jeanne D'Arc, and it is this name that is used in the text of this edition, to maintain a sense of the story's authenticity. The title of this volume, however, is *Joan of Arc* because of the name's familiarity to readers in the English-speaking world.

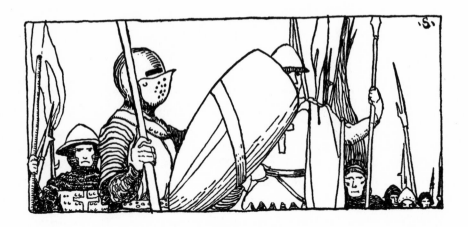

INTRODUCTION

The most remarkable aspect of the story of Joan of Arc is that from its brilliant beginnings to its soul-shattering close it is based entirely on the experiences of a real teenager in the fifteenth century. No dramatist's romantic imagination has ever exceeded the wonder of the brief and tragic tale of the peasant maid who became the savior of France. This historical novel, originally written early in the twentieth century by Lucy Foster Madison closely follows written accounts of the time. Everything revealed about Joan's character is based on recollections of the men and women who knew her, and much of the dialogue was recorded during her lifetime.

Even in her earliest days, there was a quality that set Joan apart. For one thing, she seemed graver and more devout than other children. Although she lived in an age when religion was a passionate and vital part of everyone's life, her faith imbued every hour of her day. Joan was twelve years old when she first heard her angels. After that, until the end of her life, she heard them speak to her every day, and sometimes several times a day.

The second distinctive quality about Joan was her patriotism. In Joan's childhood, the English occupied most of the French provinces north of the Loire and were trying to extend their claim over the entire kingdom of France.

The village of Domremy where Joan lived was situated on the direct route from France into the duchy of Lorraine, and the roads at that time were swarming with travelers—soldiers, swashbucklers, wandering university scholars, and vagabonds. Politics were hotly discussed by all the people who lived in that valley. Domremy was loyal to Charles, the Dauphin and disinherited claimant to the throne, but the neighboring village of Maxey supported Philip, the Duke of Burgundy, a staunch ally of the English, who hoped one day to become master of France.

Joan lived and breathed the battles of the ongoing war between England and France, which had started long before she was born and seemed to be leading to the total defeat of France. In the first period of this war, which became known as the Hundred Years' War, England was victorious. In the second period, France gave a better account of herself. Then, when Joan was a small child, a great disaster befell the French at Agincourt, where, in 1415, a small force of dedicated Englishmen, led by Henry V, slaughtered a French army ten times its size. The confidence of the French nation was destroyed.

When Joan's voices told her to come to the aid of her struggling country, she knew what they meant. When they told her to take the Dauphin to his coronation at Reims, she pledged herself to this duty. The Dauphin probably did not deserve her devotion. By all accounts, Charles was a fatuous coward, but he was also a devout believer in miracles and magic. Thus, when Joan presented herself before him, armed with the command from the Lord and ready to lead him to victory, Charles soon gave her the army she asked for.

Joan was little more than nineteen when she led the rough, disorganized French army to victory at Orléans. Dressed in her dazzling white armor, riding a coal black horse, sword strapped to her side, and bearing a great white standard painted with God and the angels, she was, in every respect, a warrior angel descended from heaven.

If her presence inspired the French, it also struck terror into the hearts of the English. Wasn't God supposed to be on *their* side? Those voices guiding Joan must belong to demons! The English were convinced they were facing a great evil spirit. In short, they were beaten by their own fear, as well as by the superior numbers of French. (Joan's troops outnumbered the English three to one.)

The intuitive military skills she displayed surprised those who knew her, but today her skills are often diminished by historians. Joan of Arc, however, apparently understood far more than she could have learned in her peasant childhood. She believed that God told her where to place the guns and how to attack successfully. However she came by it, she had an innate talent for making the correct military move.

After Joan's great victories in the field, two groups wanted to get rid of her: the English invaders and their Burgundian allies. Joan didn't know it, but two other, even more dangerous groups were also working against her: the courtiers of King Charles and the fanatical wing of the French clergy.

Charles's top man, the treacherous George de la Trémoïlle, hated Joan because she could see through his lies and corruption; the more Charles relied on Joan, the more nervous La Trémoïlle felt. Outwardly he showed Joan respect, but secretly he plotted her downfall.

The high officials of the French church were worse. The church had established itself as the sole intermediary between heaven and earth. When Joan claimed to speak directly to angels and take her instructions from God himself, the church hierarchy was outraged. If her revelations did not come through them, they said, she must be an agent of the devil.

When Joan was captured at the battle of Compiègne, her destiny tightened around her. She was turned over to church officials for trial, which meant that, if found guilty as a heretic, she could be executed. There was never any doubt what the outcome would be.

None of Joan's heroic deeds in battle can compare to the heroism she displayed during her trial. At night she was imprisoned under the most degrading circumstances; during the day she faced grueling interrogation by forty-two of France's best legal minds. And yet, without any counsel, she held her persecutors at bay for five months, answering each attack with swift and cutting responses. Every exchange was recorded by her enemies—Joan herself declared that they wrote down everything that was against her, but suppressed everything in her favor. Nevertheless, the record, which has been passed down through the centuries, speaks glowingly in her favor.

No one came to her aid. Not even Charles, for whom she had rescued a kingdom, lifted a finger to help her. To the end, Joan refused to go back on her story. On May 30, 1431, the church condemned her to be burned in the market square in the city of Rouen. At first her enemies were elated. Then, almost at once, fear set in. Had they in fact burned a saint? Twenty-five years later, another ecclesiastical court overturned the verdict and declared her innocent of all charges.

Joan of Arc performed her marvels and endured her pain over a period of less than two years. Her exploits turned the tide of the Hundred Years' War. Because of her inspired deeds, the French nation regained its sovereignty and continued to exist as a nation. Under her banners, the French army became famous for its courage and aggressiveness, and its spirit of *élan* remained its hallmark for the next five hundred years. In 1920, Joan of Arc was canonized as a saint of the Catholic Church, and remains to this day, one of history's most beloved heroines.

CHRISTINE MESSINA

New York City
1995

JOAN OF ARC

CHAPTER 1

THE CHILDREN'S FESTIVAL

"WHO-OO-EE!" The gleeful shout came from the lips of a young girl who stood, her hands cupped around her lips, on the edge of a stream that ran through the village of Domremy.

The girl was about twelve years old, with abundant dark hair and wonderfully blue eyes. For a moment she stood still, her smiling face turned up to the warm sunshine, listening for a response to her call. The Sunday morning remained quiet and still. The girl called again in a clear, sweet voice that penetrated into the farthest reaches of the village: "Who-oo-ee!"

This time the shout was caught up instantly, and many voices answered. The village wakened suddenly to life, and several boys and girls came eagerly running from cottages and joined the girl on the riverbank.

"Oh, but you're late," she cried. "It's already ten o'clock and the day will be half gone before we get to the tree. I was afraid you had left without me."

"Gone without you, Jeanne?" exclaimed one girl. "We couldn't have any fun without you. I had to wait for my mother to fix my picnic basket."

"And I!" chimed several other children in a chorus.

"Why not pack them yourselves?" demanded Jeanne, who seemed to be their natural leader. "I did my own and my brothers', too."

"Where *are* Pierre and Jean?" asked a lad.

1

"They ran back for more nuts," Jeanne said. "Here they come! Line up, and let's be off!"

Happily, the children formed a line, and began to march off toward the great oak woods, called Bois Chesnu, which stretched away toward the west. In all of France there was not a more tranquil landscape than this broad valley where the Meuse River wandered between low, undulating hills crowned with ancient oaks, maples, and birches. Although ridges of snow still clung to the hills, buds were already swelling on the bare tree branches, and new grass carpeted the fields. The rippling waters of the apple-green river sparkled in the sunshine.

Along the valley floor many hamlets and villages dotted the riverbank. The village of Domremy, with its ruined castle, monastery, and score of thatched-roofed cottages grouped about a small church, was the grayest of these hamlets, but its surrounding meadows were the richest and most fertile in the valley, and the village was famous for its vineyards in the county of Champagne.

It was a fine day in March of 1424, the fourth Sunday in Lent. On this day the children of Domremy always held a little festival around one particular tree, said to be the ancient home of fairies.

Merrily they marched toward the wood, the boys carrying baskets of lunch and the girls bearing garlands to hang on the legendary tree. The air was sweet with the smell of leaf mold that had the penetrating quality of incense. A light mist lay on the hills, and over all spread a radiant sky. The joyous party of children laughed and sang and joked as they walked, intoxicated by the mild perfumed air.

The girl called Jeanne was the blithest of them all. She skipped, light as thistledown, bubbling over with happiness. All at once she stooped and plucked a long blade of grass and held it up to the light.

"See, Mengette," she cried, showing the pale green stem to a girl near her. "How long the grass is! And how warm the sun. Oh, isn't God good to give us so fine a day!"

"He is good, yes," the girl agreed. Then, as Jeanne darted away, Mengette turned to another girl: "Jeanne is so religious," she said. "She cannot even play without talking of God. I wish she weren't so good, don't you, Hauviette?"

"Not so good?" exclaimed Hauviette. "Why, she wouldn't be Jeanne if she were not good."

"I don't mean for her not to be good, exactly," demurred Mengette. "I meant I wish she weren't so pious."

"If the priest should hear you," breathed Hauviette, shocked. "He would make you say a hundred Hail Marys!"

"And who will tell him?" demanded Mengette, anxiety flitting across her face.

"Not I, but what if anyone else heard you?"

"The others agree with me," protested Mengette. "Everyone thinks Jeanne is too pious."

"Listen!" cried one of the boys. "Whoever reaches the tree first hangs the first wreath!"

A gleeful shout went up, and everyone made a dash for the tree. Jeanne darted forward, so fleet and light of foot that she quickly took the lead. She could easily have reached the tree first, but she heard a cry from Mengette. Jeanne turned in a flash and saw that Mengette had stumbled and fallen facedown on the grass. Mengette was struggling painfully, trying to get up. Jeanne quickly ran back to her.

"Are you hurt, Mengette?" she asked anxiously. "Where's the pain?"

"In my knee," sobbed Mengette. "Run on, Jeanne. You can win the race. You were flying! Go! I'll get there when I can."

"No!" replied Jeanne. "I'll walk with you. It isn't far now, but it would seem a long way if you had to go alone in such pain. There! Lean on me."

With a sigh of relief, Mengette leaned heavily on the arm of her friend, even though Jeanne was younger and smaller than she. Slowly, with much groaning on Mengette's part, the two girls made their way to the Fairy Tree, where the rest of the party was already gathered.

The old beech tree stood at the edge of the wood, its lovely branches sweeping the ground. Once upon a time, when the Bourlemont family still lived in the castle, it had been called the "Ladies' Tree." Every spring the local maidens joined the lords and ladies of the castle to feast and dance about the tree. The castle was deserted now, for the last Bourlemont son had died without an heir. The villagers believed that the fairies had taken the tree over for a trysting place. The priest had come and chanted the gospel of St. John to exorcise the spirits from the tree, so that nothing evil could harm the little ones. And now, for its beauty and legendary charms, the children claimed the tree for their own. With bursts of song and laughter, the girls hung garlands upon its ancient branches; then joining hands, the girls and boys formed a ring and danced around the tree. The red homespun frocks of the girls and blue smocks of the boys made gay bits of color against the dark forest behind them. After the ceremony, the girls spread a cloth upon the grass and began to unpack the lunch baskets. There were nuts, hard-boiled eggs, and curiously shaped little rolls that their mothers had baked specially for this day. As the girls laid the picnic, a clamor of bells came drifting in from the villages of Domremy and Greux, chiming the midday prayer.

Instantly, Jeanne turned toward Domremy, joined her palms and bent her forehead to them. Mengette, who was sitting upon the grass beneath the shade of the beech tree, leaned over and poked Pierre, one of Jeanne's brothers, in the side.

"Do as your sister does, Pierre," she cried, pointing toward the reverent little maiden.

"Myself, I am not so devout," he answered. "My brothers and I don't feel as keenly as Jeanne does. My mother says we're lazy. But Jeanne loves the church. She is a good sister."

"And a good friend also," nodded Mengette emphatically. "She might have reached the tree and been first to hang her wreath. Instead, she came back to help me."

"Jeanne," called Hauviette suddenly, as the bells ceased to chime, "I wish we could have our festival on Thursday instead of today. Everyone says the fairies return to hold their tryst on Thursday."

"Pouf!" scoffed Pierre. "You wouldn't find them if you did come. My godfather, Jean, says there haven't been any fairies at Domremy for twenty or thirty years. So what would be the use of coming here on Thursday?"

"But *my* godmother says that one of the lords of the castle became a fairy's knight," Hauviette timidly persisted. "He kept his tryst with her under this very tree every evening. So there must be fairies. What do you think, Jeanne?"

"They come no more," Jeanne replied gravely. "My godmother, Beatrix, and the priest both say they were banished because of their evil doings."

"Perhaps they hold their meetings farther back in the wood," suggested another girl. "That may be why we can't see them."

"I'll look!" cried one of the boys, leaping up and running toward the dark forest. "If there are fairies there, I, Colin, shall find them."

"Don't go!" exclaimed Jeanne in alarm. "There are wolves and wild boars in there!"

Few people dared enter the thick, dark wood. The wolves that lived there terrorized the countryside; so greatly were the wild beasts feared that the mayors of the villages offered a reward for every head of a wolf, or a wolf cub, brought to them. A protesting chorus arose from the children as Colin threw his shoulders back and swaggered into the wood.

"Let Colin look for the fairies if he wants to," said Jean, another of Jeanne's brothers. "Let's go on to the spring."

"And so say I," chimed in another boy.

"And I. And I," agreed the others. There was an immediate stir and bustle as some of the children hastily packed up the remains of the lunch and others collected some of the wreaths from the tree. Just as they were ready to start off, there came a shrill shout from the forest: "A wolf! A wolf!" cried the voice of Colin. "Help! Help!"

The frightened children stood stock-still. Again the cry came. A babel of excited voices broke out as Jeanne bolted and ran pell-mell into the forest toward the sound of the crying voice.

Breathless, she came upon Colin standing in the midst of a blackthorn thicket. He burst into a peal of laughter as the little girl glanced about in amazement. No wolf or animal of any kind was in sight. The sound of Colin's mirth reached the ears of the waiting children; realizing there was no danger, they all ran into the wood. The mischievous boy doubled up and rocked to and fro in glee.

"I fooled you," he cried. "Look at Jeanne's face! All of you were afraid but her. How could she have helped me if there had been a wolf?"

"Shame on you, Colin," retorted Pierre. "It would serve you right if a real wolf set upon you. We shall tell your mother how you tried to frighten us."

"It was only a joke," Colin muttered, somewhat crestfallen. He had thought the others would think his jest funny, but they just stood looking at him reproachfully. "It was only a joke," he repeated lamely.

Without saying a word, the children formed a line and started off for the spring. Embarrassed, Colin followed after them.

For a while, their spirits dampened, they walked along silently, but soon enough their voices rose again in song and laughter. Those at the head of the party walked rapidly until they caught sight of Gooseberry Spring, named for the gray-green bushes that grew all around it. The stream of clear water erupted magically from the hillside, spread into a pool, then fell in a small cascade, flowing across a carpet of dark green foliage and then disappearing into the reeds and grasses. Just one drink of the crystal-pure water was thought to protect against fever for a whole year. One at a time, the children knelt by the pool and drank deeply of the transparent water. Then they spread their garlands around the spring and danced and sang as they had done before. When the sun began to drop, the tired but happy children turned their faces toward home.

Just as they reached the outskirts of the village, Jeanne and her brothers met their father, Jacques D'Arc, driving his sheep and cows home for the night. He was a sturdy, upright man, unusually strict with his children. As Jeanne and her brothers ran to help him, he greeted them: "We've company at home. Your godmother, Beatrix, has come, and two soldiers of France who have escaped from the Burgundians. Having a house by the main road has its drawbacks! Hardly a day passes that some wayfarer doesn't stop for a bite and a bed. The house is overrun."

"You know you like it, father," Jeanne said, slipping her hand into his. "Don't the travelers always bring news of what's happening beyond the mountains?"

"True enough," grumbled Jacques. "Enough complaining. We must hurry with the cattle. The night grows dark."

"And mother needs me to help," cried Jeanne, quickening her steps. "With so much company, we have a lot to do."

CHAPTER 2

THE KNIGHT'S STORY

The roof of the stone cottage started high on one side, then sloped down halfway to the ground. Two front windows allowed some light into the main room. Shovels and other farm tools leaned against the doorway of the house, and a pile of wood was stacked by the threshold. On one side of the house a little orchard bloomed with red and white flowers and pots of herbs. This was the house in which Jeanne D'Arc was born.

Next to the cottage, separated from it by only a small graveyard, stood the village church; and beyond it rose the square-towered monastery. A stream divided the cottage and church from the other houses of the village. Perhaps this accident of geography encouraged Jeanne in her belief that the church belonged more to her and her family than it did to the other inhabitants of Domremy. She had been lulled in her cradle by the sweet chime of its bells. Even now, as she stood at the door of the cottage, her hand on the latch, she paused to cast a lingering, tender glance toward the church. Inside the cottage, a tall woman stood before the hearth stirring the contents of a large iron pot hanging from a tripod; at the sound of Jeanne's wooden shoes on the threshold, she turned quickly and hastily drew the maid outside again.

7

Isabeau Romée[1] was usually a calm woman, but she was anxious about
something.

"I'm glad you've come, Jeanne," she said. "Your godmother, Beatrix, has
been asking for you ever since she arrived this afternoon. And a little while ago
two French soldiers, gentlemen both, who escaped from the Burgundians,
came asking for supper and a bed. We can feed them, but the beds are full. It
galls your father that we cannot give them a bed for the night."

"Why not, mother? Let little Catherine sleep with you, and the soldiers
may have our bed. I can sleep on the floor in front of the fire."

"But you're tired, little one, and tomorrow we'll be down at the river all day
washing clothes. You need a good rest."

"I'll sleep well on the hearth, mother," answered Jeanne cheerily. "If those
men have just escaped from prison, they've had nothing but the cold stones of
a dungeon to lie upon. Do let me have my way."

"Truthfully, I'd be sorry to refuse them. You have a good heart, child. Go
out now and bring in a bundle of wood for the fire. The night grows chilly.
Then you can lay the table while I bring a new loaf of bread from the outdoor
oven."

Isabeau watched her child carry a large bundle of logs into the cottage.
"Dear one," she said quietly. "Always ready to give up your comfort for others.
May Our Lady watch over you."

Jeanne threw the wood into the great fireplace with its large white stone
mantel. Near the hearth sat the elderly Beatrix, holding in her lap Jeanne's
younger sister, Catherine; on the far end of the hearthstone two men sat
dozing. Jeanne embraced her godmother warmly, then drew up the wooden
table before the fire. She set the table with a tall flagon of pale wine, wooden
cups, and a knife to cut bread. She glanced shyly at the two battered soldiers
whose threadbare velvet cloaks barely covered their rusty armor.

One man was about thirty-five and the other looked about ten years
younger. A thin trickle of blood seeped through the steel sleeve of the younger
knight's right arm.

It took a moment for Jeanne to muster the courage to approach him. "You
bleed, sir," she said, touching him gently on the shoulder.

---

[1] Jeanne's mother was called Isabeau Romée of Vauthon. Vauthon was her native village. It was the custom for a
woman to retain her maiden name after marriage.

"Eh? What?" The young man started quickly awake. "Oh! The wound? It's only a scratch."

"It should be dressed," said the girl with concern. "I don't like to see French blood flow."

"She's right, Bertrand," interjected the older man, now also awake. "A fresh wound tingles and burns, and we may have more scrapes before we reach Chalons. Here, I'll play your squire and help unbuckle your armor."

The young man named Bertrand, protesting all the while, stood up and let his friend help him remove his armor and roll up the sleeve of his doublet. Jeanne brought a basin of water and gently washed the blood from the wound. This wasn't the first time a wounded soldier had been cared for by Jeanne's family, and the young girl performed her task skillfully, first applying a warm compress of oil and then deftly bandaging the arm with clean cloth.

"Thank you, maid," Bertrand said gratefully. "It does feel better. What's your name?"

"Jeanne, sir."

"I'll remember it. Who taught you to dress a wound?"

"My mother, sir." Jeanne blushed at speaking so openly with a stranger.

"You have a gentle touch. If my arm doesn't heal quickly, it won't be your fault."

Jeanne blushed again and withdrew quickly to her godmother's side, taking the basin with her. Isabeau, carrying a large round loaf of black bread in her arms, came back into the kitchen, followed by Jacques, loaded down with another armful of wood. They were a hardworking, devout couple who brought up their five children—Jacquemin, Jean, Pierre, Jeanne, and Catherine—to love work and religion. Jacques D'Arc was a man of some substance in Domremy, the chief man in the village after the mayor. But times were hard for everyone, and the family, like others in the village, lived simply and frugally. Even so, they always had enough to offer hospitality to poor wandering monks and other needy travelers who were so common in the land at that time.

Isabeau emptied the stew from the iron pot onto a large platter which she carried to the table. "Sit, gentlemen, and eat," said Jacques. "You must be hungry. And thirsty, too!"

"You're right!" cried the elder knight, coming eagerly to the table. "We haven't eaten since morning, and even then it was a meager bite. Bertrand, that stew smells good!"

"Indeed it does, Louis. I'll do justice to it. The Duke of Lorraine doesn't feed his prisoners on food like this!"

"You were prisoners of the Duke of Lorraine?" asked Jacques, as he and his guests sat at the table. The women and children stayed near the hearth, waiting for the men to finish eating before they had their own supper.

"For these many months," said Louis. "It's a miracle that we ever escaped."

"Will you tell us about it?" asked Jacques. "We all belong to the party of King Charles here, and we'd like to hear a good tale."

"We know who you are, Jacques, or else we would never have stopped here. Domremy is known to be for King Charles."

"For Charles and France," said Jacques. "Except for one man, the entire village is against the Burgundians and the English invaders, even though we're situated well within the territory that the Duke of Lorraine handed over to the English."

"That's good to hear. I'm happy to tell you about our escape. The adventure began last August when I, Louis de Lude, and Bertrand de Poulengy here, set out from Chalons with six other soldiers. We were on our way to the town of Tours to purchase new armor. We traveled at night, sticking to the back roads and going around the towns occupied by the enemy; on the eleventh morning we could see the walls of Tours in the distance. The sun was up and all the gates of the town were wide open; the country folk were passing through carrying milk and fruit for the market. We all let out a joyous cry and spurred our horses forward. But joy died on our lips, for suddenly the gates swung closed, and we were left stranded outside, along with a few desperate market people. The watchman appeared on the ramparts, shouting something we could not understand, and the country people ran forward, crying out in terror. We wheeled our horses around, and over the green shoulder of a low hill we saw a dozen bright points reflecting the morning sun. Even as we watched, the points lifted and became spears. Ten, twenty, thirty, still they came, until we could no longer count them. We turned to dash back the way we had come, and more spears sprang up in front of us. In a moment they were upon us. We fought hard, but we were trapped and outnumbered.

"It's hard to know precisely what is happening in the thick of battle. Yells and wild cries filled the air; there was a huddle of falling and rearing horses, of flickering weapons, of thrusting men, and hand-to-hand combat. When it was over, I looked about me; of our little band only three men remained: Bertrand, myself, and a man named Jean Laval. We had fallen into the hands of Sabbat, the plundering bandit of the whole region. Sabbat robbed the bodies of our dead comrades, and took all the money we had saved for new armor.

"Then, instead of taking us to his main fort, he carried us back into the hills and cast us into a pit, where he held us for ransom. He let us keep our armor because it was old and worthless anyway. We remained in the pit for three months, barely surviving on bread and water. It was the bread of sadness and the water of affliction. Jean died of his wounds, but Bertrand and I came through.

"Then one day some of the duke's men passed by the pirate's den on their way to Lorraine. The bandits set upon them, but the duke's men beat them back and took them prisoner. They carried us along with them, all the way to the duke's palace at Nancy, where we were thrown into a dungeon and once again held for ransom. We lay in that vile dungeon for weary days and then long months that sapped our strength. Every day we watched for a chance to escape. Finally, one evening the old jail keeper brought our bread, but no water to drink. Bertrand cried out loudly for water. When the old man, momentarily confused, turned back for the water, we instantly sprang upon him. We tied him up with his own jacket, then taking his keys we boldly set out through the courtyard. We could hear the sounds of laughter coming from inside the palace; creeping closer to the walls we could see that the Duke of Lorraine was having a birthday party. It was a perfect night for an escape.

"Unnoticed by the careless guards, we placed a ladder against the ramparts and climbed up. But just as we reached the top, the guards spotted us, and rained a shower of arrows on us as we scrambled over the wall; Bertrand was hit in the arm. We dropped down the outside wall, landing on the edge of the moat. We crept along in the dark, staying close to the walls so the archers on top couldn't see us.

"They must have thought we had fallen into the water, for presently the hue and cry died down. When all was silent, we cautiously crossed the moat, afraid of the cold, dark water but desperate to reach the other side. We climbed the far shore, free men again. We obtained horses—well, I needn't tell you how—and made for safe territory. And that, Jacques, is our story. A common one in France today."

"Ay, too common," agreed Jacques, shaking his head. "Truly, France has fallen upon evil days."

"Indeed. And we owe it to Queen Isabella of Bavaria, who made that infamous treaty of Troyes in which she disinherited her own son, the Dauphin, and made Henry V of England heir to the French crown."

"She lost us France," agreed Jacques.

The younger knight spoke abruptly: "I was there at Troyes when that treaty was signed four years ago. I remember the day well. The streets and ramparts of the town were filled with people waiting to see our poor mad king, Charles VI, as he was brought from his rooms to sign the treaty. The Dauphin, his only son, was there, looking like death; the kingdom to which he was the rightful heir was being given away to the English king.

"His mother, Queen Isabella, dominated the dreadful proceedings, flaunting a gown of blue silk damask and a coat of black velvet lined with ermine. At the conclusion of the ceremonies she set loose into the air flocks of singing birds.

"Now, mad Charles is dead, and Henry is dead, too. Henry's infant son will be King of France when he comes of age; in the meantime, his English uncle, the Duke of Bedford, holds the crown for him. And the Dauphin, the man who should be king, hides in retreat. Isabella lost us France. The shameless woman."

"Have courage, Bertrand," said Louis. "Remember the prophecy of Merlin, the soothsayer: 'Though a woman should lose France, from the Bois Chesnu in Lorraine a maiden shall come to redeem it.' "

"It's just an old tale. How could a maiden save France? I don't believe it."

"I don't believe it, either," said Jacques. He laughed outright. "Why, the oak wood is at the edge of this very village," he said, jerking his thumb over his shoulder. "This is one prophecy that won't come true."

"Laugh if you will," said Louis. "God makes all things possible. As for me, I would be happy to see a woman come to the aid of France.

"But now I'm tired and it's been a long time since I've slept in a real bed. My friend, Jacques, if you have such a thing as a bed here, please take me to it."

"This way, gentlemen." Jacques lit a candle and led them to an upstairs room, while Isabeau gathered her children around to say their prayers, after which the family went to bed.

But Jeanne lay down on the stone hearth in front of the dying fire.

CHAPTER 3

THE WAVES OF WAR REACH DOMREMY

Life for the people of France in 1424, the year our story begins, was hard. War with England had gone on for more than a hundred years and the kingdom had disintegrated into weakness and poverty. There was no unity among the people or provinces.

The mad King Charles VI had signed the Treaty of Troyes, which disinherited his own son. To bring himself into line to inherit the French crown, Henry V of England had himself adopted by King Charles. And to make his position even more secure, Henry married Catherine, the daughter of Charles and Isabella.

Thus, when Charles VI died, Henry, already the King of England, would also become King of France; any children born to Henry and Catherine would likewise inherit the English *and* the French thrones.

By fusing England and France into a single crown, the war that had lasted a hundred years was expected to come to an end. But in 1422, Henry and Charles both died.

The English, led by the Duke of Bedford, Henry's brother, continued their invasion of France, occupying one territory after another. The Duke of Bedford acted as regent of France, holding the crown until Henry's infant son came of age and could assume authority over England and France.

13

Surprising as it seems, the English claim in France was supported by some Frenchman. At this time there were warring factions throughout France. After mad Charles VI died, his disinherited son, the Dauphin, declared himself king, but he was not universally supported by his own people. Various dukes and princes of France tried to consolidate their own power and raised armies loyal to them personally, rather than to the French state or crown. The Duke of Burgundy and his followers, known as Burgundians, supported the English; the Duke of Armagnac and his followers, called the Armagnacs, supported the Dauphin.

Throughout France many causes vied with each other for the people's support, and roving bands of armed men struck the population at will, robbing their way from one end of the country to the other. The villagers of France lived in a constant state of fear that their livestock, crops, property and homes, even their lives, could be snatched from them without warning by marauders sweeping the countryside. In preparation for attack, many villages had secured areas where the people could hide. Lookouts kept watch for the glitter of lances and tried to give ample warning to the people so they could gather their cattle and retreat to safety.

The valley of the Lorraine and Champagne rivers was as unsettled as any in that difficult time, but eventually it was decided that its inhabitants were directly subject to the Dauphin who called himself King of France, Charles VII, although he had never been officially crowned. The valley was the main road to Germany, and also the frontier between the lands of the king and his principal enemy, the Duke of Burgundy.

All the villages near Domremy, except one, supported Charles. The valley had always suffered cruelly from war, and life at Domremy was one of perpetual alarm. All day and all night a watchman was stationed on the square tower of the monastery and the people were ready to fly at a moment's warning.

Still, in the midst of these anxieties, the men planted and reaped, women spun and wove, children played and sang, and rural people continued to practice their occupations. Inside the house of Jacques D'Arc, life seemed calm and serene. March passed, as did April, and soon it was May. The trees were masses of foliage, the meadows were dotted with wildflowers, and the green water of the winding river was almost hidden by dense clumps of rushes growing along the banks. The Valley of Colors, as the Romans had called this valley, was so radiant, fragrant, and flowery in this beautiful May weather that it easily deserved its name.

"Jeanne," said Jacques D'Arc one morning as his daughter rose from the breakfast table and took her usual place before the spinning wheel, "you cannot spin today. I need Pierrelot in the field, so you must watch the sheep. If we do not get the sowing done soon, we cannot reap a harvest."

"Very well, father," Jeanne said. Taking along her distaff, which would allow her to prepare thread for spinning while she watched the flock, she went outside to lead out the sheep. Most villagers kept their sheep in sheds attached to the house, but the D'Arc family kept their animals in a separate building. It was still early, but she had a long way to take the sheep to the uplands for grazing, so she needed to get an early start.

By the time Jeanne arrived in the meadow, Hauviette and Mengette were already on the upland with their flocks. They also had their distaffs, and soon the three friends were seated together near the oak wood, pulling the threads for spinning, chatting gaily. All three girls kept a careful eye on the browsing sheep, knowing well the value of the flocks they tended.

On this sparkling spring day, it seemed as though the whole village was out, so many men, women, and boys were sowing the fields or busy in the vineyards on the hill slopes. The morning had almost turned to noon when the quiet of the peaceful scene was broken by a hoarse shout from the watchman on the square tower of the monastery: "The Burgundians! The Burgundians are coming! To the fortress for your lives!"

As his voice died away, the bells of the church took up the alarm. Those same bells that celebrated births, tolled for the dead, and summoned people to prayer now noisily pealed in a harsh and terrifying clamor.

Instantly the fields and vineyards were full of commotion and confusion. People ran everywhere shouting to others. Men, women, and children ran frantically toward the village, carrying their farm tools, and driving the cattle before them. From the cottages emerged the old men and women who no longer worked in the fields but cared for the young children and the houses. The old people and the children carried whatever they could manage from the cottages and ran toward the castle.

At the first alarm from the watchman, Jeanne, Mengette, and Hauviette sprang quickly to their feet. Mengette and Hauviette dropped their distaffs and ran toward the fields where their elders were, forgetting everything but their own safety. But Jeanne stood still, a small frown wrinkling her forehead. Sheep are nervous animals, and the flock had lifted their heads and were beginning to bleat piteously. If they bolted into the plunging, bellowing cattle, nothing could be done to control them. If they should break and run to the forest they would be devoured by wolves. And if they became scattered in the meadow they would be captured by the attackers. Either way, her father would be the loser. She hesitated for only a moment and then, clear and sweet, she sounded the shepherd's call: "Cudday! Cudday! Cudday!"

Her voice rose bell-like above the confusion. The old leader of the flock recognized the tones of his shepherd, and started toward her. Jeanne turned, and started toward the village, stopping frequently to sound the call: "Cudday! Cudday! Cudday!"

And quietly, confidently, the leader followed her, bringing the flock with him. Halfway to the village Jeanne met her brother, Pierre, who came running to her, breathless and panting: "Father says to leave the sheep, Jeanne."

"No, no," she replied. "I can bring them in safely."

At this moment Jacques D'Arc's voice rang out loudly: "Leave the cattle and sheep, friends! Make for the castle! The enemy is upon us."

The terrified people glanced down the road from which the raiding party was approaching. There was little time to reach the fortress and, as Jacques D'Arc had seen, it couldn't be done without dropping everything. Leaving the animals, the villagers broke into a run, while Jacques ran to his children.

"Father, I know I could—" began Jeanne, but her father interrupted her.

"Don't talk, just run, little one. There is no time to lose."

The castle stood on an island in the Meuse River. The abandoned building had a large garden surrounded by a wide, deep moat. This had once been the home of those ladies and lords who in olden days had danced around the Fairy Tree. The last of the lords had left the property to his niece, who lived far away in Nancy. Wanting a place to retreat from the attacks of marauders, Jacques D'Arc and a neighbor, on behalf of the villagers, had leased the castle from the lady for a term of nine years.

On this bright May morning, the approach of the marauders was too rapid to allow the people to do any more than reach the castle in safety. Jacques D'Arc and his two children were the last to cross the drawbridge, which was instantly drawn up, and the gate was closed. They were safe, for the fortress was a place that ten could hold against ten hundred.

Through holes in the castle walls, the terrified villagers watched as the spoilers rode screaming into the village. Some rounded up the cattle and sheep, others hitched oxen to carts and drove them to the middle of the village, while still others piled the furniture from the cottages into the carts. Silently the villagers watched while the hearths of their homes were torn up and mantels demolished as the raiders searched for hidden treasure. Even the church was pillaged. Then, to complete the misery of the people of Domremy, the plunderers applied the torch to the houses.

Women wrung their hands, some dry-eyed, others with sobs and cries at the sight of their blazing homes, while men gnashed their teeth, enraged that they were powerless to prevent the disaster. Finally the raiders departed, carrying whatever they could away with them.

As soon as the plunderers passed from view, the villagers rushed out of the castle and across the drawbridge to fight the flames that were consuming the village. Some of the cottages were too far gone to be saved, but after the flames were extinguished a few houses remained that could be inhabited again with some thatching to their roofs. Among these was the house of Jacques D'Arc.

CHAPTER 4

THE AFTERMATH

Anguish filled the eyes of Isabeau Romée as she crossed the drawbridge from the castle and walked slowly with her children to the ruined village of Domremy. Other women shed bitter tears or shouted out their misery to the heavens. Isabeau's was the deeper grief that knows no tears.

The village and its surroundings were desolated. The enemy had plundered, ravaged, and burned every building. Whatever they could not carry off, they destroyed. The newly sown fields were trampled and the blossoming orchards burned. Houses that had been rescued from the flames were badly damaged; the entire village and the neighboring village of Greux had been sacked and pillaged. How were the people going to live?

As Isabeau stood in front of their cottage, her husband came up to her. "We still have the house," Jacques said. "We can thatch the roof and soon be living inside again. We will send to our market town of Neufchâteau for bread and grain. Do you have the money?"

"Yes, Jacques," Isabeau answered, taking a bag from the folds of her gown. It contained a small sum of money saved for just such an emergency. Jacques took it and his face brightened.

"Come now, it's not so bad," he said. "We'll send right away for the grain so we can resow the fields and will buy bread so we can live. We shall do well."

18

"Yes," Isabeau agreed, but she looked sadly at her children. Then she turned to Jacques in a passionate outburst: "In all your life, Jacques, and in all my life, we have known nothing but war. Must my children also live their whole lives in the midst of strife? Must they too sow only for soldiers to reap? Build only for enemies to burn? Be hunted like wild beasts and killed if they cannot pay ransom? Must they have nothing to count on, neither their property or their lives? Oh, Jacques, must France always be torn by war?"

"You are beside yourself with sorrow, Isabeau," said Jacques gently. "This is no time to give way. There is much to be done. All we can do is take up our burden and do the best we can. The issue lies with God."

Isabeau pulled herself together sharply. "You're right," she said. "It's no time for grief. There is much to do. Jeanne, take care of your little sister while I see if there is anything left. We need to find food for many."

Blinking back her own tears, Jeanne took her weeping little sister to a tree and sat down, drawing the child into her lap. Pierre followed them, while Jacquemin and Jean went to help their father. Soon Mengette and Hauviette joined the D'Arc children, and presently all the boys and girls of the village found their way there, whispering comforting words to each other and to the smaller children they cared for. Children are flexible and it wasn't long before their fright wore off. The young people began to tell about their experiences in subdued but excited tones.

"I saw a Burgundian as big as a giant," declared Colin. "If I had a crossbow and bolt, I would have killed him."

"Oh, you were just as afraid as the rest of us," said Pierre scornfully. "Why, even the men did not try to fight, the enemy were so many. And if they could do nothing, neither could you."

"The men could not fight without weapons, Pierre," Jeanne said quickly. "They had none in the fields."

"I shall be a warrior," Colin boasted. "I shall wear armor and ride a horse, and I shall help drive the English out of France."

Jeanne looked at him with sparkling eyes. "Yes," she cried eagerly. "That is what should be done. Oh! I would like to go, too. Why don't they stay in their own country?"

"You?" Colin began to laugh. "You're a girl, Jeanne D'Arc, and girls don't go to war. They can't fight."

"I could." A determined light came into Jeanne's eyes, and she set her lips in a firm line. "I know I could." At this the other children joined in Colin's laughter, and the boy cried gaily: "I'd like to see you. Oh, wouldn't the English run when they saw you?"

Jeanne began to answer, but just then she heard her mother's voice calling. So, shaking her finger at Colin, she rose obediently and started for the cottage. At the cottage door her father stood gazing intently at a long rod that he held in his hand. Jeanne touched him lightly on the arm.

"What is it, father?" she asked gently. "Are you grieving over the cattle and our goods?"

Her father looked up, startled.

"Yes, my little one. But not so much about that as the future burden we now bear. This rod is the tally stick with which we tote up the taxes owed by Domremy and Greux. I don't like to think about it. It will seem too heavy after the misfortune that has come upon us."

The village elder had many responsibilities. It was up to Jacques to summon the mayor and aldermen to council meetings, to tell the people of the plans and decrees, to organize the lookouts both day and night, and to guard any prisoners. It was also his duty to collect taxes, rents, and dues. An arduous job at any time, but doubly so in a ruined country. Jeanne knew her father was responsible for collecting the taxes, but she had never realized how distasteful this task was for him. She looked curiously at the tally stick.

"Why does it have notches, father?" she asked.

"To show the amount due. There are two tallies: one shows what the peasants pay to their landlords; the other, called the royal tally, shows what the landlords pay to the king. Here at Domremy we are directly subject to the king and pay the royal tally. Sir Robert de Baudricourt, the captain of Vaucouleurs, has told me that the Dauphin needs money badly. But it will be hard to pay the tax after what has happened here."

At this moment, Jacques D'Arc did not look his best. His clothes were dusty and grimy with soot, and his face and hands were filthy from fighting the fires. But through the soot and grime shone the light of compassion for the burden that the village would have to bear. Jeanne did not see the soiled clothing or the blackened face and hands; she saw only that her father was troubled beyond the loss of his goods and cattle. She threw her arms around his neck and drew his face down to hers.

"I wish there were no tax, father," she said.

"I do, too, my little one," he sighed. "But wishing will not make it so. You are a comfort to me, Jeanne. But your mother is calling. Let's go to her."

Hand in hand they went into the house, where Jacques deposited the tally stick in a corner. Isabeau met them, a smile lighting her face.

"See," she cried, holding up a huge loaf of black bread. "It was in the back part of the oven and the thieves missed it. Take it to your playmates, Jeanne, and give a piece to each of them. Children get hungry and it will be a long time before we have bread from Neufchâteau!"

Jeanne took the loaf gladly and hurried to her playmates. Yesterday the children considered bread ordinary, but today its appearance in Jeanne's hands was greeted with cries of joy. No one had eaten since early that morning, and they fell upon the precious loaf eagerly. Jeanne divided the large loaf into many equal pieces, and the children passed the pieces among themselves. Soon the youngest began to cry for more. Jeanne had expected this, so she had not eaten her share. Now she quietly divided her share among the smallest, giving each a little bit. Then Pierre pulled her by the sleeve.

"You haven't had any," he said. "And I—I have eaten all of my share."

"That's fine, Pierrelot." Jeanne smiled at him reassuringly. "I can wait until the bread comes from the market. Let's go on to the castle now. Mother said everyone is to sleep there tonight."

"But there are no beds," whined Colin.

"No, Colin, there are no beds, but floors are better than the fields. It would be dangerous to sleep outdoors because of the wolves."

"Wolves?" Colin whitened visibly, and the children huddled closer together. "I didn't think of wolves. Is there really danger?"

"The men are worried because some of the cattle and sheep were trampled to death and their carcasses may draw the wolves. We'll sleep in the castle until the roofs of the houses are repaired."

The arrangements were as Jeanne had said. The nights were to be spent inside the castle, while the days would be spent rebuilding the village and resowing the fields. With this plan agreed on, the peasants resignedly took up their lives. For no matter how adverse fate may be, life must go on and misfortune must be faced and overcome.

The months that followed tried the endurance of the unfortunate citizens of Domremy. Food was scarce everywhere. From early spring until harvest, the stock of food in a rural community is always at its lowest, so even though many villages of the valley shared their provisions with their unfortunate neighbors, their own needs had to be taken into consideration. Famine reared its ugly head in the villages of Greux and Domremy, and many people died of hunger.

One day Jacques D'Arc gathered his family together. On the table was a single loaf of bread and next to it a pail of water. He looked at them sadly.

"This is our last loaf," he said, "and we have no more food. So this is our last meal for now. We will eat today, and tomorrow we must do as we can. Be thankful therefore for what we have."

He cut the loaf into seven parts, giving a portion to his wife first, then one to each of his children except Jeanne. Hers he kept beside his own. When all had been served he turned to her.

"Come here, my little one," he said.

There was something in his tone that Jeanne did not understand; timidly, she went to his side. Jacques put his arm around her.

"Have you eaten today?"

Jeanne blushed, and hung her head, but she did not reply.

"You haven't," he said. "Yesterday Pierre saw you give all of your portion to your sister. The day before you kept only a small part for yourself, giving Catherine the rest. Is that right?"

"Yes, father, but I go to the church and pray and then I do not need food." Jeanne took courage as she said this, and raising her head looked at him bravely. "I don't feel very hungry."

"Fasting is good for the soul, child, but too much is bad for the body. Let me see you eat your share."

"But, father," she protested.

"Eat," he commanded.

When Jacques spoke in that tone, his children knew resistance was useless, so silently Jeanne ate her portion. Her father watched her eat, until every crumb was swallowed. She did not sit down at the table, but went to the open door and gazed down the road through eyes filled with tears. Her heart was very full. Father and child were very close, and she knew that he suffered because of his family's misery. She gazed out at the valley wishing that she might do something to help him.

The valley had regained much of its beauty. The trees were leafy once more, the fields green with new crops, and the gardens abloom with the promise of later abundance. However, black gaps still stood among the houses, ugly reminders of the pillaging marauders. As Jeanne stood leaning against the door, something down the road caused her to jump violently.

"Father," she cried.

"What is it?"

"Cattle and sheep are coming down the road. They look like ours!"

Jacques sprang to his feet and ran to the door. One look and he shouted: "They are ours! Friends, neighbors, come and see! The cattle have come back."

From the cottages the people ran, incredulity turning to wild excitement as they saw the animals they had thought were gone. The animals were being herded by a number of soldiers who were commanded by a young knight. From him they learned what had happened.

When the lady who owned the castle heard of the raid, she protested to her kinsman, the Count of Vaudemont. She was still the lady of Domremy and Greux, and she considered the destruction of the villages a personal wrong done to her.

The chief of the raiding band had delivered his plunder to the Château of Doulevant, which was under the protection of that same Count of Vaudemont. When the Count heard the lady's complaint, he sent the young knight and his soldiers to reclaim the animals and booty and return them to their rightful owners.

With tears and cries of joy, the villagers welcomed the knight and his party. They had brought food, too, so life began to brighten quickly. Only the older, wiser villagers shook their heads ominously, worrying what troubles tomorrow would bring.

After that the days passed quietly in the valley with war everywhere around. And Jeanne grew and blossomed as the lily grows out of the muck of a swamp.

CHAPTER 5

JEANNE'S VISION

Summer gave way to autumn and winter; winter turned into spring, and then again it was summer. Though there were raids in distant parts of the valley and wild rumors and false alarms, Domremy was mercifully spared a second attack. A strict watch was still kept from the monastery tower, but by and large village life had resumed its tranquil aspect. The men worked in the fields and vineyards, women spun and wove and looked after their households, and children played and tended the herds and flocks on the common meadow.

One warm afternoon in late July, Jeanne, with some of her playmates, was on the uplands watching the flocks nibble the short green grass. The boys and girls were scattered over the pasture, but Mengette and Hauviette sat with Jeanne under the shade of a tree. The three friends were never very far apart, and as usual their fingers were busy with the threads of their distaffs.

It was a delicious afternoon. The warm air was soft and balmy, fragrant with the perfume of wild linden flowers. In the fields the ripening wheat rippled in the breeze like a yellow sea, and scarlet poppies added great splotches of color. The Meuse flowed sluggishly through dense reeds and bushes, almost hidden by the foliage. A lovely scene, for the Valley of Colors was never more beautiful than in summer. A busy scene, too, for men and boys were working in the fields and vineyards, either cutting the ripened grain with their long scythes or tying up the vines, heavy with bunches of grapes.

"The sheep are getting restless," Jeanne said, as she noticed that some of the animals were beginning to stray apart from the others. "They have nibbled the grass clean here. It's time to move them."

"And I'm getting sleepy," said Mengette with a yawn. "We've been here since early morning. If I keep on pulling threads from this distaff I'll do like Colin over there and fall asleep in the grass."

"He shouldn't sleep when he has the sheep to attend to,"said Hauviette, shaking her head. "They might stray into the vineyards or the forest, and he'd never know where they had gone."

"He knows we're watching," said Jeanne. "I think he depends on us to look after them, even though his flock is the largest one here. We should wake him up before we move our sheep away."

Jeanne got up as she spoke and went quickly over to where Colin lay stretched out on the grass. She had grown taller in the past year, "shot up like a weed," her mother said. Her expression had become more thoughtful, and her eyes seemed larger and brighter. She seemed to be puzzling over many things, but still retained her gaiety and high spirits. The sleeping boy opened his eyes drowsily as she shook him.

"Wake up, Colin," she said. "Wake up and listen to what I am telling you. We're going to take our sheep into another field. You have to wake up and look after your flock."

But Colin pulled away and settled down for another nap. Jeanne shook him again vigorously.

"Wake up you lazy boy," she cried. "What will your father say if something happens to the sheep? We're going to move ours."

Colin sat up reluctantly, muttering and rubbing his eyes. He seemed so drowsy that Jeanne thought she should goad him to action.

"Colin, a cluster of linden flowers is growing on the edge of the forest. They're very pretty and I'm going to pick them. I heard your mother tell you to bring her some flowers from the fields. I'll race you to see who gets to them first."

"It's too hot to run," he murmured. "It's just like you to want to race when it's hot. I'd rather sit still."

"But you have to wake up," persisted Jeanne. "Come on! You have never beaten me at a race and you can't do it today."

"Aw! I never tried very hard," grumbled Colin, slowly getting to his feet. "I'll run, but I'd much rather stay here. I don't see why you want to pester a fellow anyway. And why do you want to move the sheep anyway? They'll do well enough right here. Where did you say the flowers were?"

"Over there." Jeanne pointed toward a large cluster of yellow linden flowers growing near an oak thicket on the edge of the wood. These flowers grew abundantly all around the village. "Girls," she said, turning toward her friends, "Colin thinks he can beat me to that bunch of linden blossoms."

"The idea," laughed Mengette teasingly. "Why, he can't beat any of us, not even little Martin who is half his size. We'll all run just to show him. Line up, everybody. Come on, Martin. We'll start on the count of three. Get ready! One—two—three—go!" And laughing merrily they were off.

Now the children often ran races together when they tended the animals on the uplands. Jeanne was very fleet of foot and this afternoon she ran so swiftly and easily that she seemed to have wings. Reaching the flowers well ahead of her companions she bent over and inhaled their perfume, feeling a sense of rapture that she had never known before. Hauviette was the next to arrive.

"Oh, Jeanne," she cried, gazing at her friend with admiration. "I never saw anyone run the way you did. Why, your feet scarcely seemed to touch the ground."

"Jeanne always runs as though she were flying," panted Mengette, now coming up next to them. "Anyway. I'm glad that Colin didn't beat us. He's way behind, and here is Martin coming up next. Shame, Colin," she cried, laughing, as the boy finally lumbered up to them. "Not only did Jeanne beat you, but Hauviette, Martin, and I did also. All of us got here before you."

"I wasn't awake enough to run well," explained Colin, defending himself.

"Jeanne," broke in little Martin suddenly, "go home. Your mother wants you. I heard her calling."

"Mother wants me? Why, that's strange. She never calls me when I'm out with the flock. Something must be wrong."

"Maybe so," the boy said. "Anyway, I heard her calling, 'Jeanne! Jeanne!' Just like that."

"Then I must go to her," cried Jeanne. She turned and quickly ran to the cottage. As Jeanne came rushing through the door, her mother looked up with surprise from her sewing.

"Why, child, what brings you home so early?" Isabeau asked. "Has anything happened to the sheep?"

"Didn't you call me, mother?"

"Call you? No. What made you think I called you?" Isabeau asked sharply. "You should never leave the sheep alone on the uplands. The other children have their own animals to care for without worrying about yours."

"Martin told me that he heard you call me," Jeanne said. "Maybe he was playing a trick on me because I beat him and Colin in a race. I'll go back to the sheep." She started to leave the room.

"Martin is naughty," exclaimed Isabeau with some irritation. "Stay, Jeanne. Pierre has just come in from the fields and he can go to the sheep. You can help me here with the sewing. Take this garment and finish the seam while I attend to Catherine. She hasn't seemed well lately. Go out into the garden where it's cool and sit in the shade."

Jeanne obediently took the garment her mother held out and went into the garden. She was quite skillful at sewing. Her mother did exquisite needlework and was teaching her daughter to sew well, also.

It was quiet in the garden, quieter than on the uplands where the children laughed and sang songs. Here there was only the twitter of birds, the rustle of leaves in the breeze, and the humming sound of bees. It was so quiet that soon some small birds, seeing that they had nothing to fear from the maiden, flew down from the apple tree and began to peck at the grass at Jeanne's feet. Jeanne smiled and sat very still so as not to frighten them. A skylark rose from the grass in the meadow beyond the orchard and in a burst of song flew up into the air, mounting higher and higher until it was just a black dot in the sky. Still singing, the lark began to descend, circling as it gently floated earthward.

Jeanne had let her work lie in her lap as she watched the flight of the bird; now she took it up again and began to sew steadily. All at once something made her look up.

Something had changed in the atmosphere. What it was she could not tell, but she was conscious of something she did not understand. She glanced up at the sky, but there was not a cloud. The sky was as serene, as dazzling, as it had been all day. Bewildered, she picked up her sewing again and tried to go on with it, but she could not. She lay the garment down in her lap and once more glanced about. As she did, she saw a light appear between her and the church. It was on her right side, and as it came nearer it grew brighter.

The light was dazzling. Jeanne had never seen anything like it. Thrilled, but too frightened to move, she closed her eyes. And then, from the midst of the radiance, came a sweet voice, sweeter than the chimes of the bells she loved so well. It said: "Be good, Jeanne, be good! Be obedient, and go often to church. I called you on the uplands, but you did not hear. Be good, Jeanne, be good."

That was all. The voice stopped. The light faded and gradually ceased to glow. Jeanne drew a long breath, and fearfully lifted her eyes. There was nothing there. The garden looked the same as before. The little birds still pecked around her feet, and the leaves still rustled in the breeze. Could she have been dreaming? she asked herself.

At this moment, Isabeau called to her from the door of the cottage: "Take Catherine for a few minutes, Jeanne," she said. "I don't know what ails the child. Why, what's wrong, my little one? Is something bothering you? You look upset."

Jeanne began to answer. She was going to tell her mother about the wonderful thing that had happened, but something in Isabeau's expression made her stop. Whatever she may have seen, Jeanne was unable to tell her mother.

Isabeau said again, "Is anything wrong, Jeanne?"

Jeanne only shook her head and said quietly, "No, mother."

"That trick Martin played on you has upset you," complained Isabeau. "You ran the race and then ran home thinking that something was wrong with us here. It was a mean trick, although he was only teasing. I'll speak to his mother about it. The boy spends too much time with that naughty Colin."

Jeanne was startled. The voice had said that it called her on the uplands. Could that be what Martin had heard? If so, then she hadn't been dreaming. It had really happened. She spoke timidly to her mother: "Perhaps he didn't mean to trick me, mother. Perhaps he really thought he heard you calling me."

"How could he, when I didn't call?"

Isabeau hurried into the kitchen, while Jeanne, still wondering what had taken place, took her little sister into the garden and sat down.

CHAPTER 6

JEANNE'S HARSH WORDS

Partly from shyness and partly from fear of ridicule, Jeanne did not tell anyone about her strange experience in the garden. But she often thought of what had happened, and she wondered what it meant. One day, when Jeanne and her friends were down at the riverbank doing the wash with the women of the village, Mengette remarked on her faraway look.

"What has come over you, Jeanne?" said Mengette. "I have spoken to you twice but you haven't answered. Has your mother been scolding you?"

"Mother scolding? Why, no!" Jeanne glanced up in surprise. "Nothing is wrong, Mengette. I was just thinking."

"About what?" When Jeanne didn't reply, Mengette lowered her voice and said, "You're thinking too much, Jeanne. You're not like your usual self, and everyone has noticed. When we come to wash, we always laugh, sing, talk, and have a good time, but you do nothing but mope." Mengette gave the clothes she was washing a vicious thump.

"Well, I haven't moped so much that my clothes aren't clean," retorted Jeanne, holding up some linens for inspection. "Mengette, those poor clothes will be beaten to a thread if you pound them much harder."

Mengette let her paddle drop and pushed back her hair with wet hands.

"I'd be happy to beat them to a thread just to hear you laugh again. Now come closer, and I'll tell you something that Hauviette told me last night. I don't want anyone else to hear."

The two girls were soon deep in conversation punctuated by peals of merriment. All along the bank of the river, the women and girls knelt over their washing tables, talking as they worked, or sometimes singing rounds. As Mengette said, the pleasure of washing was in meeting the other women and girls; they chatted, laughed, and exchanged news between the thump, thump of the paddles, which could be heard all along the valley as they beat and turned and dipped and turned again the coarse garments of their families. Work that would have been irksome when done alone was lightened by the communion and fellowship of friends.

In spite of the heat of the day, it was pleasant by the river. Bluebells and tall white plumes of spirea grew among the greenish white mignonette and rosy meadowsweet, embroidering a delicate tapestry of color against the vivid green valley. The smell of new-mown hay made the air fragrant and hills and meadows smiled under a cloudless sky. Finally the washing was finished. The sun was getting low behind the Domremy hills when the last snowy pieces of linen were stretched on the grass to bleach; when they were dried, the women folded them into large wicker baskets which they lifted onto their backs. As the other women started homeward with their burdens, Isabeau lingered to speak to her daughter.

"Leave the tables and paddles," she said. "I'll send the boys back for them later. You've done enough for one day. Do you know where the lads are?"

"Since the hay was all cut, father told them to take the afternoon for themselves. I think they've gone fishing downriver."

"I hope they don't meet the Maxey boys anywhere. When boys from our side of the river meet those from the Lorraine side, there is always a fight. I don't like it."

"It's because the boys from Domremy and Greux are Armagnacs and those from Maxey-sur-Meuse are Burgundians," said Jeanne. "How can they help fighting, mother, when even grown-ups fight their enemies when they meet?"

"True. It's no wonder they fight when there is so much fighting in the land." Isabeau sighed. "I wish there were no war. But let's not speak of it. Since the boys are somewhere along the river, they must pass the bridge to come home. Wait here for them and tell them to bring the tables and paddles home. I'll go ahead home to get supper started."

"Very well, mother," Jeanne agreed. So while her mother went back to the cottage, the girl rinsed off the washing tables and drew them up on the banks. Then she sat down near the bridge to watch for her brothers.

She didn't have long to wait. Suddenly there were shouts and cries from the Lorraine side of the river and Jeanne's brothers, Jean and Pierre, followed by other Domremy lads, came running at full speed. Chasing after them came a passel of Maxey boys, hurling insults and stones at their fleeing adversaries.

Jeanne could see a long, deep gash bleeding freely from a wound on Pierre's head. At the sight of the streaming blood, she burst into tears. She couldn't stand the sight of blood, and fighting frightened her. Then, Gerardin d'Epinal, a Burgundian, came across the fields. He was the only man living in Domremy who did not belong to King Charles's party. He laughed as he saw the Domremy boys running away from the Maxey boys. Knowing how loyal Jeanne was to the Dauphin, he teased: "That's the way the Burgundians and English are making the little Dauphin run. Soon he will be forced out of France into Spain, or perhaps Scotland. Then Henry will be king of both England and France."

At that comment Jeanne grew white. Her tears stopped and she stood up very straight and looked at him with blazing eyes.

"I would rather see you dead," she said in low intense tones. Then, after a moment, she crossed herself and added: "That is, if it were God's will, Gerardin d'Epinal."

Long afterward, when Gerardin d'Epinal retold the story, her words became famous as the only harsh words Jeanne D'Arc ever used in her whole life. For now, Gerardin went on his way, saying lightly: "You shouldn't take things so seriously, Jeanne."

By this time, the Domremy boys had reached their own side of the river and were safe from further attack. They gathered around Jeanne.

"Why did you speak to Gerardin that way, Jeanne?" cried Jean.

Jeanne hung her head. "I don't know," she answered. "Yes, I do. It was because of what he said about the Dauphin and also because of the cut in Pierre's head."

With that she put her arm around her brother. "Does it hurt much?" she asked. "Let's wash it off before we go home. Mother doesn't like to see blood."

"And neither do you," exclaimed Pierre, noting her pale face. "Don't bother about it, Jeanne. It doesn't hurt much." He shrugged his shoulders with pretended indifference.

"Mother will be upset when she sees you've been fighting," Jeanne continued.

"We didn't mean to," broke in Jean quickly. "We came to the river to fish, but some of the Burgundian boys came down to the other side and began calling us names, saying that we didn't dare cross over and fight. So we ran back to the village to call the other boys to help us. But when we got back to the river, we couldn't see anyone on the other side. So we crossed the bridge to the Lorraine side anyway, and—"

"They set upon us," interrupted Pierre excitedly. "They were hiding in the bushes and behind trees, and as soon as we reached the opposite bank they threw themselves on us."

"And did the Domremy boys give a good account of themselves?" asked Jeanne. "And how did you get the gash, Pierre?"

Jean looked embarrassed. "I did it," he said. "Like Oliver did to Roland in the *Song of Roland.* We were all so tangled up, we couldn't tell which were our boys and which were not. So I thought I was hitting one of them and instead I hit Pierrelot on the head. But I made up for it afterward, didn't I, Pierre?"

Pierre laughed and nodded. "So did I," he said. "I knew Jean would feel bad about hitting me, so we both made the Burgundians pay for it. Are you finished with the washing here, Jeanne? Shall we carry the tables and paddles home for you?"

"Yes, we're finished. Mother said you should bring the tables and paddles, but since you're hurt, I'll help Jean carry them."

"Why, it's only a scratch," cried Pierre. "And you've been washing all day. I'll carry my share. Now let's be getting home. I'm hungry as a wolf."

"So am I," declared Jean.

Supper was waiting when the young people reached the cottage, and the boys told the story of the ambush over again to their father and mother, who listened sympathetically. In the midst of the recital Jeanne slipped out and crossed the garden to the little church for evening prayers.

The church was empty except for the priest. Father Frontey smiled as Jeanne entered; he could always be sure of one parishioner, whatever the weather. Jeanne knelt in prayer before the statue of Saint Catherine, the patron saint of young girls. Then she took her seat as other people began to come in for the service.

Father Frontey led them through a short benediction service, and afterward Jeanne, feeling comforted and refreshed, walked back out into the garden. A sweet coolness veiled the evening air, and the darkness was soft and agreeable after the glare of the afternoon sun. Presently through the darkness came the light she had seen before. A light so bright, so glowing in its radiance, that Jeanne sank to her knees in awe. She was not as frightened as before, but she still did not dare lift her eyes. Trembling she waited for the voice. As it spoke the bells of the church began to ring: "I come from God to help you live a good and holy life," it said. "Be good, Jeanne, and God will help you."

That was all. The light faded gradually, and when it was gone Jeanne rose to her feet.

"It was the voice of an angel," she whispered. "The voice of an angel, and it spoke to me."

From that time forward Jeanne D'Arc had no doubt that an angel had spoken to her. For some time she stood wondering at the miracle, then slowly and thoughtfully she went into the cottage and straight to her own room.

This room was on the side of the cottage facing the church. From her window she could see the red light of the sacred altar candle glowing inside the darkened church; clasping her hands Jeanne knelt and said her prayers. It seemed to her that Heaven itself could be touched through the window of that little church.

CHAPTER 7

FURTHER VISIONS

After that the Voice came frequently. Again and again Jeanne heard it speaking to her, mostly when she was in the fields or the garden. In time the heavenly radiance took the shape of a man, with wings and a crown on his head. He seemed to be a great angel, surrounded by many smaller ones. Jeanne recognized him as Saint Michael, the archangel who was the warden of heaven, the angel of judgment and leader of the Heavenly Hosts. She had often seen his image on a pillar in the church, a handsome knight with a crown on his helmet, wearing a coat of mailed armor and holding a lance in one hand. Sometimes he was pictured balancing scales. In one ancient manuscript it was written that "the true office of Saint Michael is to make great revelations to men below, by giving them holy counsels."

A long, long time ago, Saint Michael had appeared to the Bishop of Avranches. The archangel commanded the bishop to build a church on Mount Tombe, on the spot where he would find a bull hidden by thieves. The site of the building was to include the whole area trampled on by the bull. According to this command, the bishop built the Abbey of Mont-Saint-Michael-au-Péril-de-la-Mer.

The vision that Jeanne saw was so noble and so majestic that at first she was afraid of it. But the great archangel spoke so wisely and tenderly that her fear

34

subsided. One day he said to her: "Saint Catherine and Saint Margaret will come to you. They are appointed to guide and advise you in everything you must do, and you shall believe what they say to you."

Jeanne heard this news joyfully, since she loved both of these saints. Saint Margaret, the patron saint of all nurses and various textile workers, was highly honored in the kingdom of France. And just across the river a church had been built in honor of Saint Catherine, for whom Jeanne's little sister was named.

Both saints were martyrs. Jeanne had heard their stories many times from her mother, so she eagerly awaited their coming. Saint Margaret and Saint Catherine first appeared to her on a Saturday, the day on which the Virgin Mary is traditionally honored. Jeanne had made a pilgrimage up the hill and through the woods to the shrine of Our Lady of Belmont, near the old Fairy Tree. With her savings Jeanne had bought a candle to burn on the altar and she carried wildflowers to make the holy place as fragrant as the forest. After placing her candle on the altar and laying the flowers on the shrine, she slowly started down the hill again. Near the Gooseberry Spring she knelt for a drink of the crystal-pure water. It was very quiet and shady in the clearing around the spring. The day was warm, and after her drink Jeanne sat down on a natural seat formed by the gnarled roots of a tree. Her hands rested loosely in her lap, her head drooped, and she was lost in thought. All at once she sensed a marvelously sweet aroma all around her, a perfume unlike any she had ever smelled before. She lifted her head and drew in a deep breath, glancing around to see the blossoms that were so fragrant.

She heard a slight rustling of leaves among the trees, and from above there came an unearthly light. A look of rapture came over Jeanne's face. She rose, and crossed herself devoutly, then bowed low before two shining figures, dressed like queens. Around their necks they wore rich and precious jewels, and on their heads were golden crowns. So bright was the light emanating from them that Jeanne could not look at them directly, but she knelt and kissed the hem of their garments. Gravely the saints spoke, telling their names. Their tones were so soft and sweet that the sound filled Jeanne with happiness.

"Daughter of God," they said, "rise and listen. We come to teach you how to live so that you may be prepared for your mission."

They continued speaking to her, but soon the light began to dim. Jeanne caught at their garments: "Oh, don't leave me," she cried. "Take me with you."

"No," came the answer. "It is not yet your time. Your work is yet to be done."

With these words, the forms disappeared, and Jeanne stood weeping.

After this, the saints visited her nearly every day. She met them everywhere, most often in the little garden close to the church, but also in the woods and near the spring. Soon she began to call the visions "my Voices," for their voices were always more clear to her than their appearance. Their figures and faces shimmered vaguely in the bright light that announced each visit, but Jeanne could always hear their words plainly.

In the weeks that followed, Jeanne locked her secret in her heart. She felt set apart, governed by a divine guidance. She put aside the gaiety of girlhood and lived a simple, devout life, helping her mother, obeying her father, and doing what she could for everyone. Her piety and devotion deepened. She became so good that everyone in the village noticed the change in her and loved her the more for it.

Jeanne gave whatever she had to the church: flowers for the altars, candles for the saints, and loving service to everyone.

"Jeanne is an angel," her mother remarked one day to Jacques. "There is no one like her. So good, so obedient, she never gives me a bit of trouble. And she takes such good care of her little sister! Catherine has been fretful and sickly all summer, but Jeanne can always calm her. I don't know what I would do without her. Other mothers envy me. They say there isn't another girl so good in the valley."

Jacques D'Arc frowned. "She is too quiet," he said. "Haven't you noticed, Isabeau? She no longer dances with the other children. And she doesn't play games, either. And all that praying and church-going! There is too much of it."

"Jacques!" exclaimed Isabeau. "How can you say that? The priest commends Jeanne for her devoutness."

"Then why is she so quiet?" Jacques demanded. "Is someone secretly teaching her to read and write?"

Isabeau shook her head emphatically.

"She doesn't know A from B, Jacques. Everything she knows is what she has learned from me. She knows her prayers and the stories of the saints, things that every child should know. She is skillful around the house, and excellent at sewing and spinning. There is nothing wrong, Jacques. But I wish there were less talk about bloodshed and battles. Sometimes I think it would be better if we didn't live on the main road where every passerby brings the latest news of the war."

On the road that passed by the front door of the D'Arc family tramped foot soldiers, cartloads of weapons, and men-at-arms mounted on horseback. Fugitives from the wars stopped regularly at the house to rest and eat and tell stories of great suffering. Isabeau had grown to fear the glitter of lance points. It isn't always the real assault and plundering that saps people of their courage, but the constant threat of these frightening events.

"The children hear too much of battles, and the state of France," she added.

"Don't worry about that. Such talk makes no lasting impression on children, Isabeau. It's good for them to know something of the world beyond this valley. I wonder if Jeanne might be ill."

"There is nothing wrong with the child, Jacques," Isabeau said. "She would tell me if there were. She is just becoming more thoughtful as she grows older, that's all."

"I don't like it," grumbled Jacques, shaking his head. "I fear that something is wrong. It's not right for a young girl to be so pious. Is that a priest turning in from the highway, Isabeau?"

CHAPTER 8

JEANNE RECEIVES A GIFT AND AN ANNOUNCEMENT

Isabeau glanced out the door and saw a Franciscan monk approaching the cottage. "It's one of the Gray Friars," she exclaimed, "and I haven't started supper. I must hurry, for he may be hungry."

"Let him go on to Neufchâteau," grumbled Jacques. "It's only five miles farther on and the Franciscans have a house there. They can feed him."

"Don't be silly, Jacques. The poor man may be exhausted. If he were a soldier you'd welcome him."

"If he were a soldier he would have something to say worth hearing," retorted Jacques. However, as the monk approached the door, Jacques stood up and greeted him politely.

"Peace be with you, my son," the friar said humbly. "For the love of God, will you give a poor brother of the Order of St. Francis something to eat and a bed for the night? I have traveled a long way."

"Come in, father," Jacques said brusquely. "Supper will be on the table soon, and we have a bed for you."

"Thank you, my son. A blessing on you and your house." The monk spoke so gently that Jacques's manner softened. He threw the door wide open and offered him a seat.

38

The friar had scarcely seated himself when Jeanne entered, bringing him a jug of fresh water and a cup.

"You must be thirsty, good father," she said.

"I am, my child," the monk said, drinking the water gratefully. "I have traveled many miles, all the way from Rome."

"From Rome?" said Jacques, surprised. "Hear that, Isabeau? The monk has been to Rome. Hurry with the supper, he must be hungry."

Jacques himself filled up the priest's cup with water and brought him a small stool to support his feet. Anyone who had made a pilgrimage to Rome was exalted in the eyes of all men.

Jeanne quietly helped her mother prepare supper and smiled as she watched her father bustle about the friar. Soon they were all eating with hearty relish. In return for food and lodging, travelers were expected to regale their hosts with the latest news and tales of their adventures. Thus, after supper, the seat nearest the fire was given to the monk, and the family gathered around him.

The Franciscan began by describing his pilgrimage to Rome in great detail, and spoke of visiting Colette of Corbie, a famous nun who was believed to have healing powers. Isabeau, who was very pious, asked timidly: "Do you possess any relic that has been touched by Sister Colette?"

"I wish I did," said the friar. "However, I do have a ring made by a holy man that is supposed to be a charm against the falling sickness."

Jacques looked up with quick interest. At that time, epilepsy was one of the most frightening sicknesses that could befall anyone. "May we see it?"

The friar drew a small brass ring from beneath his robe. It was an ordinary-looking ring. It had no stone, but on its sloping sides were engraved three crosses and the names Jesus and Mary. Such rings were common in France; sometimes, instead of holy names, they were engraved with figures of saints or the Virgin Mary. Any ring or relic that was said to protect against disease appealed to the imagination of poor peasant people, and above all else they desired to possess, or even touch, such a precious thing in the hopes that its virtues might pass to them. Jacques looked at his wife, and she spoke his own thoughts: "Would you sell this ring, good father?" she asked.

"I cannot sell it. It does have healing properties, even though it's only a trinket compared to holy relics."

Jacques handed the ring back to him, regret showing plainly on his honest face. "I'm sorry to hear that. My little one here has no charm against the falling sickness and I'd like to buy it for her. She hasn't been herself lately."

The friar looked at Jeanne, who had sat listening with shining eyes to his stories. Then he smiled.

"If it's for this child who, without being asked, brought me water when I was weary and thirsty, I will sell it," he said. "No, wait. I won't sell it, but if you'll give a small donation to the convent being built for the Sisters of St. Claire, then I'll gladly give it to you. I know it will prevent the falling sickness."

The priest smiled at Jeanne again. Looking at her sweet, pale face he felt certain that she would never fall ill.

Jacques drew his daughter to him, and taking the ring from the friar placed it on the third finger of her left hand.

"Do you like it, my little one?" he asked.

Jeanne's eyes lit up with pleasure. She had never had a ring and to her it was very precious. "Is it really for me, father?" she cried.

"Yes." Jacques nodded, pleased that she liked the trinket. He drew several coins from his pocket and gave them to the priest. "The ring is given to you by both your mother and myself, my child," he said. "May it protect you from all ills."

Jeanne threw her arms about her father's neck and kissed him, then she ran to her mother and kissed her also.

"It's so pretty," she cried. "And see! It has the two most holy names engraved on it."

"Let me see," said Pierre. "Sometime I'll give you a ring all by myself that shall be prettier than this."

Jeanne laughed. "As though any ring could be prettier. There couldn't be one, could there, Jean?"

"Never," Jean said, shaking his head emphatically as he examined the ring. "I like it better than the one Mengette wears."

The talk went on around the hearth, sometimes of the saints and their miracles, sometimes of the war and the state of the kingdom. It was late when everyone at last went to bed.

Jeanne was delighted with the gift. It was unusual for peasant families struggling to live through the hard days of constant warfare to give each other presents. The next time Jeanne's saints appeared, Saint Catherine graciously touched the ring and Jeanne's joy was unbounded. She would often gaze at the ring adoringly. But while the ring might protect her against epilepsy, it did not bring back her joyousness.

Jeanne was very grave and thoughtful at this time in her life. She continued to think of others, plan for others' benefit, and sacrifice herself for the welfare of others. She still tended to the sick and helped the poor, and gave up her bed to any homeless traveler. But even though she performed her duties with sweet exactness, she was quiet and abstracted. Her saints were coming to her with greater frequency now, and they constantly spoke to her of a mission.

"What can they mean?" she asked herself. "What is it that I'm supposed to do?" Weeks passed before she was finally told.

The lovely summer merged slowly into autumn, the season when heavy rains begin to fall. Rivulets of water rushed down from the hills, swelling the Meuse River into a deep, rapid torrent of water. The river overflowed its banks and shallow lagoons dotted the fields. The clouds grew lower, leaning sullenly against the hills. Fog came down thick and clinging. Soon the river was edged with frost, and snow and sleet pounded across the valley. It was winter. The warm, green hills were covered in white, gleaming palely whenever the weak winter sun broke through the scattered clouds. Few travelers passed along the road now, and the people living in the dismal gray villages were forced to depend upon themselves for news and social contact.

Life in the house of Jacques D'Arc appeared to go on as before. No one suspected that Jeanne visited with saints and angels, or that she walked with her ears alert for her Voices to tell her about the divine mission. Jeanne continued to visit with her friends Mengette and Hauviette, often spending the night with one or the other. Both girls noticed something unusual about her behavior.

"Everyone says that you're very good, but you're also odd," Hauviette confided one day when the three girls were spending the afternoon together.

Jeanne glanced up from her spinning. "And what do you say, Hauviette?"

"I say you're better than any of us," answered Hauviette quickly. "Still, there is a change in you, Jeanne. You're not so lively as you were. You never dance or race with us, or play as you used to. What's the matter?"

"I know what it is," cried Mengette. "She goes to church too much and prays too often. When the sexton forgot to ring the bells she reproached him because she loves to pray."

"But don't you like to pray, Mengette?" asked Jeanne.

"Oh, yes. But I don't give the sexton cakes to make sure he rings the bells on time. Are you getting ready to be a saint?"

Jeanne blushed scarlet at this, and didn't answer.

"Oh, leave her alone," said Hauviette. "Perhaps she doesn't feel like playing or dancing."

"That's it," said Jeanne suddenly, giving her friend a grateful glance. "I just don't feel like it anymore."

"Then we won't ask you any more about it," declared Hauviette, who loved Jeanne dearly. "And we won't tease you about it, either. So there now, Mengette!"

"Oh, if she doesn't feel like it, that's different," exclaimed Mengette, who in her own way was also fond of Jeanne. "But I wish you did, Jeanne. Games aren't nearly as much fun without you. But I won't say any more about it. Maybe you'll change your mind later."

The two girls didn't mention the matter again, although the change in Jeanne became more and more marked as the days went by. Winter was almost over when at last Jeanne learned what her mission was to be.

It was a cold morning, and Jeanne had gone to early mass, which was her usual practice. Few people were present, and the church was cold and dark. Father Frontey smiled tenderly when he saw the small figure in its usual place and Jeanne's heart glowed in the sunshine of his approval. After church she started on her short walk home across the courtyard, feeling in an exalted frame of mind. To her, going to mass was like eating bread and meat. Then, all at once, the light came.

This time it was more splendid than ever before, glowing with hues that stained the snowy ground with rosy tints. From the dazzling radiance emerged the form of Saint Michael, clothed in transcendent grandeur and holding a flaming sword high above his head. Around him gathered bands of angels, the heavenly hosts whose leader he was. At the sight of his great majesty Jeanne felt a shiver of fear run through her; she sank trembling to her knees and covered her face with her hands.

Then from his lips came the tender and familiar sound: "Be good, Jeanne, and God will help you." Her fear and her trembling subsided.

With infinite gentleness the archangel began to speak to her of France, and the "pity the King of Heaven had for it." He told her the story of her suffering country, how the English invader had taken over the capital city of Paris; how he had gained all of the country north of the Loire; how France, battered from the outside, was also torn and bleeding on the inside from the ferocious feud between the Duke of Burgundy and the disinherited Dauphin; how great French noblemen robbed their own country when they should have defended her; and how bands of mercenaries roved and plundered the countryside. He told her that the Dauphin, the rightful king, would soon be forced to flee the country, and the French nation would no longer exist.

The young girl's heart, already sad over the woes of her distressed country, swelled almost to bursting as she heard the story told from angelic lips. The "great pity" that he spoke of went straight to her heart, and she felt it in every chord of her sensitive nature. The great angel concluded abruptly: "Daughter of God, it is you who must go to help the King of France, and it is you who will give him back his kingdom."

Jeanne sprang to her feet, astounded.

"I, sir? I?"

"You must travel forth into France to do this. Haven't you heard that France, ruined by a woman, shall be restored by a maiden? You are the Maid."

Terrified and weeping, the girl fell down before him.

"Not I, sir. Oh, not I. I cannot be."

"You are the Maid," he said again.

When she at last looked up, Jeanne found herself alone.

CHAPTER 9

THE CHARGE IS ACCEPTED

"You are the Maid."

Over and over Jeanne repeated the words. It was unbelievable that she had been chosen for such a divine commission. She was a poor, uneducated girl, with no friends in high places. She knew nothing about war, or the king's court, or politics. Why, she didn't even know exactly where the court was. Common sense told her that she could not be the one chosen to restore the king to his rightful place. True, the ancient prophecy of Merlin the Magician said that a maid would come from this very region to save France. But she couldn't be the one. It was impossible!

The great archangel came again and again bearing the same message. Time after time he said: "Daughter of God, you will lead the Dauphin to Reims where he may receive his rightful crown."

Again and again Jeanne meekly protested and replied tearfully: "I am but a poor girl, sir. I am too young to leave my father and mother. I cannot ride a horse or even lift a lance. How could I lead soldiers in the field?

"You will be told everything you have to do," the archangel replied.

As time passed, and Jeanne grew older, two great principles gradually grew up within her until they filled every fiber of her being: the love of God, and the desire to do something great to help her country. The burden of France lay heavy upon her. Her heart ached and she could think of nothing but her country's suffering.

The voices of her heavenly visitors grew stronger and stronger; the more ardent their message, the holier and more heroic Jeanne's soul became. She began to see how the miraculous suggestion was possible. France lay bruised and bleeding under the heel of the English invader. Truly, only a miracle could help her country now.

Although Jeanne still resisted, she was always thinking of how the assigned task might be accomplished. Months passed. Then, one day in May of 1428, she made up her mind. She was sixteen now, strong and graceful and of extraordinary beauty.

It was a Saturday, and as was her custom Jeanne set out for the chapel of old castle to visit the statue of the Virgin Mary. Jeanne walked through the neighboring village of Greux and then climbed the hill above the town. The path was overgrown with grass, vines, and old fruit trees. The chapel stood on the deeply forested brow of the hill. Jeanne found herself alone that day, the only worshiper. She fell to her knees before the statue, and remained in prayer for a long while. Then, feeling comforted and strengthened, she rose to her feet and left the chapel. She stood on the wooded plateau, gazing thoughtfully off into the valley below. She was waiting for something.

Her uplifted face reflected all the serenity and purity of her spiritual nature. She did not have long to wait. Jeanne was no longer afraid of her visitors, and when Saint Michael appeared Jeanne knelt and reverently kissed the ground upon which he stood.

"Daughter of God," he said, "you must go to the court now. You must go. You must."

For a moment Jeanne said nothing. She knew that the command must be obeyed. She had sought out her saints that day to tell them she accepted their charge. But when she thought of leaving her father and mother, her friends, and her village, her courage faltered. She made a last faint protest: "I am so young," she said. "So young to leave my parents. I can sew and spin, but I cannot lead soldiers. If God wills it, then I—" Her voice broke and she bent her head low in submission.

At her words, the wonderful light burst into a marvelous brilliancy. The kneeling maiden was drenched in its dazzling radiance, and she was filled with a soft, warm glow. In that instant, the faith was born in her that she could accomplish anything her Voices commanded. That belief never left her again. When the archangel spoke again he addressed her as a sister: "Rise, daughter of God," he said. "This is what you must do: go at once to Robert de Baudricourt, captain of Vaucouleurs, and he will take you to the Dauphin. Saint Margaret and Saint Catherine will help you."

Jeanne rose to her feet, no longer the timid, shrinking peasant girl, but Jeanne D'Arc, Maid of France, with her heart and soul dedicated to her country. The time had come for her to go forth to fulfill her incredible destiny.

She knew now that God had chosen her, and that through Him she could win back France from the enemy and set the crown on the head of the rightful king.

It was late when Jeanne finally made her way down the hill path and on to the fields of Domremy. She passed Pierre working in one of the meadows. As he wielded the hoe, he sang a verse from the *Song of Roland*, the poem every Frenchman knew by heart.

> Our bravest men lie dead on the fields;
> Well may we weep for fair France
> Which her noble barons have betrayed.

Jeanne felt thrilled as she heard it. Did Pierre too feel for their suffering country? She ran up to him and threw her arm across his shoulder, singing with him:

> In life or death, let's think the same,
> That gentle France never be brought to shame.

Pierre smiled at her. "How you sing, Jeanne. As though you'd go out and fight for France yourself."

"I would," she replied quickly. "Wouldn't you, Pierrelot?"

Something in her tone of voice made Pierre look at her keenly. "How your eyes shine," he said. "Somehow you seem different. What is it, Jeanne? Is it the song?"

"Partly," she said.

"It does make a fellow's heart leap." Pierre spoke thoughtfully. "It always makes me feel like dropping everything to go out to fight the English and the Burgundians."

"We'll go together, Pierre," Jeanne said softly. "We—"

"What's that about fighting?" demanded their father, who had quietly come up to them. "We'll have no more of that kind of talk. Pierre, that field must be finished by sundown. Jeanne, your mother needs you in the house. There's no time for dawdling and singing, you two."

"Yes, father," they replied. Jeanne started at once toward the cottage, and Pierre bent to his hoe.

Pierre quickly forgot about his conversation with Jeanne, but Jacques D'Arc was troubled by what he had overheard. The following morning he came to breakfast, but was too worried to eat. He pushed back from the table without touching his food.

"What ails you, Jacques?" Isabeau asked. "You shouldn't start the day on an empty stomach."

"Shall I get you some fresh water, father?" Jeanne asked.

Jacques turned upon her quickly, scowling. "I dreamed about you last night," he growled.

"Of me, father?" Jeanne faltered, shrinking away from him.

"I dreamed I saw you riding in the midst of men-at-arms."

At this both Jean and Pierre laughed.

"Jeanne with soldiers?" exclaimed Jean. "Why, she would run at the sight of a lance."

But their father wasn't laughing. According to his belief, there was only one way to interpret the dream. Many women followed soldiers in those days, but they were thought of as bad women. Jacques brought his fist down on the table with a loud thwack. "I'd have you boys drown her in the river than have such a thing happen," he roared. "And if you won't do it, I'll do it myself."

Jeanne turned pale. Instantly, she realized that she must not tell her father of the mission assigned to her. He would never believe her.

At this point, Isabeau broke in. "How you talk, Jacques. What a bother to make over a dream. Come now! Eat your breakfast and forget about it."

But Jacques only repeated his words fiercely: "I would drown her rather than have a daughter of mine living among soldiers."

Jeanne glanced at her brothers. Their faces were grave now, for they understood their father's meaning. Suddenly a sense of isolation came over Jeanne and she felt as if she were no longer part of her own family. Tears ran down her cheeks. To hide her grief, she rose quickly and ran to her room.

One at a time, the children knelt by the Gooseberry Spring
and drank deeply of the transparent water.
Page 6

The saints visited her nearly every day. Often they
appeared in the little garden.
Page 36

CHAPTER 10

THE FIRST STEP

From this time on, Jeanne's family began to notice an even greater change in her bearing and appearance. Her eyes glowed with an inner light and her serene expression seemed to illuminate even the coldest morning. She was still simple in manner, but her shrinking timidity had vanished. She carried an air of authority and purpose about her. She walked tall, as if she were a leader on a divine mission, which in fact she was. None of this was planned by Jeanne. All she thought about was how she could accomplish her task. There were three things she had to do to save her country.

First, she must go to Robert de Baudricourt at Vaucouleurs.

Second, she must win back France from her enemies.

Third, she must lead the Dauphin to Reims, the historic place where all of France's kings were crowned.

She knew what she must do, but had no idea how to do it.

Vaucouleurs, the principal town of the region, lay some twelve miles north of Domremy. Its governor, Robert de Baudricourt, was well known in the valley. He was a blunt, practical man who had married two rich widows in succession, which gave him a certain amount of authority in the district. He was also a man of the sword; Baudricourt had been bravely fighting in the reckless wars in and around Lorraine since he was old enough to bear arms. His coarse and domineering personality made him an ideal soldier for his time. Jacques D'Arc had had dealings with Baudricourt the year before when Jacques appeared before Baudricourt to represent the village of Domremy in a local dispute. Jacques had told his children many tales of the rough captain. Knowing his reputation, how could Jeanne approach such a man?

She knew her father wouldn't help her on this mission. Nor would her mother go against her father's will. Neither of her parents would allow her to travel to Vaucouleurs alone. One by one, she considered every citizen of Domremy, trying to think of someone who might help her. She sadly rejected every one. Clearly, she must bide her time.

"But I can't wait long," she thought. "God wants me to go."

At this point, fate intervened in the person of Durand Lassois, Jeanne's cousin by marriage, whom she called uncle because he was so much older than she. Durand came to Domremy on a visit, and Jeanne knew at once that here was the help she needed. Durand lived in Bury le Petit, a hamlet on the river nine miles from Domremy, but only three miles from Vaucouleurs.

Jeanne took him aside and asked him to take her home with him to visit his young wife, who was Isabeau's niece. Durand, who was fond of Jeanne, quickly agreed.

"Aveline hasn't been well, Jeanne," he said. "She'll be so happy to see you."

Jacques D'Arc objected at first, but Isabeau overruled him. "It will be good for her to get away for a while, Jacques," she said. "The child needs a change. I wonder why we didn't think of sending her there ourselves."

"Only for a week, then," said Jacques.

"A week is better than nothing," said Durand. "Don't worry, Jacques. We'll take good care of her."

So a few days later Durand and Jeanne started for Bury le Petit, taking the hill path beyond Greux. As they walked through the forest, fragrant with the breath of spring, Jeanne said abruptly: "Uncle Durand, while I'm at your house, I want you to take me to Vaucouleurs to see Robert de Baudricourt."

"You want me to do what?" he asked, open-mouthed.

"Take me to Vaucouleurs to see Robert de Baudricourt."

"What for?" he demanded, staring at her hard.

"So that he may send me to France to lead the Dauphin to Reims, that he may be crowned king there."

A bewildered expression came into Durand's honest face. He passed his hand across his brow.

"Perhaps we're walking too fast," he said gently. "Your mother said that you haven't been feeling well, and sometimes the sun plays tricks on the mind."

Jeanne wasn't surprised at his response. "I'm not crazy, uncle," she said, "and I don't have sunstroke. Have you heard the prophecy that a woman would lose France, but a maid would save France?"

"I've heard it," admitted Durand slowly. "What are you trying to say, Jeanne?"

"I am that maid, uncle. I shall save France." She spoke in a tone of quiet conviction.

Durand took a long breath and stared at her. He had known Jeanne all of her short life. He knew of her good deeds, her purity and truthfulness; he knew that her only fault was going to church too often. Now, as he looked into her clear eyes and observed her calm manner, he knew that she believed what she said. Whatever the nature of her affliction, she wasn't mad.

"You must believe me, uncle," she pleaded. "Haven't I always been truthful?"

He nodded.

"I am telling the truth now. God has called me to win back France from her enemies, and to lead the Dauphin to be crowned at Reims. I've been instructed to ask Robert de Baudricourt to escort me to the Dauphin. But I have to reach Vaucouleurs. Will you help me?"

Durand was speechless. Jeanne told him everything, all about her heavenly visitors and her mission. She spoke with such sincerity and assurance that, in spite of himself, Durand believed her. It was an age when many people did believe that angelic hosts visited the pure and good.

Durand suddenly said, "All right. I'll take you to Vaucouleurs. Your father won't like it, though. Have you thought of that?"

"I know, uncle, but it is the will of God. I must go," she said.

Durand crossed himself. There was such a look of exaltation about Jeanne's whole person that he felt as though he were in church.

"I'll take you, Jeanne," he repeated. "But don't say a word about this when we reach my house. Neither Aveline nor her parents would believe you."

"Many people won't believe me, uncle." Jeanne sighed, and thought of her own dear ones at Domremy. "Even Robert de Baudricourt won't."

"Then why go to him for help?"

"I was commanded," she answered. "Later he will believe."

So they agreed on their plan and completed the journey to Durand's home. Durand Lassois and his young wife lived with her parents. Aveline's mother was Isabeau's sister. Both mother and daughter were so happy to see Jeanne that they kept her close to them for most of the week. Finally, on the fourth day, Durand Lassois found an excuse to go into nearby Bury le Petit and invited Jeanne to walk along with him.

"Go ahead," Aveline said. "But don't stay away too long."

Jeanne's heart was beating hard as they left Bury le Petit behind, and set out on the short, three-mile walk to Vaucouleurs. Although she had lived all her life in this valley, she had never seen the grim little fighting town where Robert de Baudricourt stubbornly held off the Burgundians.

The hills pressed down almost right on top of the walled town; inside the walls, low buildings clustered around the base of a hill upon which stood a church and the captain's castle.

Jeanne and Durand climbed one of the narrow streets leading up to the castle. As usual, the gates were open, allowing anyone to enter. Soldiers were scattered about the courtyard, laughing and talking as they polished their armor and sharpened their swords. They cast curious glances at the rustic countryman and the fair girl crossing the courtyard, but allowed them to pass into the antechamber of the castle.

"Shall I speak to Sir Robert first?" asked Durand. He felt awkward and uncomfortable entering the castle, and secretly he hoped that the captain would refuse to see them. Jeanne shook her head.

"Let's go together, uncle," she said. Turning to the page who stood at the entrance, she said, "Go to Sir Robert and tell him that Jeanne, the Maid, comes with her uncle and would like to speak with him."

"Wait here," the page said pertly. "My master is eating."

"Take the message now," Jeanne said firmly. "My Lord's business is important and must be attended to now."

The insolent youth's manner became more respectful, and he bowed quickly and started off. He returned shortly, saying, "The captain says you may come in. This way."

They followed him through a long, winding passageway into a large banquet hall. There, at a long table that ran the full length of the hall, sat all the officers of the garrison. At the far end of this table, raised up on a platform, was another, smaller table. Here, four men sat eating, one a brawny, gray-haired man whom Jeanne knew at once was Sir Robert.

Durand Lassois felt shy and ill at ease among so many noblemen; he stopped just inside the door, awkwardly twirling his cap in his hand. But Jeanne, who used to tremble and blush in front of strangers, walked up to the head table.

The captain gaped when he saw her step boldly forward. She was wearing the ordinary red homespun frock that all peasant girls wore, and her abundant hair was hidden by a close-fitting white cap. But her beauty shone out. Seeing her, Robert de Baudricourt softened his usually harsh voice: "Welcome, child. What do you want from me?"

"I'm here because the Great Sire told me to come to you, Sir Robert," she answered fearlessly, "so you may tell the Dauphin to get ready for his coronation."

Sir Robert was shocked. He leaned forward and looked keenly into Jeanne's face. She continued calmly: "It is the Great Sire's wish that the Dauphin become King of France. He has sent me to lead him to his crowning."

A moment of silence followed this startling announcement. The officers dining at the table looked embarrassed, their faces full of pity for the demented girl.

"And who is this Great Sire?" asked Sir Robert.

"He is the King of Heaven."

Now it so happened that the men had just been discussing the war. Rumors were flying that the English were preparing to attack the region south of the Loire valley, and the Burgundians were set to attack that little wedge of loyal territory in which Vaucouleurs lay.

That a young peasant girl, accompanied by her rustic uncle, should calmly tell them that she was ready to straighten out the complex difficulties of distressed France seemed like a huge joke. Sir Robert gave out a great shout of laughter and his men laughed along with him. He was not a sentimental man, but he liked a good joke, and the rafters rang with his coarse laughter. When his merriment subsided, he turned to Durand.

"Is this girl your daughter?" he asked.

"No," replied Durand, shaking in his boots. "She is the daughter of Jacques D'Arc."

"So?" Sir Robert looked at Jeanne with new interest. "I'll tell you, the girl is daft; clean daft. Whip her and send her home to her father."

Whip her? Durand Lassois turned a startled glance upon the captain. Whip Jeanne, who was so good and sweet? Frightened, he grasped Jeanne's arm.

"Come," he whispered. "Let's go now."

But calmly, courageously, Jeanne faced the captain.

"I'll go, Sir Robert, but I shall come back. You are the one the Great Sire chose to take me to the Dauphin. My Voices have said so, and so it is."

They knew she must be mad, but even so, the captain and his men were impressed by the girl's quiet gravity and noble bearing. Without saying another word, they allowed Jeanne and Durand Lassois to leave the room.

CHAPTER 11

A TRYING TIME

At the end of the week, Durand Lassois took Jeanne back to Domremy. Their trip was not a happy one. Word of their visit to Sir Robert had gotten around; the soldiers at the garrison had spread the story to the townspeople, and from there the story had leaked out into the countryside, and eventually to Domremy. The whole valley buzzed with talk of Jeanne's claim that she would lead the Dauphin to his crowning. By the time Lassois and Jeanne reached the village, an enraged Jacques D'Arc was waiting for them at the cottage door.

"What's this about visiting Sir Robert de Baudricourt?" he demanded. "Why did you go there? What business did you have?"

Jeanne faced him bravely. "I had to go," she said calmly. "It was commanded. Sir Robert has been chosen to give me soldiers to accompany me to the Dauphin, so I may then lead him to his coronation. I am to save France, father. It is commanded by the King of Heaven."

Her father's jaw dropped. He stood staring at her, then turned to his wife with a groan.

"She's lost her senses, Isabeau," he cried. "Our daughter's wits are wandering. This is what happens with so much church going and prayer. I'll have no more of it."

"Shame on you, Jacques. It's not the church's fault. She's been listening to too many stories about bloodshed and war, right here at home. I warned you about it."

"I don't care what caused it," Jacques said vehemently. "I want no more of this talk about the Dauphin. And no more visits to Vaucouleurs. Do you hear me, Jeanne?"

"Yes, father," she answered quietly. "I don't want to disobey, but I must do the work the Lord has asked. Let me tell you—"

"No! Tell me nothing," cried Jacques. "Go to your room and stay there for the rest of the day.

"Listen to me," he added, turning to make a sweeping gesture that included his wife and sons, "wherever Jeanne goes, one of you will go with her. Give her no chance to go off with any band of roaming soldiers. I'd rather she were dead."

Jeanne, weeping bitterly at his harsh words, obediently went into her own little room. Jacques D'Arc now turned fiercely on Durand Lassois.

"And you, Lassois! Why did you let her go to Vaucouleurs? You knew I wouldn't like it. And you knew it would cause talk. Why did you permit it?"

"Yes, I knew all that, Jacques," responded Durand, shifting uneasily from one foot to the other. "But Jeanne really believes that she has received a divine command to go to Sir Robert. I think she would have gone to him no matter how hard I tried to stop her. Wasn't it better that I take her there myself?"

"He's right, Jacques," Isabeau said. "The child is clearly daft, and you can't argue with a crazy person. What's past is past. She's has been to Vaucouleurs, and it cannot be undone now. What we can do is to protect her against any future wanderings."

Isabeau was as distressed as her husband, but in order to reassure him she tried to speak calmly.

"True enough," muttered Jacques. "I suppose you had to do what you did, Durand, but I still don't understand."

"I don't think Jeanne is out of her senses," Durand said. "Remember the legend that a Maid from the Bois Chesnu will save France? It might as well be Jeanne as anyone else. She is holy enough."

"Ridiculous! Isabeau is right. Jeanne's been listening to too many tales of war and legends about the wonderful Maid. It can't be her. She is only a peasant girl, and she's never even ridden a horse or carried a lance. Don't let such wild talk addle your wits, too, Durand. Now, tell me everything that happened at Vaucouleurs. The village rings with gossip of the affair. I want the whole truth."

Durand Lassois told Jacques and Isabeau the whole story. Facing Jeanne's disbelieving parents had shaken his confidence, but he tried to tell the tale with sympathy for his niece. Jacques listened in stony silence; then, when Durand had finished, he leaned his head on his arms.

Jacques D'Arc was an honorable man, esteemed in his village. He was fond of his children and brought them up strictly. He himself aspired for nothing out of the ordinary and wanted his children to grow into conventional and upright men and women. He did not for a moment believe that his daughter had received a divine command. He didn't know about Jeanne's heavenly visitors, and wouldn't have believed in them if he had known. He thought that somehow Jeanne had taken it into her head to travel with soldiers and he feared she would become a bad woman. The mere idea filled him with pain. At last he lifted up his head.

"She told Sir Robert she would come back?" he asked.

"Yes, Jacques. She believes that she has been commanded to do so. She told you that. Jeanne will do whatever she thinks God wants."

"She's deluded," Jacques said curtly. "Do you really think the captain would listen to her if she went back?"

Durand thought it over. "No," he said. "I don't think he'll pay any attention to her."

Jacques brightened. "Good," he said. "She won't be going anywhere if I can prevent it. I'll guard her well."

After that, Jeanne's every move was carefully watched by a member of her family. Her father, who had always had a soft spot for her, was now always severe and harsh. Her mother, too, though never cruel, often spoke sharply. Isabeau knew her daughter's pure heart too well to believe ill of her, but she did think that Jeanne's wits were wandering. However, as she watched Jeanne continue to perform her customary duties with care and exactness, she worried even more. What could be wrong?

Except for Mengette and Hauviette, everyone in the village avoided Jeanne. Whenever she appeared in the narrow streets, villagers bent their heads together, gossiping and pointing their fingers. Jeanne could hear them whispering: "There goes she who is to save France." "Jeanne D'Arc says she is to lead the Dauphin to his crowning."

It was a bad time. On the outside, Jeanne appeared serene and untroubled, meekly submitting to the gossip and jibes of her neighbors. But when she was alone at night, she shed many secret tears over these jeers and taunts. Life would have been unendurable without her Voices.

"Be patient, daughter of God," they said. "It will not be long. All will be well. Your time will come soon."

One day, after being stung by some remark he had heard against her, Jacques scolded Jeanne severely. The Maid looked sad and despondent.

"You mustn't be angry with your father, Jeanne," said her mother. "He is cut to the heart, and grieves over you."

"I'm not angry," Jeanne answered sadly. "I know he doesn't understand. You don't understand either, but someday you will." Jeanne, who loved her parents dearly, had often tried to explain herself to them, but they wouldn't listen.

"We understand too well," responded Isabeau. "Jacques is afraid you'll try to see Sir Robert again. I've told him you won't." She gave Jeanne a questioning glance.

"I must, mother. It is commanded."

"Jeanne, stop such talk," exclaimed her mother sharply. "Where did you get such ideas? The neighbors say they've seen you alone at the Fairy Tree hanging wreaths, and that you met a wicked fairy there who put a curse on you. Is it true?"

"If there are fairies, mother, I have never seen them. And I haven't carried wreaths to the tree in years. The only wreaths I carry are the flowers I bring to the altar of Our Lady in the Chapel of Belmont, or to our own church here."

"Then why are people talking so?" asked her mother fretfully. "If you would stop talking about helping the Dauphin, perhaps this gossip would stop. Your father is distressed over your stubbornness. He's even asked the priest to exorcise the evil spirit from you."

"Did my father do that?" exclaimed Jeanne, tears springing to her eyes.

"Oh, it won't happen." Isabeau herself had interfered. In fact, she was as worried about her husband as she was about Jeanne. "Father Frontey refused," Isabeau continued. "He said your soul was as pure as a lily, whatever the state of your wits."

Isabeau paused again and looked at her daughter. She was puzzled and a little awed by Jeanne's new attitude. Then she went on abruptly: "I was married when I was your age, Jeanne."

"Were you, mother?" A light smile stirred the corners of Jeanne's mouth. She knew what was coming next.

"Yes, and Mengette has been engaged since Easter. She is going to be married after the harvest."

"She told me, mother."

"Of all the girls your age, you and Hauviette are the only ones who aren't married or engaged. Hauviette is a little younger than the rest, so she has some excuse. But you are sixteen and quite old enough to have a home and husband of your own."

"Mother! You mustn't speak to me of marriage. I cannot marry until my task is finished. I have promised my Voices."

"Don't be silly! A home and husband to look after will make you forget these silly ideas. I've told your father. Be reasonable. I know someone who would be perfect—"

"Not while France writhes in agony under the heel of the invader," Jeanne said firmly, turning to leave the room.

"Whether you like it or not, you shall be married," cried Isabeau. "Your father has decided. Your future husband comes to see you tonight."

Jeanne was stunned. She never dreamed her parents would go so far. She quietly answered: "I've pledged my faith to my Lord. I cannot give it to any man until His mission is completed. It's no good talking about it." Again she started to leave the room.

"Nevertheless, Colin de Greux is coming here this evening," said Isabeau, thoroughly exasperated with her daughter.

Colin? The merry nature that lay just below Jeanne's grave demeanor surged up and her eyes twinkled. Suddenly, she laughed outright. Her mother glanced at her quickly, surprised and relieved.

"There! That's better," she said. "He'll be here after supper."

"It doesn't matter, mother."

There was something in Jeanne's tone that disturbed Isabeau, but at least things seemed to be turning out better than she had hoped. She was determined to make the best of it.

Colin de Greux did come calling right after supper. He was grown up and nice-looking, still the same easygoing, clownish sort of fellow he had always been. Ordinarily, Colin would never have been Isabeau's first choice for Jeanne, but she was desperate to find her daughter a husband. Most of the

village lads had grown shy of Jeanne because of her extreme piety, and now the
gossip made them even shyer than before. Right now, given Jeanne's fanciful
behavior, her parents had decided that marriage to Colin, who could be easily
manipulated, was better than no marriage at all.

Jeanne immediately saw through all this and was determined to make short
work of the marriage plan. When evening came, she took a hoe and went into
the garden. This is where Colin found her, working hard among the artichoke
plants.

"How do you do, Jeanne?" he said sheepishly.

"Very well indeed, Colin." Jeanne continued hoeing vigorously, seemingly
absorbed in her task.

Silence fell between them. There was something about Jeanne's manner
that made the young man uncomfortable.

"It certainly is warm out here," he finally said.

"Perhaps you'll be cooler in the house," Jeanne said sweetly.

"But the whole family is in there," Colin said, and looked toward the bend
under an apple tree. The young men and women of Domremy were always
permitted to sit together when the suitor was approved by the parents.

"Why, yes, Colin, you'll find all the family in the house. Did you wish to see
them?"

"No, I don't wish to see them," he said angrily. "I wish to talk to you,
Jeanne."

"I'm listening." Jeanne finished the row she was hoeing, and moved over to
the next. The tall heads of the artichokes nodded stiffly between the two
young people.

"Your father said I could talk to you. But how can I talk while you're
hoeing?" he exclaimed.

Jeanne laid down the hoe and looked directly at her old playmate. "Colin,"
she said seriously, "mother told me you were coming and why. But it's no use.
I cannot marry. There are plenty of other girls in the village who would gladly
marry you."

"I don't want any other girl but you, Jeanne. I've always liked you, and you
know it. Besides, your father—"

"You cannot marry a girl against her will, Colin, and I shall not marry you. I
am speaking plainly so you will understand that I'm serious and stop wasting
your time."

"But your father says you will," the boy muttered.

Without a word Jeanne turned away and ran into the church. She was safe there because her mother wouldn't allow her to be disturbed if she was at prayer. Sulkily Colin went back into the house.

Colin didn't give up his courtship. Encouraged by Jeanne's parents, he frequently came calling after supper. Somehow all of his pretty speeches, along with his confidence, shriveled when he came face to face with Jeanne. For her part, Jeanne went serenely about her business, ignoring her father's demands and her mother's pleading to marry the lad.

The days sped by.

CHAPTER 12

A DEFEATED SUITOR

A new rumor soon displaced interest in Jeanne D'Arc, her mission, and Colin's wooing. It was said that Antoine de Vergy, Governor of Champagne, had received orders from the Duke of Bedford, the English regent, to raise an army and bring the city of Vaucouleurs under English rule. The rumor was confirmed when de Vergy and his men marched out from Champagne, laying waste to all the villages in their path. Domremy and Greux lay in the southern part of the targeted area, between Bar and Champagne, and was directly in the line of attack. Threatened again with a disaster, the people of the two villages held a meeting to decide how best to protect themselves.

Men, women, and children gathered in front of the little church to discuss the situation, and their faces showed they fully understood the menace. Their liberty and property were all in danger, even their very lives; everything would be swept away by the ravaging Antoine. The nearness of the danger made them numb, but it was the numbness of despair. Resistance was out of the question. What could they do?

"Why not retire to the castle?" asked Father Frontey. "It's been a refuge before. Isn't it a secure stronghold?"

"We are afraid it isn't, father," responded one man. "Antoine boasts that we cannot hold it against him, since he knows a secret passage to enter whenever he chooses. We have searched for the passageway but we cannot find it, although we're certain it exists."

"Then what can we do?" asked the priest.

"We can do this," answered Jacques D'Arc, suddenly elbowing his way through the crowd until he stood by the priest's side in full view. "We can gather our furniture in carts and drive our cattle and sheep in front of us to Neufchâteau. The town belongs to the Burgundians, so it will be safe from English attack, but its sympathies are with the Armagnacs."

"That's it, Jacques!" "Well said!" the villages cried in a chorus of approval. "When shall we go?"

"Better today than tomorrow, friends," shouted Jacques. "Better now than later. We don't know when they will be upon us."

"Right, Jacques," came the cries of agreement. The people hurried to gather up their goods and cattle. It was all disorder and confusion as men and boys ran to the fields for the flocks and herds, which were quickly driven into the main road; women stripped their linen chests and cupboards, quickly piling their furnishings into oxcarts.

Isabeau cried as she worked, for she knew if they ever returned they might find the cottage burned and the village devastated. She had always known war. Her mother and her grandmother had known it. For ninety-one years battles had raged, and the end was not in sight. France was a wreck, a ruin, a desolation. Throughout the land there was nothing but pillage, robbery, murder, cruel tyranny, even burning of churches and abbeys. Seeing her mother's grief, Jeanne went to her and put her arms around her.

"Don't be sad, mother," she said. "Before many more years have passed, the war will end. This is the last time you will ever have to flee from your home."

Isabeau brushed away her tears and looked at her daughter. "Why do you speak this way, Jeanne?" she asked. "It's as though you knew the future."

"Yes, mother, I do know. It will be as I say. Now, let's get the rest of the furniture into the cart. Father is getting impatient."

Isabeau felt comforted. She dried her eyes and perked up. Jacques came in and seeing Jeanne so helpful spoke gently to her in his old, tender manner. Jeanne's heart felt lighter than it had since her return from Bury le Petit.

The animals were already in the road; the oxcarts piled high with the belongings of the villagers were drawn up behind them. The women and children stood ready, waiting for the word to depart. Suddenly, a man-at-arms rode among them, crying: "Go! Go while there is time. Vaucouleurs has been attacked and Antoine is leading a group of men this way."

Before the villagers had time to ask questions, he was gone. With despairing looks at the homes they were abandoning, the people of the village started toward Neufchâteau, a market town five miles to the south of Domremy. The day was very hot, and the refugees wearily followed the road through fields of wheat and rye, up vine-clad hills, to the town, where each family searched for lodging. Jacques took his family to an inn kept by a woman named La Rousse.

Only a few hours later, Antoine de Vergy's men swept into Domremy and Greux, and both villages were destroyed.

For Jeanne, the days that followed were tranquil and happy. As she had in Domremy, she now drove her father's animals to the fields around Neufchâteau and tended his flocks. She also helped La Rousse around the house. And when she was not helping her hostess or tending the cattle, she was in church.

During the first few days of their stay in the market town, Jeanne saw Colin frequently, but to her great relief he did not press his attentions on her. Then after a while she did not see him at all.

One day, after dinner in the large common room, the inn's few guests had separated into small groups. On a gray day the large room, with its dusky walls and blackened beams, would have looked gloomy, but on a day such as this the midsummer heat and bright sunshine made the darkened room seem cool and restful.

Jeanne sat quietly in the nook of the huge projecting chimney, waiting for the guests to leave so she could clear away the dinner. There came a knock at the outside door at the far end of the room. Before Jeanne could reach it, the door swung open and a priest entered. Always reverent in her attitude toward priests, Jeanne bowed before him.

"Would you like to eat dinner, father?" she asked.

"Later, my child," he replied. "First, I want to speak with a maiden called Jeanne, the daughter of Jacques D'Arc."

"I am she," said Jeanne in astonishment. "What do you want with me, father?"

At that moment Isabeau and La Rousse entered the room. La Rousse hurried forward to welcome the newcomer, but she paused, stopped by his words: "I come from the Bishop of Toul, Judge of the Ecclesiastical Court having jurisdiction over Domremy and Greux. He commands you, Jeanne, daughter of Jacques D'Arc, to appear before him to show cause why you should not marry Colin de Greux."

Through the large room the lingering guests buzzed among themselves. Everyone it seems had heard something of Colin's courtship.

Jeanne stood dumbfounded. So this was what Colin had been up to, she thought. And what about her parents? Were they part of this scheme? She turned and looked at them searchingly. Isabeau could not meet her daughter's eyes, but Jacques met her glance steadily. Father and daughter gazed into each other's eyes, Jeanne with sorrowful reproach, Jacques with grim determination. Then slowly Jeanne turned to the priest.

"When does the bishop wish to see me?" she asked.

"Two days from now. If you cannot show why your pledge to Colin should not be kept, the pledge stands and you shall be married at once."

Jeanne nodded in acknowledgment and started to leave the room. Isabeau ran to her.

"It's for your own good, little one. Now you will always be near us. And Colin will make a kind husband."

Jeanne did not answer. As she passed through the door she heard her mother say: "She is as good as married, Jacques. She is too shy, too gentle, to protest against it. She will do whatever the bishop tells her without question."

"Don't be too sure of that," said La Rousse before Jacques could reply. "These gentle maids have a way of turning at times, and Jeanne has spirit."

"She has always been obedient, and will be now," said Jacques with confidence. "Except for this wild fancy of going to the Dauphin, she has always been dutiful."

"Sometimes the gentlest maid will turn if pressed too hard," La Rousse repeated.

And this was exactly what happened. Jeanne was filled with sorrow that her parents should take Colin's side in trying to force her into marriage. Briefly, she despaired, for it was against her nature and training to protest against those in authority. And then her soul rose up against it.

"I will not be forced to marry," she decided suddenly. "I will go to Toul and tell the bishop the truth. I will go."

Then she heard her Voices. "Go, daughter of God, and fear nothing, for we will help you."

Jeanne was up before dawn to prepare for the journey. She knew that the main gates leading from the inn's courtyard would still be closed, but there was a small door at the back of the inn that opened directly into the street. Jeanne reached the door unseen and went out. It was thirty miles to Toul, a dangerous journey on foot through the war-torn countryside; she might be set upon at any moment by roving bands of armed men. But Jeanne had the courage of desperation. She feared the marriage more than anything else, and if she did not protest in person there would be no getting out of it. Knowing that her saints were with her, she made the long trip in safety, arriving that evening at Toul, footsore and weary but with a peaceful heart.

Many churches graced the old town and, according to her custom, Jeanne at once went to a chapel and prayed before a statue of the Virgin Mary. Then she went to find food and lodging. She soon found shelter with a humble family, and since she was never idle wherever she was, she immediately made friends by helping around the house and sewing and spinning. The next morning she went to see the bishop.

Colin was already in the chapel, where the bishop was sitting. The youth's self-satisfied expression turned to surprise when he saw Jeanne, for he had never supposed she would appear to contest the action. Many people from Domremy were present to act as Colin's witnesses.

Colin told the bishop that Jeanne had been betrothed to him since childhood. Jeanne was amazed to hear the villagers affirm that they knew such an engagement existed. After they had spoken, the bishop turned to the girl and said kindly: "And where is your counsel, my child?"

"I have none, Your Excellency." Jeanne raised her eyes to the bishop's. "I need none. I only have to speak the truth, isn't that so?"

"That is all, but—" The bishop paused and looked attentively at the slender maiden. She did not look like a peasant, either in her bearing or in her appearance. And she did not have the manner of someone who would give her word and then disregard it.

"Proceed," he said. "Let her take the oath. Put both hands on the Bible and swear that you will answer truthfully the questions that will be asked."

Kneeling before him, Jeanne laid her hands on the Bible, and said simply, "I swear."

Then she recited her name, her country, and the names of her parents, godmothers, and godfathers.

"And now, my child, tell me about this promise of marriage to Colin de Greux," the bishop asked.

"I never promised to marry him or any other man," she answered.

"Have you witnesses to prove this?"

"There are my friends and neighbors, Your Excellency. They will speak for me."

The judge leaned forward. "They have spoken against you, child. Didn't you hear them say that they knew of your engagement to Colin?"

"Yes, sir, but I would like to question them."

"Go ahead," he said. "It is your right."

So, one by one, they were recalled to the stand while Jeanne asked three questions of each of them:

Had he seen her at any of the dances or merrymakings with Colin?

Had he seen her at church, or any public place, with Colin?

Had he ever heard her, Jeanne, speak of being engaged to Colin?

To these questions the witnesses all had to answer "No."

"Your Excellency, if I were betrothed to this man, wouldn't I go with him to church, to dances, or to other public places?"

"It would seem so, my child; but why would he take this action if he didn't have cause?"

"I have always found my greatest happiness, sir, in going to church and in prayer. And I have received a command from my Lord, the King of Heaven, to perform a certain task. Because of that I went to see Robert de Baudricourt of Vaucouleurs to give him a message. Because of this journey, my parents, who do not believe in my mission, thought that my senses were wandering, and decided that marriage would be a good thing to cure my fancies.

"So they encouraged Colin to call on me. The first time he visited I told him it was no use, for I would not marry him. Neither him nor any other. Isn't that so, Colin?"

She turned to the youth so quickly, asking the question with such abruptness, gazing steadily at him, that Colin, taken unawares, nodded unthinkingly. The bishop spoke instantly: "Colin de Greux," he said sternly, "this maiden speaks the truth. It is our opinion that she has given you no promise. Tell me whether it was from this maiden, or from her parents, that you received a promise of her hand in marriage."

"It was from her parents," Colin confessed sullenly.

"And not from her at all?"

"No, Your Excellency."

"She has promised you nothing, and your action against her is dismissed. You, young man, and her parents also, would do well to let the girl alone. She is a good and pious person. And I do not find that her wits wander at all, for without any professional counsel she has established her case. Go in peace."

Jeanne thanked him tearfully and with a full heart began her trip back. She had beaten Colin and defied her parents' wishes. How would they receive her?

Filled with this thought, she trudged the thirty miles back to Neufchâteau.

CHAPTER 13

FAREWELL TO HOME

To Jeanne's surprise her family and friends welcomed her warmly. Some Domremy people who had been Colin's witnesses had gone ahead of her, and by the time she arrived back in Neufchâteau all the village folk had heard the story. They seemed to be on her side. After all, not only had she conducted her case without any help, but the bishop had commended her and spoken sharply to Colin. That poor boy was now the laughingstock of his neighbors.

Isabeau folded her daughter in her arms and held her close to her heart. She shuddered thinking of the perilous journey Jeanne had made rather than submit to an unwelcome marriage. Jacques spoke to her with something like pride in his voice. For the first time these good people understood that their daughter was different from other girls and that she should be treated differently. More than once Jeanne caught her parents looking at her with curious, puzzled expressions, as if they weren't certain she was still their own child.

La Rousse was happy with the outcome of the affair, and wished Jeanne to stay with her indefinitely. But neither Jeanne nor her parents would agree to this. After two weeks, the family returned to Domremy.

They found that Antoine de Vergy had completely destroyed the village. The governor had been enraged to learn that the villagers had escaped with their cattle and belongings, depriving him of booty and ransom, and in retribution he had ravaged and burned with even more fury than usual. Only a few cottages were left standing. The crops were entirely destroyed; the monastery with its square watchman's tower, once as proud as a fortress, lay in a heap of blackened ruins. The church was also burned, so that Domremy folk had to walk to Greux to hear mass.

But at least the people still had their flocks and herds and their furnishings. And it was summer. Bravely, with patience forged by long suffering, they began to rebuild and repair their homes. While the work went on, they lived in the castle.

Terror reigned over the countryside; misery and discomfort were everywhere. Yet somehow life went on. The summer ended and the first days of autumn came, and along with it news reached them that Orléans, the strong, independent city called the center of the Loire valley, was under siege by the English. If Orléans fell, France could not be saved.

The English made a mistake when they attacked Orléans, for it belonged to another Charles, the Duke of Orléans, whom they were holding prisoner. Customs of war dictated that a prisoner's property should not be violated. This attack was considered unprecedented treachery, and Domremy buzzed with talk as travelers related horror tales of what was happening at Orléans. They said the English had built fortified towers all around the city and entrenched themselves there in great strength. No one could get through and the inhabitants of the city were starving.

"It's outrageous," declared Jacques. "A great villainy."

"A great villainy." Jeanne repeated the words to herself. She was intensely loyal to all of the royal family, and best of all loved this Charles, the gentle poet. Sorrowfully, she sought comfort from her Voices.

"Have no fear, daughter of God," they said consolingly. "You shall save Orléans. Your time has come. Go into France, and overcome the siege that threatens the city. Go, daughter of God. Go!"

The Voices urged continually. But soon the valley was shrouded in the cold white garb of winter, and there seemed no way for Jeanne to leave the village. Although she never said so, she also dreaded leaving her home and family. Her upbringing would not permit her to disobey her parents lightly. And Jeanne knew they would never give their consent. To obey her Voices, she must go against her parents.

Her parents didn't watch her closely anymore. Jacques respected her now, and hoped she had given up the idea of going back to Vaucouleurs. Jeanne knew all this.

Her parents also knew she still had her mission in mind, for Jeanne talked about it freely. Jeanne knew what she had to do, and longed to get started. Again and again, she asked her Voices for advice. They absolved her from obedience to her parents. God's command was higher, they said, and it was this command that she must obey.

Certain as to her mission, nothing could change her mind. She looked for every means to accomplish her purpose.

The old year faded into the vale of discarded years, and January of 1429 ushered in the new year. Jeanne was now seventeen years old. The sixth of January was cold and stormy, but if it was bleak and wintry outside, inside the cottage it was cheery and comfortable. In the afternoon, the family gathered around a great fire, each one busy with household chores. Jacques and his eldest son, Jacquemin, were mending a harness; Jean and Pierre were shelling corn for the cattle; little Catherine was polishing the copper and pewter implements, while Jeanne and her mother sewed and spun. Suddenly, they heard the crunching of wheels on the frosty snow, followed shortly by a loud "Hallo!" Jacques laid down his work.

"Now who can that be visiting in such weather? Open the door, Pierre, and see who's there."

But Jeanne was already at the door and opened it wide to the visitor. Her eyes lit up as soon as she saw the man standing there.

"Come in, Uncle Durand!" she said. "You look cold."

"I feel cold!" Durand Lassois hurried over to the fire. "Jacques, you're a lucky man to be close to the fireside today. Pierre, will you take care of the oxen? The poor brutes are nearly frozen, and so am I."

"You look it, Durand," Jacques said. "Here, come closer to the fire. Isabeau, a hot drink will warm him up. Welcome, Durand, welcome! It's a cold day."

"It is," agreed Durand, rubbing his hands before the blaze.

"And how is Aveline?" Isabeau asked, as she placed a hot drink before him.

"She's not well, and the baby is fretting. That's why I've come. Aveline's father is also sick and her mother is looking after him. So Aveline hopes that Jeanne might come to stay for a while. Will you let her go, Jacques?"

Jeanne listened anxiously for her father's answer. She didn't believe he would consent to the trip. Jacques was silent a long time, but finally he said slowly: "I think she can go, Durand. It's been dreary here all winter and the work heavy. She may go and stay with you three weeks to help Aveline. That is, if her mother agrees."

"Why, yes," Isabeau said quickly. "With a young baby Aveline needs some-one with her to look after things. And it will give Jeanne a chance to hear all the latest news."

Jeanne was amazed that her parents so readily let her go. Obviously, they didn't expect her to try to see Robert de Baudricourt again. Or perhaps they were sure Sir Robert would send her home if she did call on him.

Jeanne got little sleep that night. She knew she was going to deliberately disobey her parents, but there was no other way. As soon as Aveline was better, Jeanne had decided to go to Vaucouleurs. She knew this was the last night she would ever spend in her own home.

"I would rather be torn apart by wild horses than disobey my parents," she said to herself. "But God commands it, and I must go."

Her destiny called, and she followed the summons. All earthly ties must be subservient to her great purpose. Suffering France must be saved, and her mission was to give aid. Her time had come.

The next morning, Jeanne said good-bye to her parents, brothers, and little sister. Her loved ones may have wondered why she said farewell so tenderly when leaving for such a short time. But she dared not speak of her mission. Jeanne passed from her father's house for the last time and climbed into the cart.

Mengette, whose home was nearby, was at the window as Durand Lassois's cart passed. Jeanne waved to her, crying, "Good-bye, Mengette. God bless you."

All through the village she saw faces of friends and neighbors appear at their windows, or on their doorsteps, and waved good-bye to each one. As they drew near the home of Hauviette, Durand slowed down for her to call good-bye to her friend. But Jeanne shook her head.

"I cannot speak to her, uncle," she said almost choking on her tears. "My heart would fail me, for I love her too dearly to say good-bye."

They passed slowly out of the village. As they passed through Greux she saw Colin standing in one of the narrow streets. Jeanne leaned out of the cart to call to him.

"Good-bye, Colin," she said. "God give you good fortune."

"Where are you going?" he asked. He had been avoiding Jeanne since the meeting at Toul.

"I go to Vaucouleurs," she dared to say. "Good-bye."

"To Vaucouleurs?" repeated Durand Lassois as they left Colin behind. He turned to look at Jeanne. "But what about Aveline?"

"I won't leave her as long as she needs me, uncle."

"I know that, Jeanne." He swung his long whip across the oxen's backs as he spoke, and the big animals swung into a trot.

Jeanne turned to take a last look at the valley she was leaving forever. She gazed at the thatched roofs of the village; at the ice-bound river with its rushes coated with frost; at the forest, bare and leafless; at the snow-covered hills and white shrouded meadows; at all the familiar objects of her youth. She gazed until her eyes were blinded by tears.

And so down the Valley of Colors for the last time passed Jeanne D'Arc.

CHAPTER 14

VICTORY OVER DOUBTING HEARTS

Jeanne stayed with Aveline until she was well again. Now nothing stood in the way of her going to Vaucouleurs.

"Jacques won't like it, Jeanne," Durand Lassois protested feebly. "Neither will Isabeau."

"I must go, Uncle Durand. If I had a hundred fathers or a hundred mothers, if I were the daughter of a king, I would still have to go. It is commanded."

Durand knew that both Jacques and Isabeau would be angry with him for helping her, but he made no further objection. Jeanne could not be persuaded to change her course, so he got ready to travel. Perhaps, like Jacques, he expected Sir Robert to send her home. At any rate, Durand was cheerful enough when they started out to Vaucouleurs.

"You will come back with me, won't you, Jeanne? We're going only for the day, aren't we?"

"No, uncle. I shall stay in Vaucouleurs until Sir Robert gives me soldiers to take me to the Dauphin."

"And if he won't? What then?"

"He will in time, Uncle Durand. My Voices have said so."

Durand Lassois sat silently. He was somewhat in awe of his young niece, especially when she had that look of exaltation on her face, as she did this morning. He felt as he did when he heard the church bells ring. But he had more to consider than the spiritual side of things. He was the one who eventually would have to tell Jacques. After a while he asked, "Where will you stay in Vaucouleurs? Have you thought of that?"

"Why, yes, uncle. Mother has a friend who lives in the town, Catherine le Royer. I'm sure she will put me up for my mother's sake."

"Good," said Durand, feeling quite relieved. "I know Catherine, and her husband, Henri, too. He's a wheelwright. They are good and pious people."

Soon they reached the little walled garrison nestling among the low hills, and again Jeanne and Durand Lassois climbed the hill upon which the castle stood. And once again they were ushered into the great dining hall where they found Sir Robert as before, seated at dinner with his officers. However, there was no smile on his face this time. He looked gravely at Durand, still awkward and ill at ease, and then at Jeanne, dressed in her usual red homespun dress and white cotton cap.

"Well, my little maid, what brings you here this time?"

Jeanne curtsied low before answering: "My lord captain, God has commanded me many times to go to the gentle Dauphin, who is the true King of France; he shall give me soldiers with whom I shall relieve the siege at Orléans, and I shall then take him to Reims for his coronation. And you, sir, must take me to him. It is commanded."

Robert de Baudricourt sat silently regarding the maiden. She was so earnest, so apparently sincere in her demand. Was she inspired by heaven? Or possessed by the devil? He didn't know how to answer her. His own situation was precarious. When Antoine de Vergy had raged through the valley the previous summer, he had overwhelmed the garrison town, and Sir Robert had promised to capitulate. He had not yet turned the town over to de Vergy's control, but the day of surrender was set. If by some stroke of luck the garrison could be relieved before the fixed day, the promise would cease to be valid.

Sir Robert's condition was serious. If he didn't get help, he and his people would be caught in the coils of the enemy. Any suggestion that would help the Dauphin come to his aid, however farfetched, was something to listen to. He didn't really believe the maid could help, but—

"I need to give this some thought," he said at last. "Where are you staying? I want to speak with you further concerning the Dauphin."

A stir of surprise circulated among the men. Their captain addressed the maiden as his equal!

"With Catherine le Royer, the wheelwright's wife, sir," Jeanne answered.

"I will speak with you again," repeated Sir Robert. Jeanne and Durand Lassois, understanding that the interview was over for the time being, left the dining hall.

Catherine le Royer welcomed Jeanne warmly, at first for Isabeau's sake and then for her own. In a few days Jeanne had completely won the heart of her hostess with her gentle ways, her skill in sewing and spinning, and her earnest faith. Together they attended church, spun, sewed, and busied themselves around the house. Sometimes Jeanne climbed the hill to the royal chapel that stood next to the captain's castle. There she knelt and said her prayers before a wonderful statue of the Virgin Mary.

News of her mission spread through the town and surrounding countryside. People flocked to see her, and those who came believed. This was the girl appointed by God to save France. Every day a little mob hung about the cottage door simply to see Jeanne come and go, chiefly to church. From every lip came the saying, "France lost by a woman shall be restored by a maid from Lorraine." And the excitement grew.

Again and again Jeanne visited Robert de Baudricourt, each time saying, "I must reach the Dauphin. It is the will of the King of Heaven. I must go even if I go on my knees. My lord captain, in God's name, send me to the Dauphin."

But Sir Robert, although he continued to listen, remained deaf to her pleadings. He admitted that he was impressed by her intensity and sincerity, but he could not believe. How could a young girl, fair and lovely as this peasant maid, save France? The thing was absurd. And yet, what if it were true? And so the matter rested, day after day.

Jeanne wept bitterly over the delay. She believed so implicitly in her Voices that she couldn't understand why others did not also believe. Her fame grew and soon spread beyond the valley. One day, as Jeanne was on her way to church, a young soldier pushed his way through the crowd that routinely gathered to see her.

"Well," he said jokingly, "what are you doing here? Are we all ready to turn English?"

"I'm here to ask Sir Robert to take me to the Dauphin. But he doesn't listen to me. Nevertheless, I must reach the Dauphin if I have to wear my legs out to my knees."

Her answer was given with such complete seriousness that the young knight was impressed. He spoke more gently than before: "Haven't you heard? The Dauphin has promised his little son, Louis, to wed the infant daughter of James, the King of Scotland. King James's wife, Margaret, is on her way to France with an army of six thousand men.[1] I don't think the Dauphin needs your help!"

"Even so, I must go to the Dauphin. No king or duke or wife of the King of Scotland can restore France. I alone am commanded. Truly, I would rather be at home spinning by my poor mother's side. But I must go, for the Great Sire has commanded."

"Who is this Great Sire?" he asked.

"He is God, the King of Heaven," she answered.

The young soldier was moved. In spite of himself he suddenly believed. He stretched out his hands and laid them between hers.

"There!" he said. "I, Jean de Novelonpont, commonly called Jean de Metz, pledge you my word as a knight that with God's help I will take you to the Dauphin."

"You will, sir?" cried Jeanne joyfully.

"On my word of honor I promise it. When will you start?"

"Now is better than tomorrow; tomorrow is better than the day after," she told him, her face flushed with smiles. This was the first gleam of hope in all the weary days of waiting.

"I will get ready at once," he said. As he started to leave, he turned: "What clothes will you wear?" he asked hesitantly.

Jeanne smiled, recognizing the difficulty she would have if she wore women's clothing while traveling with men. She knew that if she were to live among soldiers she must change the dress she wore.

"I will dress as a man," she answered promptly. "It will be more acceptable."

De Metz nodded his approval, and went on his way. Joys, like sorrows, come in bunches. Soon after, one person after another came to believe in Jeanne. In

---

[1] "Margaret did not come to France until seven years later. The six thousand men never did come. Jeanne did."
—*The Maid of France*, Andrew Lang

a few days another knight approached her. He was older and more serious than de Metz.

"Have we met before?" Jeanne asked.

"I don't think so," he replied. "I would remember if we had. Wait a minute! Aren't you the girl who dressed my wounded arm at your father's house in Domremy?"

"It's possible, sir. We took in many travelers."

"It is!" he said. "I am Bertrand de Poulengy. My wound healed quickly because you took such good care of me. And now you are here with a mission? Can you do as you say? Can you relieve the siege at Orléans and bring the Dauphin to Reims for his coronation?"

"Not I, sir, but my Lord, the King of Heaven, will do it through me. I am only his humble instrument."

"Tell me about it," he said. "I have talked with Jean de Metz, but I want to hear about it from you yourself."

Jeanne talked freely to him, as she did to anyone asking about her mission. When she was finished, Bertrand de Poulengy placed his hands in hers, just as de Metz had done, and pledged his knightly allegiance to her.

Even though the knights were now ready to set forth with her, they still couldn't leave for Orléans without Sir Robert's consent. Jeanne grew impatient. Orléans couldn't hold out forever.

"In God's name, Sir Robert," she cried one day in exasperation when she met him by accident at the foot of the hill, "you are too slow making up your mind. Today a battle has already been lost near Orléans. Send me quickly before the worst happens!"

"How could you know that?" exclaimed Sir Robert.

"My Voices told me," she answered. "I must be sent at once."

"I'll see," he said. "If it's true, then you shall go. But are your Voices evil or good spirits?" Without waiting for her answer, he abruptly turned away.

The next morning, as Jeanne sat quietly spinning with Catherine le Royer, the door opened suddenly and Sir Robert, accompanied by Jean Fournier, the parish priest, came in. Sir Robert signaled Catherine to leave the room, and Jeanne found herself alone with the two men. The priest sprinkled holy water around the room and upon Jeanne herself, saying in Latin: "If you are evil, go away; if you are good, come closer."

Jeanne was hurt when she understood his words, for he was giving the formula used by priests to exorcise evil spirits. If Jeanne was possessed by evil spirits, the priest expected to see her struggle and writhe about in an effort to escape the room. But Jeanne remained calm and serene. She displayed no agitation or frenzy. On the contrary, she fell on her knees and bent her head before the priest. Father Jean stretched out his hand and blessed her.

"The spirit that fills her cannot be evil," he said to Sir Robert. With that, the two men turned and left the cottage as suddenly as they had come. Jeanne burst into tears.

When Catherine came back into the room she found the girl still sobbing. "Father Jean shouldn't have done that," she cried. "He has seen me every day at church and heard my confession. He should know the kind of person I am."

Catherine put her arms around Jeanne to comfort her. "Don't cry," she said, "he only did it to please the captain. Now that Sir Robert knows for certain that you are not possessed by evil spirits, he will help you."

Catherine was right. Assured that Jeanne was not possessed by evil, Sir Robert then knew that the power in her must be good. At last he made up his mind to help her. He had already sent a secret message to the Dauphin, telling of the maid, her mission, and her piety. He was waiting to receive permission from Charles before starting Jeanne on her journey.

But Jeanne didn't know this. She grew more restless, longing to be about her work. Everywhere she looked there seemed to be nothing but obstacles to her mission. One day Durand Lassois came to see her, bringing news from Jacques and Isabeau. Since Jeanne could neither read nor write she had asked the priest to send her parents a letter asking for their forgiveness. In the letter the priest had also described her good deeds and saintly ways, adding details about her daily life that he thought would set their minds at ease. Now Jeanne listened eagerly as Durand told how her parents had received the letter.

"The whole countryside is talking about you, and they already knew how you were living and what you were doing. Jacques is still not reconciled to your leaving home, but he said that as long as you lived a good life you had his blessing and forgiveness. Isabeau wept when she heard the letter, but she sends her love and prays that you will quickly fulfill your mission and return home again."

"I wish I could, Uncle Durand," she sighed. "But there's one obstacle after another. I would like to be home with my mother, and if my work were done I could be. The time is so short. I cannot wait any longer." She bowed her head and wept. Suddenly, she wiped away the tears and turned to Durand with a new idea.

"Uncle Durand," she cried. "Will you take me to the Dauphin?"

"You mean walk there?" he asked, amazed. "It's nearly 150 leagues!"

"Even so, I must go! If Sir Robert won't give me soldiers, I must go without them. Will you go with me?"

"Yes," he said at once. Jeanne didn't notice the smile lurking in his eyes. Lassois was a practical man and he knew the plan was impossible. He hoped that his niece would realize the folly on her own. "I'll get my friend Alain to go with us," he said. "It's a dangerous journey even with soldiers for escort. When do you want to start?"

"At once," cried Jeanne. "The sooner, the better. When I've relieved Orléans and the Dauphin is crowned, I can go back home. Believe me, I will not leave my parents again. Go, get Alain, and let's start!"

After Durand Lassois left her, Jeanne got ready to travel, dressing in a man's tights, a sleeveless padded vest, with a coat over it. By the time Lassois returned with Alain, she was ready to leave. The three set out on the road to Orléans. Just outside town they stopped at the roadside shrine of St. Nicholas, where Jeanne knelt briefly in prayer. When she rose to her feet all of her restless impatience had left her.

"I was wrong, uncle," she told Lassois. "It is not proper to go to the Dauphin like this. We must turn back."

Durand Lassois grinned broadly.

"I told you, Alain," he cried. "I knew we would be turning back."

Jeanne looked at him in astonishment. "How did you know?"

"Why, the Dauphin wouldn't receive you in such humble company. But if you arrive escorted by knights, with the blessings of Sir Robert, it will be easy to get his attention."

"I see," Jeanne sighed. "I was wrong. We will go back to Vaucouleurs."

After this venture Jeanne had more patience than before, and soon her patience was rewarded. One day a messenger from the Dauphin rode into town bringing a letter of consent to the captain. Sir Robert immediately sent for Jeanne.

"It seems your information is correct," he said. "There was a battle near Orléans. The Battle of Herrings was lost at Rouvray. The Dauphin's messenger says that Charles will receive you. You start for Chinon in a few days."

"I have traveled many miles, all the way from Rome," said the monk.
Page 39

There was no smile on his face this time.
Robert de Beaudricourt looked gravely at Jeanne.
Page 75

Overjoyed, Jeanne ran back to tell her friends the good news. The impossible had happened: she would be taken to the Dauphin, just as she had demanded, and at the appointed time.

The sweetness, simplicity, and sturdy purpose of the Maid had won the hearts of all the citizens of Vaucouleurs. Everyone now knew of her great mission and everyone was prepared to help her. They took it upon themselves to purchase new masculine clothing for her, which included a new jerkin, a nicely fitting doublet, hose, and spurs. Sir Robert gave her a horse. Jeanne took off her white cotton bonnet and let down her long dark hair. She sighed only once, then Catherine cut her hair in a round pageboy. Dressed in her new clothes, a velvet cap on her head, she was ready.

Her escort included Jean de Metz and Bertrand de Poulengy; the Dauphin's messenger, Colet de Vienne; a bowman named Richard; plus two lancers who served the knights. The men had heard that enemy soldiers were nearby and suggested that Jeanne wait a little longer. But she was not afraid: "In God's name, fear not, and take me to the Dauphin. We have waited long enough."

On the twenty-third of February, Jeanne's little band of friends joined the townspeople assembled at the city gate to watch the departure. The women trembled and wept as they looked at the girl, so young and fearless. One cried out, "How can you go when it is so dangerous? The enemy is everywhere!"

Jeanne turned a happy face toward them and answered serenely: "I am not afraid of enemy soldiers. My path is safe before me. If we encounter the enemy, my Lord God will make way for me to reach the Dauphin. I was born for this purpose."

Sir Robert was also present at the gate. As he gazed at the bright face of the maiden, his grim heart was touched. He made Jean de Metz dismount and kneel before him. "Swear that you will deliver this maiden whom I place in your care safely and surely to the Dauphin."

"I swear," de Metz answered solemnly.

From each and every man the captain took the same oath. Then, belting his own sword around the girl's slender waist, he said, "Go! Come what may!"

And off into the mists that enveloped the meadows of the valley rode the gallant little company, down the road toward Chinon.

CHAPTER 15

STARTING THE GREAT ADVENTURE

Thus began the strangest ride that was ever made. A thousand perils lay ahead: great rivers to be crossed; great forests infested by wolves to be traversed; trackless spaces of hostile country to be covered.

Jeanne knew all the risks but, happy in the knowledge that she was at last on her way to the Dauphin, no danger seemed too formidable. She wasn't afraid of marauding bands; nor did she worry about the conduct of the soldiers who traveled with her. A great peace filled her soul. Her work had begun. How it would end she neither knew nor asked; she only knew what she must do. So lighthearted did she appear that Bertrand de Poulengy wondered at it. Jeanne noticed him looking at her with curiosity.

"What is it, sir?" she asked.

"It will be a hard, tiresome ride," he answered.

"I know."

"To sit in the saddle so long is exhausting. Are you accustomed to riding?"

"No. I never rode at all until I came to Vaucouleurs."

"I can hardly believe that." He looked with frank admiration at the slight, erect figure sitting on her horse with confidence. "You ride as though born to the saddle. It's a good thing, because this journey will tax your endurance. We stop tonight at the Abbey of St. Urbain, but after that our only bed will be the open fields. We must avoid the roads and towns held by the English. It will be dangerous."

"What do you fear, sir?"

"That we shall never reach Chinon," he answered gloomily. "There are only seven of us. What can so few do if we're attacked?"

Jeanne turned a smiling face toward him. "Have no fear," she said. "My brothers in Paradise will watch over us."

"Can you really do what you say?" he asked.

"I can do what I am commanded to do. It's been four years since my Voices first told me that I must deliver France from her enemies."

But Poulengy and the rest of the company, now that they were actually on the road of this wild adventure, were losing some of their confidence. Perhaps the girl really was a witch. They could be hanged if they brought a witch to court. Doubts and misgivings assailed them as they rode forward.

Far into the night they rode before stopping at the old Abbey of St. Urbain on the right bank of the Marne River. Jeanne was glad to lay her weary head upon a simple cot, but she was up early the next morning to attend mass. Then she and her companions set off again. Crossing the Marne by the St. Urbain bridge they pressed on toward Chinon.

They were in more dangerous territory now, so they proceeded more stealthily. Poulengy and de Metz were experienced soldiers and accustomed to such expeditions; they knew how to travel quietly through the back roads without gaining attention. Some days were sunny, with the nights clear and full of moonlight. Others days they rode on through rain and sleet and even snow. Jeanne was always cheerful, always confident, always good-humored.

Her men-at-arms were hotheaded, hot-hearted soldiers of fortune, neither overly scrupulous nor overly pious, but they learned to respect the young girl in their charge. It was a feeling that combined chivalry and religion. She was so devout and clean-spirited that they held her in reverence. If they did not altogether believe in her visions, they did believe in her goodness, her purity, and her faith. In time they came to think of her as a saint.

"Truly, Bertrand, she comes from God," declared de Metz one day after returning from a nearby town where he had gone looking for food. The company dared not enter the village for fear of being discovered. Everyone in the whole countryside knew by now that the Maid of Vaucouleurs was on her way to the Dauphin under escort, and the knights feared an ambush from the enemy. "She hasn't much money, but she gave me alms to give to the poor in the village. She does this whenever we draw near to a town."

"She is a saint," agreed de Poulengy. "I think she must be inspired. How else could she withstand the journey the way she does? She may seem a little weary when we stop for a rest, but when we start again she's as cheerful as on the very first day."

"It's as though she received bread from Heaven for her meals. I've been on many wild marches, but this one has been the most grueling. I'm afraid we might be ambushed, Bertrand, and I would rather die myself than see her harmed."

"I agree, Jean. But I'm not sure that the others do. I overheard Richard, the bowman, talking with our aides this morning. They talked about the marvelous way the maid has withstood the journey, but say that a mere maiden couldn't be so strong. They think she's a witch. We must be on guard in case they try some trick against her."

"Can't they see she is one of God's saints?" exclaimed de Metz. "I'll tell them a few things—"

"No, Jean," counseled the older man, laying his hand lightly on his friend's arm. "Don't be too quick to judge. Not so long ago we had our own doubts about the maiden. The aides may intend no harm at all, but I thought you should be prepared. Let's say nothing just now, but watch and wait."

"You're right, Bertrand." De Metz lowered his voice. "But if they try anything—" He paused, touching his sword meaningfully.

Poulengy nodded, and the two knights returned to camp. They were marching by night now, and resting during the day. Their camp lay between two hills sloping down to the banks of a swollen stream. Though a cold rain was falling they were afraid to light a fire. Huddled together in the chilly woods the little party ate their cold meat and bread in silence. After the comfortless meal they all lay down on the wet ground to get what rest they could while Richard the bowman stood watch. They were aroused suddenly by a wild shout from the archer: "The English! The English are upon us!"

Instantly the two knights and the Dauphin's messenger leaped to their feet and, swords drawn, threw themselves in front of Jeanne. She sat up calmly as the men breathlessly awaited the approach of the enemy. The two aides were about to run when Jeanne spoke in her grave, sweet voice: "Stay. I tell you, in God's name, there is no danger."

At this, Richard, seeing that she was unafraid, burst out laughing. In a bound Jean de Metz reached him and grabbed him by the throat.

"Dog!" he cried, shaking him violently. "We have enough to fear without you giving false alarms! That shout of yours may still bring the enemy to us. I'd like to throw you in the river."

"I did it to scare the witch," muttered Richard, his face white as he eyed the swollen, rushing stream. The water was dismally cold and very deep. "I meant no harm."

But de Metz, enraged by the word "witch," lifted him bodily. Jeanne's soft voice stopped him.

"Wait, friend," she said. "The joke was badly timed, true, but it was only a joke. He can't frighten or harm me. No one can until I have fulfilled my mission. Let him go."

"Do you hear that?" De Metz let Richard slide slowly to the ground. "If it weren't for her you'd be drinking deeply of that water. See that you behave better or I'll go hard on you. Or anyone else who tries any more tricks."

De Metz glared so fiercely at the whole company that the men visibly shrank back. There were no further attempts to frighten Jeanne during the rest of the journey, and from then on no one was more devoted than Richard the bowman.

On they rode, and still on. Through gloomy woods, by hazardous highways, and over swollen rivers the seven made their way. On the morning of the tenth day they came into Gien, a village situated on the Loire River, about forty miles north of Orléans. At last they had reached friendly territory, and the danger was now almost over. Jeanne and her knights talked freely of her errand, and the news spread rapidly that a girl had come from the region of Lorraine to lift the siege of Orléans and lead the Dauphin to Reims. Messengers from Gien slipped through the blockade that surrounded Orléans and carried the story into the besieged city. Its commander, the Count of Dunois, sent two of his officers on to Chinon to ask the Dauphin to send the Maid to help him.

The news concerning Orléans was desperate. The Battle of the Herrings, fought at Rouvray, had been a disastrous defeat for the French. Orléans would fall at any time. After a brief rest at Gien, Jeanne and her company rode tirelessly on.

Now that the hour was near, Poulengy and de Metz were filled with anxiety at seeing the Dauphin. Charles and his councilors might think they were all fools, and the knights would be a laughingstock. By now they were so used to confiding in Jeanne that they told her about their misgivings.

"Don't worry," she assured them. "The Dauphin will receive us graciously."

Since they were in friendly territory they did not expect to encounter danger from the English, but there were politicians around the French court who were not happy to hear about a wonderful Maid who was coming with help from Heaven and the Holy Saints. There were also bandits on the highways, robbing and killing travelers, no matter what side they were on. One band of mercenaries lay in ambush waiting for Jeanne's little company to come by. Their intention was to capture and imprison her, hoping the Dauphin would pay for her rescue.

Jeanne rode fearlessly in front of the little company while the knights followed close behind, keeping a keen watch on the deep woods that edged both sides of the road. Suddenly, a party of wild-eyed men burst from the right side and surrounded them, yelling and thrashing their swords. The knights reeled and met the onset head on; then high above the noise of screams and clashing swords sounded Jeanne's voice, clear and bell-like: "Hold! Let's not spill French blood while the English wait for us at Orléans. Stop, friends! It's not God's will that you kill each other."

Involuntarily the men stopped, their swords still raised in midair. The bandit leader turned a searching, curious glance toward Jeanne. She met his gaze calmly. There was something so pure and unearthly in her look that the man's eyes dropped, and he hastily crossed himself.

"Pass on," he said. At this sign his comrades fell back, and the seven rode on in safety.

Bertrand leaned over and whispered to Jean de Metz, "Did you see that? Those rascals were helpless when she cried out. Truly, the child is sent from God."

"She is, Bertrand, but I didn't need this to prove it. Think of all the dangerous miles we have traveled without a mishap of any kind. It's nothing short of miraculous."

Jeanne heard them talking and smiled.

"Marvel not," she said. "God clears the way for me. I was born for this."

And so they came to the green slopes of Fierbois, from which they would proceed to Chinon, where the Dauphin waited.

CHAPTER 16

JEANNE COMES TO HER KING

Jeanne sent a message to the Dauphin, asking for his permission to enter the town, for her knights could go no further without his consent. She dictated the following letter to a scribe:

Gentle Dauphin—I have ridden a hundred and fifty leagues to bring you aid from our Father, the King of Heaven. I have much good news for you, and beg that you will allow me to tell it to you in person. Though I have never seen you, I would know you in any disguise among a thousand. May God give you long life.

—Jeanne the Maid

The Dauphin's messenger, Colet de Vienne, carried the letter to Chinon. They had to wait at least a day for the answer to come back, so Jeanne had the pleasure of hearing mass in the village church, which was dedicated to Saint Catherine, one of her daily visitors. This was Saint Catherine's most famous sanctuary, for here she received multitudes of pilgrims and worked great miracles. Since the beginning of French history, Saint Catherine had inspired national worship. Jeanne lingered lovingly in the chapel, hearing three masses and listening with delight to the stories of the saint's miracles.

The following day, the messenger de Vienne was back with permission to proceed on to Chinon. As they mounted and rode toward the town, Jeanne's heart beat fast. At last she was going to the Dauphin, and her heart sang for joy.

The nearer they drew to Chinon, the poorer the country became. For lack of money the Dauphin had to move often, and his court had been stripped bare. Many stories were told about his extravagance and consequent poverty. It was a poor prince to whom Jeanne was going.

On March sixth, eleven days after leaving Vaucouleurs, Jeanne and her party entered Chinon. It was the fourth Sunday in Lent, Laetare Sunday. Jeanne thought about far off Domremy: the boys and girls, the youths and maidens, all would be going to the Fairy Tree and the spring. They would be eating their hard-boiled eggs and the special rolls their mothers had kneaded. Her brothers, Pierre and Jean, would be there. But Jeanne didn't let her thoughts wander long, for she was at last in Chinon.

The walled town was built on a meadow beside the Vienne River. Behind it rose a high perpendicular ledge on which the castle stood, the finest in the realm of France. Behind these proud walls there breathed the Dauphin to whom she had been impelled to come by a miraculous love. Jeanne looked up at the castle with a longing glance, but she had to wait for permission to enter. She turned her attention to the town.

Narrow lanes of overhanging houses crowded against the hill leading up to the steep castle buttresses. Jeanne and her company stopped at an inn in the town and waited. It was Lent so the spits for roasting meat were idle. Without eating, Jeanne retired to the room given her, and spent the next two days in prayer while she waited to hear from the Dauphin.

Then the messenger Colet de Vienne came with a command for the two knights to come up to the castle to answer questions about the Maid. Bertrand was angry.

"Does the Dauphin want this, or is it the command of George La Trémouïlle? Some say that the Dauphin's favorite cares nothing for France, and only wants the Burgundians to get their share so they can pay him off."

"I wouldn't say that Charles is not master of his own Court," Colet replied warily. "Although some say that La Trémouïlle doesn't want an inspired Maid to arouse the Dauphin from his laziness. The Dauphin's other advisers also want to know more about the damsel before she reaches him. It's on their advice that he has sent for you."

"But he has the letter from Sir Robert de Baudricourt, the captain of Vaucouleurs, vouching for her," de Poulengy said heatedly. "It's just one more delay, and we're running out of time. Jean and I believe she can save Orléans. We believe she's been divinely commissioned to do so."

"Then why fret about telling the Dauphin what you believe?" asked Colet. "He questioned me and I spoke freely. I told him of her goodness and the safety of our journey through hostile territory."

"You're right," de Poulengy said. "Why worry. But it seems to me that if I were the Dauphin I'd jump at the chance to help so distressed a kingdom."

"That's what worries us all, Bertrand," said Jean de Metz. "Everyone who cares about the Dauphin and France. La Hire, the fiercest soldier of the Armagnacs, says, 'Never was a king who lost his kingdom so gay as Charles.' But lead on, Colet. Charles the Dauphin commands us, and we must go. Perhaps good will come from it after all."

"Perhaps. Deputies from Orléans are already here in Chinon praying that the Dauphin will send her at once."

"Now that is good news," said Bertrand. "I feel much better now. Come, Jean, we go!"

Seldom has any king deserved greater contempt than Charles. Lazy, idle, and cowardly, he was the puppet of his worst councilors. He threw away most of his money on luxurious living. But, at that time, no matter how weak a king was, his bodily presence was important to his people, for Charles the Seventh was the image and sacred symbol of France.

In his favor he was very devout and his piety was sincere. He was generous to others, as well as to himself. He had pity for the poor. From time to time he seemed to realize that, despite his helplessness and incompetence, he was still the man who ought to do all. But he was weak, a slave to his favorites and advisers, blind to their deceits and defects, willing to put up with anything from them. And it was these councilors who intended to ruin Jeanne.

Soon de Poulengy and de Metz returned to the inn to report to Jeanne the outcome of the meeting.

"It's a shame that the Dauphin doesn't govern alone," said Bertrand with disgust. "But, oh, no, the whole royal council must agree before he will see you. Some of his councilors claim your mission is a hoax. Some say you are a witch. Yet others want him to see you. Yolande, Queen of Sicily and the Dauphin's mother-in-law, openly says that since Sir Robert de Baudricourt recommended you so highly, and since you have risked the journey through many miles of hostile territory, the Dauphin ought to at least hear you. In my opinion, Yolande is the best adviser and the best soldier the Dauphin has. So there the matter rests. But he should consent to see you."

"He will, sir. Have no doubt. He will hear and see me soon."

"Perhaps, in time. But before that time comes, certain priests and clerks, experts in telling good spirits from bad, are to examine you. They're following us, aren't they, Jean?"

De Metz nodded. "They're coming now," he said.

"In God's name, why don't they let me go on with my work?" exclaimed Jeanne.

They heard steps outside the door and the innkeeper entered, bowing low before several imposing clergymen and their clerks.

Jeanne stood up and curtsied. The visitors looked surprised when they saw that the renowned Maid was a mere girl. The senior bishop spoke for them: "Are you the maid who has come from Vaucouleurs?"

Jeanne nodded.

"You have made that long perilous journey to speak with the Dauphin?"

"Yes, sir."

"You seem very young for such a dangerous and exhausting march. You don't look a day over sixteen."

"I'm seventeen, sir."

"It's said you have a message for the king."

"Yes, sir."

"Tell it to us. We will carry it to him."

Jeanne stood up even straighter and looked at them calmly.

"I cannot, sir," she said. "It's for the Dauphin alone to hear. To him, and to no one else, will I tell it."

"Maiden," said the bishop, "the king has many councilors who are wise and learned men. They don't think he should see you until he learns the details of your mission. If you have an important message for him, you should tell it to us first. That is, if you wish to see him."

"Is not the Dauphin his own master? Isn't it up to him to decide who shall see him?" demanded Jeanne.

The bishop looked confused. "Certainly," he said hastily. "But he relies on certain people to discover who is worthy to enter his presence. Tell us why you wish to see him."

Jeanne stood still for a long moment, as if waiting for something; then suddenly her face was transfigured with joy, for the light shone beside her. She bowed her head and the Voice that she waited for spoke: "Tell him of your mission, daughter of God," it said. "Lift your head and answer boldly. We will help you."

Jeanne raised her head, and said quietly, "My Voices have given me permission to speak," she said. "Two commands have been to me by the King of Heaven. First, to relieve the siege of Orléans; the other, to lead the Dauphin to Reims that he may be crowned there."

The bishops listened with amazement. They had neither seen the light, nor heard the voice. But they knew the girl had received some kind of message.

"Those are marvelous commands, my child," the bishop said. "What sign can you give us to prove you can carry them out?"

"I'm not here to give signs," cried Jeanne, her impatience flaring up. "Give me men-at-arms, and I'll show you."

"Then tell us how you received the commands."

Jeanne never liked to talk much of her visions, but she told them a little about her experience. The priests questioned her about her religious habits, how often she went to church and took the sacraments of communion and confession. She answered simply and freely. At last, the clergymen left, charmed by her sincerity and modesty.

As evening fell, the Count de Vendome, one of the nobles of the court, arrived at the inn to take Jeanne to the Dauphin. The time had come at last. De Vendome scrutinized the girl: she was dressed like a page, in a simple gray jacket and black tights, and on her head she wore a little black cap with a silver brooch; the sword given her by Robert de Baudricourt hung by her side. At a glance she might easily have passed for a boy. The nobleman admired her slender, erect posture, but his words were grave: "You don't mean to see the Dauphin dressed in that garb?" he asked.

"This and none other, sir," she answered cheerily. "For in this garb I shall carry out my mission."

So, led by the Count de Vendome and followed by her two knights, Jeanne started for the castle. They made their way up a broad winding path to the rocky ridge along which the great walls of the ancient castle stretched. From the drawbridge high above the wide, deep moat, swirling with dark water, the whole town and valley could be seen. Just within the gate soldiers rested and played dice, although darkness was falling quickly now. As Jeanne and her escorts crossed the drawbridge, the soldiers stopped their games and a murmur ran from lip to lip. Everyone in Chinon had heard of her.

"It is the inspired Maid from Vaucouleurs, coming to see the king."

Suddenly, one soldier came up close to Jeanne and peered impudently into her face.

"By all the saints," he said, "it's a pretty wench!" he cried. "May God send more such witches to Chinon. I—"

Angrily Jean de Metz swept him out of the way.

The soldier wrathfully cursed de Metz.

"Oh, do you curse God?" said Jeanne sadly. "You who are so near death?"

The man stood as if turned to stone. Some of his comrades began to gibe at him, and he turned on them in a rage.

"Do you think I care what a mad woman says?" he shouted. "I defy her and her prophecies." He laughed loudly and leaned back heavily against the low wooden fence of the drawbridge. Suddenly the fence railing gave way, there was a crash, and down and down he plummeted. The deep waters of the moat closed over him.

The frightened soldiers looked in awe at Jeanne and her companions, who were already walking up the broad steps of the king's residence. When she heard the crash, Jeanne turned.

"What has happened?" she asked.

"Nothing," answered de Metz quickly, fearing that she would be upset at the news. "Part of that old fence along the bridge snapped."

Without knowing that her prophecy had been fulfilled so soon, Jeanne passed on into the great hall where she was to meet the Dauphin. The room was crowded with curious onlookers. At the end of the vaulted room an enormous fire blazed in a white stone chimney, its firelight reflecting on the polished oak floors.

Veteran soldiers, councilors, priests and bishops, and many fair ladies dressed in royal finery were gathered to see the sorceress. A throng of the noblest lords and ladies of France, dressed in crimson and azure velvet and cloth of spun gold, looked with amusement and surprise at the girl before them. There was Jeanne, dressed in her young man's attire, with her hair cut round like a page's. In turn, Jeanne cast her eyes around the room and saw a brilliant mob of vivid color glowing in the flaring flames of the many torches that lit the room. The fans of the ladies fluttered; their high headdresses towered above the men; a thousand unfamiliar colors and shapes combined to dazzle and confuse the eye.

But Jeanne was neither dazzled nor confused. She looked about her and saw the skepticism on the faces around her, but paid them no heed. Instead she stared at the figure seated on the throne.

The Count de Vendome touched her arm gently. "Kneel," he whispered. "The king is before you."

But Jeanne did not kneel. She continued to look at the figure seated on the throne, and knitted her brows thoughtfully. Then she turned around and looked searchingly among the courtiers crowding the room. A low murmur ran through the crowd as Jeanne suddenly moved toward a group of courtiers. Pushing them aside, she knelt before a soberly dressed young man hiding behind them.

"God give you good life, gentle Dauphin," she said.

"I am not the king," he said. "He sits on the throne."

"In God's name, gentle Dauphin, it is you and no other." Rising from her knees, she continued, "Fair Dauphin, I am Jeanne the Maid. I am sent to you by the King of Heaven to tell you that you shall be crowned at Reims."

Charles stopped smiling. The masquerade planned for the amusement of the court had failed.

"How do you know this?" he asked.

"My Voices have told me. I have come to lead you to your crowning, but first I must lift the siege of Orléans. I can do it if you will give me an army. I beg you to send me at once to Orléans."

Touched by her sincerity, the Dauphin gazed at her and asked, "How do I know you can do this, Maid? What sign can you give me?"

"You will see the proof when I rescue Orléans. But I have another sign which I can tell you alone."

The Dauphin drew her into a window recess out of earshot of the courtiers. "Tell it to me now," he said.

"Gentle Dauphin, when you prayed this morning you felt a great pain in your heart."

"True," nodded Charles.

"Did you tell anyone the prayer that you made?"

"No," he answered. "My prayer concerns no one but myself."

Jeanne spoke quickly and passionately. "You prayed that if you were the true heir of France, God would protect you and restore you to your throne. But if you were not the rightful king, God would let you escape with your life into Scotland or Spain."

"That was my prayer," said Charles, astonished. "I never said the words out loud, only in my heart alone. Tell me more, Maid. Do your heavenly visitors have an answer to my prayer?"

"They do. To ease your heart I tell you that you are the true heir of France and the rightful king."

Jeanne spoke with such authority that the Dauphin smiled radiantly. He took Jeanne's hand and bowed over it.

"I believe you, Maid," he said. "Though all should doubt, I believe. You shall have your army and you shall go to Orléans."

"God be praised," Jeanne exclaimed. "May He give you long life. Give me the men soon, I beg you, so I may be about my work."

"You shall have your wish," he said gently. With this declaration he led her back to the gaping courtiers.

CHAPTER 17

THE IMPOSSIBLE HAPPENS

The next day, as Jeanne sat with her two knights discussing the audience of the evening before, de Gaucourt, former commander of Orléans, hurried in.

"Jeanne D'Arc," he said, bowing low, "I come by order of the king, who wants you to come to live in the Tower of Coudray, which is a better place for you and nearer to him. Your friends may join you, if you wish."

"Yes," Jeanne said with an affectionate glance at Poulengy and de Metz. "They have proved themselves true and faithful friends. Without their help I would never have reached the Dauphin. They believed in me even before Sir Robert did. And they shall go with me to Orléans, if they wish."

"We do wish," the knights said simultaneously. "To Orléans, and any other place that promises a fight for France."

"I wish we were on our way to Orléans now," sighed Jeanne as they left for the castle.

As they climbed up the steep approach to the castle in daylight, they could see that the long mass of embattled walls, of towers, turrets, ramparts, and watchtowers, was in fact three separate castles. De Gaucourt led them to the middle castle, where the Dauphin dwelt, and across the bridge of the inner moat. At the end of the bridge they passed through an archway into the Tower of Coudray.

They paused at the top of a stairway. Here Guillaume Bellier, the lieutenant of the tower and the Dauphin's major-domo, waited to greet them.

"You are to stay with my family, Jeanne," he said, bowing to her. "My wife comes to take you to your room."

As he spoke a pleasant-faced woman came out of an adjoining room and greeted Jeanne warmly. She looked surprised at the way Jeanne was dressed, but seemed charmed by her youth and beauty. Bertrand sighed as he saw Jeanne leave with the lady, and in a low voice spoke to de Metz: "I am happy to see Jeanne in good hands. Madame Bellier is a devout woman, and they will enjoy each other's company. It has made me sad to see a young girl without any of her own sex around her."

"Yes, but the angels visit her, Bertrand, and bring her comfort and solace like no one has ever had before. I believe that she is a messenger from the blessed saints that love France. Still, I too am glad that Madame Bellier is taking care of her."

Jeanne's rooms were in the upper story of the tower, and Lieutenant Bellier sent one of his own pages, called Mugot, to wait on her. Her two knights and their servants had rooms just below hers.

Now that the Dauphin had taken Jeanne under his wing, people flocked to see her. Clergy came to test her religious convictions; captains quizzed her about her knowledge of war; and all the lords and ladies asked questions about her mission. Many asked if the Bois Chesnu were near her home, since everyone now remembered Merlin's prophecy about the oak wood. Jeanne was eager to begin her work, but she answered all of them so patiently and was so gentle and simple that everyone she met grew to believe in her.

Every day the Dauphin had Jeanne brought to him. He was weak and timid, but her simple faith impressed him, as it impressed everyone who met her, and her trust in him gave him courage. He wished to give her armed men immediately, as he had promised, but his royal council overruled him. The councilors admitted that women who heard heavenly voices were not to be scorned, and that English kings were as ready as French kings to listen to the words of saintly men and women. Still, they advised the Dauphin to proceed carefully for fear he might be accused of using witchcraft to help himself.

In the Middle Ages it was the custom for saints to speak with kings and for kings to listen to them. But sorcery was an unpardonable sin. So, in the opinion of the royal council, Jeanne must be thoroughly investigated before they would hand her an army.

While the talking went on and on, Jeanne's fame grew. She fired the zeal of the officers who came to see her and shamed them into some hope of saving France. She charmed the ladies of the court by her modesty, and the common people told wonderful stories of her piety and exploits. To gain such renown so quickly was a great achievement for a seventeen-year-old. But Jeanne, who believed God was responsible for everything that was happening to her, only wondered why anyone would even hesitate to trust her.

One day after attending mass in the royal chapel, Jeanne turned to find the Dauphin and a young nobleman standing beside her. Jeanne curtsied to the monarch, who said, "We have brought our cousin, the Duke of Alençon to see you, Jeanne. He is very interested in the house of Orléans, since he is married to the daughter of Duke Charles."

"He is welcome," Jeanne said simply. "The more there are here of royal blood, the better."

"We think so, too," said the Dauphin. "We would like you to dine with us today so our cousin may learn more of your mission."

Jeanne bowed low, charming Alençon with her courtly manners. Then she and the young duke followed the Dauphin to the dining hall. George La Trémouïlle, the king's favorite adviser, was there. Built like a barrel, he was a heavy drinker who would lend money to the Dauphin and the other nobles at high interest. Through this practice he had put many important people in his debt.

Dismissing the courtiers, the Dauphin sat down at the table with Alençon and Jeanne. Only a month ago Jeanne was eating her meals at a peasant's table, and now she was dining with royalty. But her thoughts were not about food or dinner tables. She thought only of the Dauphin. Jeanne was obsessed with the desire to see him govern the realm wisely and well. So she talked seriously to him, asking him to live according to God's will, to be a good ruler to rich and poor, friend and enemy. If he would rule wisely and fairly, she told him, the King of Heaven would do for him what he had done for his ancestors and restore him to the highest place in the land.

Gazing into Jeanne's bright, eager young face, which was flushed with courage and glowing with celestial ardor, the Dauphin longed to do kingly deeds to be worthy of the blood of his ancestors. After the meal the little party went to the meadow by the river, where Jeanne demonstrated her horsemanship with such skill that both the Dauphin and the duke were impressed.

"That horse looks like a farm animal," said Alençon of Jeanne's mount, which de Baudricourt had bought for her. "I'll give you a steed more worthy of you."

The next day Alençon presented her with a magnificent black charger. It was the beginning of a warm friendship between the two. The duke became one of Jeanne's most enthusiastic supporters, and she grew fond of him not only because he was the son-in-law of the Duke of Orléans, but because the English had treated him badly and he wanted to fight. Jeanne measured men by that standard. She had a hearty contempt for men who sulked at court and idled away their time having fun while France was under English rule. Alençon had been held captive by the English for three years. It was said that his captors had offered him his liberty and wealth if he would join them, but he rejected the offer. Like Jeanne, Alençon was young and sincere.

Despite Alençon's enthusiastic approval, the Dauphin still did not support Jeanne wholeheartedly. His royal council, led by La Trémouïlle, urged caution. At this point La Trémouïlle was indifferent to Jeanne. He did not yet dread her power or plot against her as he would a few months later. The Dauphin's priest and other clergy examined Jeanne daily. Although Jeanne was aware that they questioned her on orders from the Dauphin, she answered discreetly about her mission.

"In God's name, why do they ask so many questions instead of allowing me to help the Dauphin?" she asked Alençon one day after a particularly long session with the bishops.

"Perhaps doubting comes naturally to them," the duke replied. "You'll have to be patient, Jeanne."

"Patient, patient!" Jeanne fumed. "Can Orléans hold out forever? Daily I pray to be free of these churchmen."

Alençon laughed, but then he saw tears in Jeanne's eyes.

"Endure a little longer, my friend," he said gently. "I believe that the end of these many questions is in sight. But in the meantime the Dauphin is sending you to Poictiers."

"And why to Poictiers?"

"The royal council think you should be examined by the learned theologians there," he explained. "They admit that they can find no fault in you, but before giving you an army they want the church to pass judgment on your inspiration. When that's over I am sure there will be no further delay and the Dauphin will send you to Orléans."

"What's the use of educated men asking me questions when I don't know A from B?" Jeanne asked. "But in God's name, if we must go, let us be going."

The next day she left for Poictiers, attended by a large company. Many of the Dauphin's court were eager to see how the peasant maid would acquit herself. Besides Alençon and her own knights, the company included veteran men-at-arms who laughed at the idea of a mere girl lifting the siege of Orléans. There were also many courtiers, some who believed in Jeanne and others looking for amusement. Yolande, the Dauphin's mother-in-law, who believed wholeheartedly in Jeanne, also traveled with the company. But Yolande's presence did not console Jeanne, who fretted because so much valuable time was being wasted.

Poictiers was about fifty miles from Chinon. It was here that men loyal to the Dauphin had come after fleeing from Paris when the capital city fell into English hands. It was also a legal center.

When she arrived in Poictiers Jeanne was put up in the house of the wealthy and distinguished attorney general, Jean Robateau. The house, which was near the law courts, had a small chapel where Jeanne went daily to pray. In the days that followed, the chapel would become a haven of refuge for her.

The Archbishop of Reims presided over a council which, in turn, appointed a special committee to investigate Jeanne. The committee included several professors of theology, an abbot, a canon of Poictiers, and one or two friars. First, the committee sent emissaries back to Domremy to look into Jeanne's past. Then, escorted by a squire, they went to interview Jeanne at Robateau's house. As they entered the house, Jeanne came to meet them. She had been subjected to so much questioning at Chinon that she was weary, and the new examination seemed needless and futile to her. While she had great respect for working priests and religious people, she had little use for the learned doctors. However, she was pleased to see the squire, a young man named Thibault, because he at least was in military dress.

Jeanne knelt quickly before the committee and then went up to the squire and greeted him like a comrade.

"I wish I had a thousand men like you," she said.

"Jeanne D'Arc," the abbot said gravely, "listen to us. We are sent to you from the king."

"I know that you're here to question me," said Jeanne with spirit, "but what's the use?"

"Why have you come to court?" asked the abbot.

"I have come from the King of Heaven to lift the siege of Orléans and to lead the Dauphin to Reims for his coronation," she answered.

"But what made you think of coming?" asked a professor of theology.

"Because my Voices told me to come."

"Your voices? What voices?"

Although she disliked talking about her visions, Jeanne realized she would have to give some explanation. The doctors listened carefully while she told them something about her revelations. She was a humble peasant maid, ignorant, simple, her hands hardened with toil, but as she told her tale she seemed to be divine.

After the committee left for the day, Jeanne went into the chapel to seek comfort from the saints who spoke to her daily. The next day the committee returned. The professor of theology spoke first: "You say that God wishes to free the people of France from their distress. If he wishes to free them there is no need for the soldiers you ask for."

"In God's name," exclaimed Jeanne with some irritation, "God will give the victory, but the men-at-arms must first do the fighting."

There was a stir among the learned men at this answer. The professor who had asked the question smiled as though he was pleased with the answer. Another member of the committee murmured: "No clerk of the court could have answered better."

Then a friar named Sequin took his turn. He spoke with the accent of Limoges, his native district.

"In what language do these voices speak to you?" he asked.

This question seemed frivolous to Jeanne. She knew no language but French, so what other language would the Voices use?

"They speak in a language better than yours," she answered, which made the other members of the committee laugh, for the accent of Limoges was a common subject of ridicule.

"Do you believe in God?" continued the friar.

"Firmly," she replied.

"Then you must know that God does not wish us to trust you without some sign that you can do what you say. We cannot advise the king to risk his soldiers on the strength of your word alone. What sign can you give?"

"I did not come to show signs in Poictiers," cried Jeanne, now thoroughly worn out. "Lead me to Orléans with a few men-at-arms and I will show you the sign. Listen, and I will tell you what will happen. I will drive the English from their siege. I will lead the Dauphin to his coronation at Reims. Paris will pledge allegiance to the rightful king, and the Duke of Orléans will return from his captivity. This is what the Voices have told me."

All of those who heard her words that day lived to see her prophecies fulfilled, all except Jeanne herself. During her life, only the first two happened.

"Why do you call Charles 'Dauphin,' instead of 'King?' "

"Because he is not king until he is crowned and anointed with the sacred oil at Reims," she answered.

Each day for the next three weeks the questioning continued. In addition to this official examination of her faith and character, many other investigations were made into her claims. She was visited by every curious person, men and women, in the whole region and asked endless questions until her story became known to the whole country.

Queen Yolande and her daughter, Queen Marie, along with their ladies-in-waiting, subjected Jeanne to a penetrating inquiry. They asked about her life in a subtle, feminine way, testing her innocence and purity. The women wanted to know why she wore a man's clothing. Jeanne told Queen Yolande: "It is the best way to dress for fighting, and while I did not choose to fight, I have been commanded to do so. Therefore, I live among men-at-arms, and this way of dressing is correct. I must wear this clothing to do what I am commanded to do."

"True," agreed the Queen thoughtfully. "You are quite right. I see it. Others shall see it, too."

Yolande was charmed by Jeanne and reported to the learned council: "It is my belief," she said, "that the child was sent from God."

All the women said so. Jeanne had the women on her side, as well as many of the members of the council who had grown to believe in her. Some of the men were disgusted with the cowardice and treachery of La Trémouïlle and the other hangers-on. These men were willing to fight for France and they were aroused by Jeanne's enthusiasm.

Meanwhile, the emissaries who had been sent to Domremy to investigate her past returned to report that they had discovered no flaw in her character. At the end of three weeks of daily examinations Jeanne was summoned before the whole council to hear the committee's judgment. Alençon, her two faithful knights, and other true friends went with her. The Dauphin and his advisers also attended, and so did Queen Yolande and many people from the town. The Archbishop of Reims presided over the council and read the judgment: "Jeanne D'Arc's character has been studied. We have looked into her birth, past life, and intentions. She has been examined by clerks, churchmen, men of the sword, matrons, and widows. Nothing has been found in her but honesty, simplicity, humility, maidenhood, and devotion.

"After hearing all these reports, taking into consideration the goodness of Jeanne D'Arc and that she declares herself to be sent by God, it is therefore determined by this council that the king should use her and that she may go with the army to Orléans."

There was dead silence as the archbishop finished reading the statement. The incredible thing had happened. The peasant maid had triumphed. To the young girl, barely seventeen, had been given the task of lifting the siege of Orléans.

Suddenly the silence was broken by a storm of applause. Charles rose and beckoned Jeanne to come to him. As she arose to obey the command, the court and the people also rose and stood reverently as a mark of homage and respect. Charles himself was moved to behave like a king. He descended from the throne and escorted Jeanne back to the throne where everyone could see her, then bent low over her hand as if she were the king and he the humble servant.

Jeanne, with tears of happiness streaming from her eyes, fell on her knees and kissed his hand. For Charles, to her, represented France—the France she had come to save.

CHAPTER 18

THE WARRIOR MAID

A wave of enthusiasm swept the land as the news of the verdict spread. France began to shake off her yoke of cowardice and rose to action. Men and arms began to filter into Blois, the nearest city to Orléans that remained in Charles's hands. Alençon and the other lords, Queen Yolande of Sicily, and cities like La Rochelle which remained loyal to Charles opened their treasuries and gave money to finance the army. An inspired young woman had been sent from God to lead France to victory against the enemy. Men took heart and prepared to go retake Orléans.

Possession of this city, which lay between the provinces that had submitted to the English and those remaining loyal to France, was crucial to Charles. Orléans would be a gathering point for his friends and a stronghold they could use to fight his enemies. The success of Charles's cause depended on its possession. If Orléans were lost for good, the monarch would have to flee the country. The outcome of the siege of Orléans would determine the fate of France, its nationality, its very existence.

A month went by before the full number of men and sufficient provisions could be gathered for the battle, but Jeanne understood that such a massive effort took time and she was no longer impatient. While she waited, the Dauphin sent her to Tours to be fitted with armor. Queen Yolande herself

103

designed the armor for Jeanne. It was to be of steel inlaid with silver and burnished to a shining whiteness symbolic of purity.

Charles surrounded Jeanne with a household appropriate for a person of her importance. She lived with Lady Eleanor, one of Queen Marie's ladies and wife of Jean du Puy; her attendants were Jean d'Aulon, a veteran from Orléans, who acted as her squire, the two knights who had accompanied her from Vaucouleurs, two pages, Louis de Coutes and Raimond, and, later, Father Jean Pasquerel, an Augustinian friar who was her priest and confessor. Jeanne accepted the household and splendid armor because they symbolically showed the people and the army that the Dauphin trusted her, which helped her mission.

For the design of her flag and the type of sword she would carry, she gave directions herself because her Voices had given her specific revelations concerning these. Charles would have given a sword to her to replace the one from Robert de Baudricourt. But she told him of another weapon that her Voices had told her to use.

"I have sent a letter to the priests at Saint Catherine's church in Fierbois asking for it," she said. "I told them that it would be found buried in the earth behind the altar. The messenger should return with it today."

"If it is there," Charles remarked, half laughing.

"It will be, Dauphin," Jeanne said confidently.

"But how will they know that they've found the right sword?"

"There will be five crosses on the handle."

The Dauphin dropped the subject, and decided to wait and see if the sword was found where Jeanne said it would be. Alençon, La Trémouïlle, and Queen Yolande were listening and waiting, too. La Trémouïlle echoed Charles's own thoughts by saying, "I should like to see this mystic sword, Your Majesty."

The monarch smiled without replying. But Alençon, reacting instantly to the mocking tone in La Trémouïlle's voice, exclaimed, "If she says the sword is under the altar at Saint Catherine's, it is there. And anyone who denies it shall answer to me."

"Easy, cousin," said Charles lazily. "There will be time enough for private quarrels after Orléans. La Trémouïlle doesn't doubt her, he only has a natural desire to witness the marvel."

At this moment, the messenger Jeanne had sent to Fierbois entered. He approached the Dauphin and presented a sword to him. Charles drew the weapon from its red velvet sheath and examined it closely. It was an ancient blade and though it had been cleaned it still showed traces of rust. On the handle, just as Jeanne said there would be, were five crosses.

"Did the priests know the sword was there?" he asked the man.

"No, sir. At first they said that Jeanne D'Arc must be mistaken. But after some looking and searching they found it just where she said, buried behind the altar. It was very rusty when it was taken from the earth, but when the priests started to clean it the rust fell away by itself. There is a great stir over the event at Fierbois and the priests had this scabbard of crimson velvet made for Jeanne to carry the sacred weapon in."

"The matter is indeed marvelous," commented Charles, laying the sword in Jeanne's hands. "But even though it is a good blade, it will need sharpening before it can be used."

Jeanne blushed. "It shall never be used to shed blood," she said. "I love it already, but it shall not be used to kill. I could not kill anyone."

Charles smiled slightly. Here was a maiden anxious to lead an army into battle, but she was saying that she could not shed blood.

"And what about your flag?" he said. "Didn't you say that you had divine guidance about it also?"

After some urging Jeanne told Charles the exact design that Saints Margaret and Catherine had dictated to her. The Dauphin had the standard painted just as she described. It was made of white linen and on its field were scattered golden lilies. In the middle God was painted holding the world and sitting upon the clouds; on either side an angel knelt, and the motto was *Jesus Marie*. This standard symbolized her mission: the lilies of France, the country she had come to save; God, who had sent her; and Jesus, the Son of Mary, her watchword. On the reverse side of the standard Charles had the artisans embroider Jeanne's symbol, a silver dove on a blue field.

The great standard was to be used to rally all of the men. Jeanne also had a personal banner and a pennant. On the banner, which she would use to gather the men for prayer, was painted Jesus Christ on the cross between the Virgin Mary and Saint John. On the pennant, which she would use to signal her guards, was pictured the Annunciation, the angel with a lily kneeling to the Virgin Mary. Jeanne declared that she would carry the great standard herself, which was unusual for a general in the field, but this was the command of her saints.

"Take the standard for God and carry it boldly," they had told her.

While all these preparations were being made, Jeanne visited Alençon's wife and mother at St. Florent near Saumur. Alençon's wife was also called Jeanne. Her father was Charles, Duke of Orléans, then nearly fifteen years a prisoner in England. Jeanne of Orléans, as Alençon's wife was called, worried now for her husband's safety.

"Don't be afraid, madame," said Jeanne D'Arc. "I will bring him safely back to you."

While Jeanne was at St. Florent, the two knights, Poulengy and de Metz, had gone on a pilgrimage to Our Lady of Puy en Velay. For this year, 1429, was the year of Jubilee, as any year was called when Good Friday and the Annunciation fell upon the same day. The years when this happened were always marked by strange and great events, and crowds flocked to the church.

The morning that the knights were to return, Jeanne was receiving visitors in an upper room of the house of Jean du Puy. Her attention was caught by a commotion in the street below; there came shouts and cries and the sound of footsteps, followed by a rush of men hurrying up the stairs. As the door was flung open a young voice cried, "Jeanne, Jeanne! Where are you? We have come to you, Jeanne."

Jeanne cried for joy as Pierre and Jean, her brothers, came into the room, followed by the two knights and Father Pasquerel.

"Oh, boys!" she cried, trying to embrace both of them at once. "When did you come? How did you get here?"

"We met the knights and Father Pasquerel at Puy en Velay, where we went with mother on a pilgrimage. Then we came on here," Pierre told her, giving her a bearlike hug.

"With mother?" exclaimed Jeanne. "Mother went to Puy en Velay?"

"Yes. She sends her love and blessing to you. She made offerings for you there," Jean said.

"And father?" Jeanne asked anxiously. "How is father?"

"He grieves over your absence, Jeanne, but he sends his blessing and love also."

"Thank God," cried Jeanne. "It's good to have you here. Now you shall be members of my household and be with me wherever I go."

The arrival of her brothers made Jeanne very happy. It was as if her home had been brought to her. Now, with Jean and Pierre by her side and the love and blessing of her parents, she approached her task with a light heart.

By the twenty-fifth of April everything was ready for the march to Orléans. Jeanne left Tours and went to the military station Blois to meet with the captains and soldiers. It was a busy scene in the little town. The roads were full of oxen, cows, sheep, and pigs all gathered to feed the troops when they occupied Orléans. The lowing cattle, bleating sheep, and riotous noise from the soldiers in camp made an uproar. Many of the captains were officers of wide renown. There was De Gaucourt, the old commander of Orléans, whom she had already met; Rais and Boussac, two marshals of France; Culent, the Lord Admiral; and La Hire, the Gascon pirate. They revered her as a saintly child, but after they met with her they said among themselves that while she would inspire the army with courage, as for war—well, when had a woman known anything about the art of war?

After meeting with all the captains, Jeanne sent the English a letter by herald:

> To the King of England and the Duke of Bedford, who calls himself regent of France; and to your lieutenants William de la Poule, Comte de Sulford, John, Lord of Talbot, and Thomas, Lord of Scales:
>
> Listen to the King of Heaven. Give to the Maid who is sent by God the keys of all the good towns which you have taken by violence in France. She is sent by God to redeem the rights of the King of France. She is ready to make peace if you will hear reason and be just toward France and pay for what you have taken.
>
> And archers, brothers-in-arms, and others who are before the town of Orléans, return to your own country at God's command.
>
> King of England, if you will not do this, wherever I meet your people in France I will make them flee. I am sent from God to drive you all out of France. If the soldiers obey, I will have mercy on them. Do not be obstinate for you shall not withhold the kingdom of France from God, the King of Heaven. Charles is the true heir, for God wills it, and so it has been revealed to the Maid. If you do not listen to the word of God and the Maid, we will chase you out of France.

The Maid begs you and bids you, Duke of Bedford, not to bring destruction on yourself.

—Jeanne the Maid

Into every part of this armed camp the girl of seventeen penetrated. Armies of that day were usually brutal; drinking, gambling, stealing, and other vices were prevalent. But even though the soldiers were rude, rough, and lawless, they adored and revered some holy things. To them the fair young girl was a saint. They adored her and talked freely among themselves about her personality and habits. She was good to the poor, confessed daily, and often heard mass three times a day; there was also a grace of purity about her as though she had descended from Heaven. So when Jeanne declared that the war was a holy war, and that all who followed her must be free of sin, the gambling and stealing stopped, and the men went to confession and received communion daily. La Hire, too, although he was a fierce ruffian, even gave up swearing, but he begged Jeanne to leave him something to swear by and she, having a sense of humor, left him his baton.

On the morning of April twenty-eighth all was ready and the army started its march to Orléans. The day was bright and beautiful. Brilliant sunlight flooded the fields and meadows full of wildflowers. At the head of the army marched a long procession of priests carrying crosses and banners, swinging censers from which smoky incense rose; their solemn chanting was accompanied by fanfares and bugles of the army. Following the priests Jeanne came on a great white charger that the Dauphin had given her. She was wearing her white armor inlaid with silver, all shining in a radiant whiteness like Saint Michael himself. With her rode her squire, D'Aulon, followed by her faithful knights, her brothers, and her priest. Behind them stretched the main body of the army, a forest of glittering spears, each division commanded by its own general. Then came the long train of carts and cattle that supported the army. As Jeanne rode by with all behind her, the citizens of the town lined up along the roadside to bless her.

Blois was thirty miles from Orléans on the same side of the Loire River as the besieged city. Jeanne's plan, which had been given to her by her Voices, was to go directly to Orléans by the right bank, and enter the city by its western gate, right past the English fortifications. Her theory about the art of war was simple: attack the main body of the enemy. But since she was unfamiliar with the countryside, she left the routing of their approach to her captains.

The English had built a line of strong fortresses called bastilles around Orléans. And these fortresses closed all the gates of the city but one. The French generals believed it would be disastrous to fight their way past these strongholds. After their experience at Rouvray the generals hesitated to come face to face with their enemies in the field. As far as they were concerned, Jeanne's main value was to stir up the troops and inspire them to fight courageously, not to plan battle strategy. So they decided to approach Orléans from the left bank of the river. They did not tell Jeanne about their new routing, letting her believe that Orléans was directly in their line of march.

After crossing the bridge at Blois they marched up the south bank and spent one night in the field. About noon the following day the army came to the heights of Olivet, two miles south of Orléans. From this vantage point the city and the position of the besieging army could be plainly seen. Jeanne looked out and immediately saw how she had been misled. Between her and Orléans lay the wide river, a broken bridge, and the camps of the English.

The generals had neglected to figure out how the army and all of its provisions could be ferried across the river under the English artillery. On the far shore the citizens of Orléans swarmed over the walls and piers of the city, trying to launch sailboats to cross the water and fetch the army. But a strong wind was blowing and it was impossible to bring up the heavy barges needed to transport men and provisions. Meanwhile the army and convoy were open to attack by the English, who could safely cross the river under the guns of their fort on the island and the bridge.

Jeanne spoke her mind plainly to the generals. She wanted to attack the fortresses of the English on this side of the river at once, and the soldiers were eager to follow her. The generals pleaded with her to hold back, fearing they wouldn't have the strength to hold the bastilles if they did succeed in taking them. The army marched upriver to a point six miles above the city. Their progress was watched anxiously by the people of Orléans; the countryside was so flat that every movement could be easily seen. When the expedition stopped, the Count of Dunois, half brother to the Duke of Orléans and commander of the city, rowed upstream in a small boat to meet it. Jeanne spurred forward to meet the hardy young man who leaped from the boat.

"Are you the Count of Dunois?" she asked.

"I am," he said. "And I'm glad that you've come."

"Are you the one who suggested that I should come by this bank instead of the other side?"

"I and wiser men than I gave that advice. We believed it was the best and safest way," he answered mildly.

"In God's name, the advice of my Lord is safer and wiser than yours." Jeanne pointed to the water running rough and fast, a strong wind following it, so that no boats from Orléans could reach them.

"You thought you could deceive me, and you deceived yourself instead, for I bring you better help than any captain ever received, help from the King of Heaven. God himself has taken pity on the city of Orléans. And with the help of God all will still go well."

At that moment the wind that was against them shifted and each vessel could now tow two others. Dunois was very impressed by this sign from God and looked at Jeanne with reverence. Taking advantage of the favorable change, he had the heavy barges towed up the river to a place where the supplies could be loaded without danger of attack. As the loaded barges floated back downstream to the city, some of the soldiers attacked the English bastille of St. Loup, preventing the enemy from firing on the flotilla and assuring the safe arrival of the supplies.

Now the Count of Dunois asked Jeanne to return with him to the city. The people were awaiting her arrival, he said, and it would give them courage and hope just to see her. But Jeanne was reluctant to leave the main body of the army, which was going to return to Blois, cross back over the bridge there, and return to Orléans by the right bank, according to Jeanne's original plan.

Jeanne was afraid to leave them. She had been deceived once, and didn't know for certain whether the captains would keep their promise to return with the soldiers. She also worried that she might lose her hold on the men if they were without her presence.

Dunois implored the captains to promise to return. They promised and then, sending her great standard on with the soldiers, Jeanne and Dunois crossed the river by barge, taking along her personal entourage and a small force of two hundred lances.

It was nearly eight o'clock in the evening when she rode into the city by way of the Burgundy gate. She was clad in full armor, mounted on the white horse, and carrying her white pennant. On her left rode Count Dunois also dressed in armor, and behind her came her entourage, with many lords and squires, captains and soldiers, all followed by some of the people of Orléans who had gone out to escort her.

At the gate were the rest of the soldiers and the men and women of Orléans. The bells of the city rang out and the people cheered and wept for joy. The Maid had come and they had every reason to rejoice. They had endured a great deal and now they felt comforted because of what they had heard about this simple maid. Through the glare of the torches Jeanne saw the sea of faces turned toward her. She stretched out her hands toward them: "Be of good cheer," she cried. "God has heard your prayers."

Everyone tried to touch her or to touch even the horse she rode. The people came so close that a torchbearer was pushed against the pennant and the fringe caught fire. Instantly Jeanne spurred forward, leaned down, and put out the flame with her mail-clad hand.

The procession made its way to the Cathedral of St. Croix. Jeanne gave thanks as she entered the church. She was in Orléans at last.

CHAPTER 19

THE HOUR AND THE GIRL

The next day Jeanne was eager to engage the enemy, and the citizens would gladly have followed her, but Dunois and the captains of the Orléans garrison wanted to wait for the army to return from Blois. Through the years of devastating war, the French people had stopped believing in themselves. It was said that a thousand Frenchmen could be beaten by two hundred Englishmen.

The first herald Jeanne had sent to the English had never returned. Now she sent another summons, demanding that the enemy surrender before the attack, and return her messenger at once. Dunois also wrote to the English, warning that if they harmed Jeanne's herald, Dunois would retaliate on his English prisoners.

The last messenger was returned at once, but the English still kept the first herald, threatening to kill him. By the rules of war messengers were always protected and never killed. But the English said this herald came from the Armagnac witch, and thus should be burned at the stake in place of his mistress.

The English thought Jeanne's letter demanding their surrender was a joke. They called her a "dairy maid" and told her to go back to her cows; they threatened to burn her if they caught her.

Despite their scornful, defiant words, an undercurrent of fear could be

Far into the night they rode.
Page 83

An inspired young woman had been sent from God
to lead France to victory against the enemy.
Page 103

sensed in their response. Both the English and the French believed that Jeanne had supernatural powers of some kind. The English believed she was an emissary of evil.

That afternoon La Hire and Florent d'Illiers, two of the captains who had entered the city with Jeanne, sallied forth with a small force of men-at-arms and some citizens. The English had established a small outpost between their main fortress and the city wall. The French troops attacked the outpost and drove the English back into the main fortress, but the English rallied and pushed them back into town.

In the evening Jeanne rode forth, the townspeople crowding around her, and stopped on the town end of the broken bridge. She called out to the enemy, courteously asking them once more to withdraw while there was still time. Sweetly and clearly her voice rang across the water, so that the English on the other side of the bridge could not fail to hear her. Sir William Glasdale —called Classidas by the French—came out on the bridge and hurled a volume of abuse on Jeanne. She was momentarily overwhelmed by his foul epithets, then, drawing her sword, she waved it above her head, crying, "Do you dare curse, Classidas? You who will die so soon without a stroke of the sword?"

Glasdale, now surrounded by his captains, retorted with such vile words that Jeanne wept bitterly. And still weeping she turned her horse and rode back into the city.

There was no sign of the army coming back. Dunois was afraid that without Jeanne the captains had been unable to persuade the Dauphin to send the army back to Orléans. He decided to go back to Blois and bring the army himself. He set out on Sunday, accompanied by Jeanne's squire, D'Aulon. Jeanne took La Hire and other captains and covered his departure, taking up a dangerous position between the Dunois expedition and the enemy. In the English towers not a man budged, not a shot was fired. So Dunois went on his way unharmed, while Jeanne returned to town. The citizens were watching for her, and as she entered the town they pressed forward and walked by the side of her charger to the cathedral, where every journey ended. Everywhere she went people crowded around her, following her every step, as if they couldn't get enough of the sight of her.

Unable to attack until Dunois came with the army, Jeanne rode out on Monday to reconnoiter the English position. As always she was followed by the captains and soldiers and a great crowd of townspeople who seemed to feel no fear in her company.

The city of Orléans was built in a loose parallelogram, its southern side bordering the banks of the Loire River. The city was protected by a strong wall from twenty to thirty feet high, punctuated by twenty-four towers. A parapet ran along the top of the wall to screen troops so they could safely stand up and fire, or drop down heavy stones and boiling liquids through openings in the wall. Outside the wall, except on the river side, ran a ditch forty feet wide and twenty feet deep.

On the river side the walls of the city rose directly from the water. A great stone bridge with arches, buildings, and fortifications spanned the river here, but the English held both the broken bridge and its huge fortress, called Les Tourelles, which was connected to the opposite shore by a drawbridge. Their vantage point from Tourelles, supported by three smaller forts, commanded and dominated the entire river border of Orléans.

The suburbs outside Orléans had been destroyed by their own residents to prevent the English from taking shelter there. The fifteen thousand homeless people crowded into the city, nearly doubling the population of Orléans and threatening all with famine.

The other three sides of the city could be penetrated through four great gates which led to and from the main roads. On the north side the Bannier Gate and the Paris Gate opened on the road to Paris. On the east side the Burgundy Gate opened on the road to Checy and Jargeau, from which the English drew many of their supplies. This road was commanded by the St. Loup tower, one of the enemy's strongest fortresses.

On the west side, the Regnart Gate opened on the road to Blois. The principal camp of the English was here, guarding the road to Blois and controlling all traffic. They could easily stop any convoys carrying supplies and food from the royal provinces into the city.

It was through the Regnart Gate that Jeanne went to make her reconnaissance. As she rode around the city at a leisurely pace, the enemy soldiers craned their necks to get a look at her, but not a shot was fired. She seemed like a shining vision, clad in white armor, riding her white horse, her head covered by a little velvet cap ornamented with nodding plumes, her dark hair flying around her face. Even as the English hurled words of abuse at her, their lips turned pale with superstitious terror.

Unharmed, Jeanne completed her survey, then led her troops back through the gate into the city, then on to the cathedral. Here Jean de Mascon, known to be a very wise man, said to her, "My child, have you come to lift the siege?"

"In God's name, yes."

"The enemy is strong and well entrenched; it will be a great feat to drive them out."

"Nothing is impossible to the power of God," Jeanne answered.

The next day an advance guard marched into the city bringing word that the French army was on its way from Blois. At dawn on Wednesday, Jeanne, accompanied by La Hire and five hundred of her men, rode out to meet the army on the Paris road. Right under the noses of the enemy they rode, but not a shot was fired from the English forts. To the English troops the slender figure in shining armor seemed supernatural.

Led by the priests chanting solemnly, headed by Father Pasquerel bearing the great standard, Jeanne and her army reentered Orléans by the Paris Gate, as she had intended to do the first time. By noon she had her army safely housed within the city's walls.

That evening D'Aulon dined with Jeanne. While they were still seated at the table, Dunois came in to tell Jeanne that Sir John Fastolf, the commander who had scattered the French in the Battle of the Herrings, was on his way from Paris with reinforcement and supplies for the English. Word was that he was only a day away.

Jeanne was joyful at the news. At last, she would have action. "Dunois," she cried, "I command you, in God's name, let me know as soon as he arrives! If you don't, I—well, I will have your head."

"I'm not worried, Jeanne," the Count replied. "I'll let you know the minute we have news."

Now, not every knight was as enthusiastic about Jeanne as Dunois, La Hire, and a few others were. It was natural for men who had been unsuccessfully defending the beleaguered city to feel jealous of Jeanne and her claims. One captain named Guillaume de Gamache was insulted by the suggestion that Jeanne should plan the attack against the enemy.

"How could a woman whom nobody knows know better than a captain how to wage battle? I am folding up my banner."

Dunois had tried in vain to placate these men. Unknown to Jeanne, those captains who had remained behind that morning while Jeanne marched out to meet Dunois had made a sortie of their own, gathering up their men to go against the strong bastille of St. Loup.

Unaware of their movements, and wearied by the early morning expedition, Jeanne lay down in the afternoon by the side of her hostess, Madame Boucher, to sleep. D'Aulon too felt fatigued, and stretched himself out on a couch to rest. All at once, Jeanne awoke with a wild cry.

"I must go against the English!" she cried. "But I don't know where." Her eyes had the rapt look they always had when she had seen her visions.

"My arms, D'Aulon! My arms!" she cried. "Quick! The blood of our soldiers is flowing. Why didn't they tell me?"

No sound could be heard from the streets on this tranquil May afternoon. But at her cry D'Aulon leaped to his feet and, without a word, began to help Jeanne buckle on her armor, assisted by Madame Boucher and her little daughter. All the while Jeanne was calling loudly to her page for her horse. Hurriedly the youth saddled the charger and brought it around to the door. As Jeanne swung herself up into the saddle, she realized she had forgotten her standard.

"My flag," she cried, and the page ran upstairs and handed down the flag through the window. With the heavy staff in hand, she spurred her horse and dashed away so fast that sparks flashed from the cobblestones under its hooves. One by one her attendants armed themselves and clattered after her.

She could hear a loud clamoring behind her as the streets filled with people shouting that the English were slaughtering the French. Straight through the town Jeanne galloped, riding toward the sound of battle, which seemed to be coming from the Burgundian Gate on the east side of the city. The gate was wide open to let in a rabble of retreating French carrying their wounded with them. Jeanne turned pale and slowed her horse.

"Whenever I see French blood my hair rises with horror," she said to D'Aulon, who by this time had caught up with her.

They pushed their way through the gate, rumbling straight through the disorganized mob of knights and archers fleeing before the English. The coup against St. Loup had proved disastrous. But as the French caught sight of Jeanne galloping through the gate, a great shout went up. The troops rallied, turned, and swept onward with her. Clear and sweet above the din of battle sounded her bell-like voice: "Friends, friends, have courage. On! On! They are ours!"

There never was anything like the response that followed. The French surged forward upon the English, who had sallied confidently out of their fortress after the original assault. Now the enemy was driven back into their bastille. The English fought gallantly, but they were no match for men imbued with divine ardor by the Maid. Everywhere the shining figure appeared in the thick of battle, encouraging and urging the men to greater efforts. In response the French hurled themselves with fury against the formidable walls of the bastille. Back and forth the tide of battle surged as the English made a desperate resistance. Back and forth until the sun began to set and with a final mighty rush the French stormed the fortress and St. Loup was taken. Before reinforcements could arrive, the fort was ransacked and burned.

Dizzy with the first victory that had been theirs in years, the soldiers and citizens reentered Orléans with banners flying, proudly displaying their prisoners and captured munitions. The city went wild over Jeanne, who had wrought the miracle. The townspeople pressed upon her as she rode by. All the bells in the city rang joyfully, and in the churches soldiers and citizens alike gave thanks to God.

At this, the end of her first battle, Jeanne wept and prayed for those who had died. She said to Father Pasquerel: "In five days the city shall be delivered; but I shall be wounded on Saturday, here." And she placed her hand on a spot between her neck and shoulder."

Her knights were now ready to follow wherever she might lead. But the next day was a holy day, the Feast of Ascension, and Jeanne's captains dissuaded her from attacking another English fortress. She herself considered her mission a holy one and saw no reason to stall, but she agreed to wait. While she went to confession and took communion, the captains held a secret meeting.

They decided to feign an attack on the strong bastille of St. Laurent, which stood on the west side of town just beyond the Regnart Gate. They expected the ruse to draw the enemy away from the line of huge forts beyond the river. Jeanne would make the feint, while the captains and their soldiers made the real assault across the river to the south.

Ambroise de Lore then summoned Jeanne to the meeting. When she came, Chancellor Cousinot himself told her they had decided to attack the great fortress of St. Laurent and she was to lead the attack. He did not mention their larger plan.

Jeanne knew he was holding something back, but she said nothing until he finished. Then she spoke quietly.

"What have you really decided?" she asked. "Why are you afraid to tell me what it is?"

"Don't be angry," Dunois said. "We can't tell you everything at once. What the Chancellor has said is true, but when the English across the river rush to the aid of St. Laurent we intend to cross over and attack their primary forts."

Jeanne let the matter rest. But the plan was never carried out. That evening she went back to the broken bridge and again called across the water to the English, telling them that it was God's will that they should withdraw from France. Then she fastened a letter to an arrow and directed an archer to shoot it into the enemy fortress on the other side of the river. "This is my last offer," she said. "I would send it by messenger, but you still hold my herald captive. Release him and I will return the prisoners we took at St. Loup."

"News from the Armagnac wench," shouted a soldier as he ran forward to pick up the letter. "Witch! If we catch you, you'll burn."

Jeanne tried to smile through her tears as she heard these insults. "I have a message from the King of Heaven, Classidas," she called back to Sir William Glasdale, the fort's commander. "The English shall withdraw; but you will be dead without a stroke of the sword."

The English hooted and jeered, and hurled taunts and foul epithets on her. Having made her message plain, Jeanne turned and rode back into Orléans.

She rose early the next morning and made her confession before mass. Then she set out, followed by her personal attendants and a multitude of citizens.

The secret of the true attack on the south bank forts had somehow leaked out. With the diversionary plan useless, Jeanne and her company headed directly for the Burgundy Gate, through which they could reach the south bank. But the captains, still intending to carry out the futile plan, blocked her exit.

Seeing armed guards posted at the gate, Jeanne cried out, "In God's name, open the gate and let us pass."

"I cannot, Jeanne," answered the captain in charge. "I have orders to keep it closed."

A shout went up from the citizens pushing behind Jeanne and they moved forward threateningly.

"You cannot prevent these people from going," cried Jeanne. "No matter what you decide, they shall prevail."

The captain hesitated. The stern faces of the citizens, determined to fight their way through the gate if necessary, told him he was in peril of his life. He threw wide the gate, crying, "Come on, I will be your captain!" And the people rushed through.

They made their way to the Loire. Across the river, lying close to the south bank, was a broad island, called St. Aignan. A little farther up the opposite shore stood the small, strategic fort of St. Jean le Blanc. In the original plan the captains intended to reach the island by boat, then lay planks across to the south shore and attack St. Jean le Blanc.

The band of citizens didn't wait for Jeanne and her men to bring horses and artillery. Instead, they immediately piled into small boats and started rowing for the island. When the English captain saw the boats coming, he abandoned le Blanc and withdrew to the larger fortress of St. Augustins, directly opposite the dominant English position at Tourelles.

The citizens landed on the island, quickly set the makeshift planks, and walked across to the south shore. When they found le Blanc empty, they were wild with enthusiasm. Without waiting for support, they marched directly to St. Augustins and attacked.

The English rushed out to meet them, slashing, slaying, and hurling taunts. Immediately the old dread fell upon the French townspeople. Panic-stricken, they fled before the enemy like disorganized rabble.

At this moment, Jeanne and La Hire, who had been having trouble getting the horses across the improvised bridge, reached shore. Seeing the French routed, they mounted hastily, and then these two, Jeanne with her banner, La Hire with his lance, charged the English. At the sight of the dazzling white figure on the white horse, the English turned and fled. The townsfolk rallied, turned, and following the men-at-arms who had finally succeeded in crossing the river, went with the Maid and the valiant La Hire, and chased the English back into their fort.

Jeanne planted her standard in the moat of St. Augustins, and the assault began. The English fought bravely, and again the French were pushed back. Jeanne was everywhere, inciting the men to greater deeds by her inspiring cries. At last, the main body of her troops came up with the artillery, and the French assault gained momentum.

Onset after onset was made. Knights vied with each other for feats of valor. A giant Englishman who gallantly defended the fort's open gate was shot by Jean, the Lorraine gunner. Instantly, Jeanne's clear, girlish voice rang out: "Enter! Enter boldly! They are ours."

In a terrible onslaught the French rushed in. A few of the English escaped by the connecting road and drawbridge to Les Tourelles. The rest were killed or taken prisoner. Great deeds had been performed on both sides, and the victory was hard won. But St. Augustins was taken. The sun was setting, and setting also was the glory of England in France. Truly, God was speaking through His Maid.

CHAPTER 20

JEANNE SHOWS HER SIGN

Worried that the men would become uncontrollable if allowed to plunder the fortress, Jeanne ordered the buildings of St. Augustins burned. In the morning, she wanted the men to be rested and ready for the attack on the major fortress of Tourelles. They would camp on the hard-won field and be in position to push the assault at dawn. Jeanne, trying to anticipate the enemy's next move, worried that the English might attack that night. She decided to sleep in the field with her troops.

But La Hire wanted her to return to Orléans for medical treatment. She had been wounded in the foot when she stepped on a piercing *chausse-trape*, a small weapon of iron with sharp spikes. Jeanne finally allowed herself to be persuaded and, with most of her captains and squires, crossed the river to the town, leaving the archers with a body of citizens on the field.

Although it was a Friday, Jeanne broke her usual fast and ate a little meat, for she was worn and weary. She wanted to build her strength for the great work that lay ahead the next day. While she was eating, a knight came to tell her that the captains were meeting in council. They had decided that their forces were too weak to risk an attack on Tourelles the next day. God had greatly favored them already, and enough had been accomplished. It would be

wiser to wait for reinforcements from the Dauphin. Orléans was well supplied
with food and they could afford to wait.

Jeanne listened to the announcement with quiet disdain.

"You have been with your council," she said, "and I have been with mine.
You may believe that the counsel of my Lord, the King of Heaven, shall
prevail. Get up early tomorrow morning, fight your best, and you shall accomplish more than you have done today."

As the knight left, Jeanne turned to her priest and said, "Rise tomorrow
even earlier than today. Do your best to stay near me, for tomorrow I shall
have much greater things to do. Tomorrow I will be wounded here." And again
she placed her hand on a spot above her right breast, between her neck and
shoulder.

Jeanne was up just before dawn, but early as it was, some of the townspeople were already waiting to see her. They had held a meeting of their own,
they said, and they were in no mood to wait for reinforcements from the king.
They had been under siege for seven months and had received nothing but
broken promises from Charles. Only Jeanne had helped them. Since God
chose to send them aid through her, it seemed madness not to accept the
divine favor. They begged her to go against the enemy that day, no matter
what the captains said.

Jeanne didn't need urging. She answered with solemn intensity: "Be of good
cheer. In God's name I will go against the English today. And the captains will
go also, and will fight with us."

The delighted townsmen departed to spread the news through the city.
Jeanne, followed by her attendants, ran down to the courtyard to mount her
war horse.

At that moment, her host Jacques Boucher came into the yard carrying a
large shad in his hand. "Stay, Jeanne. I've brought fish for your breakfast. You
need food before starting on so great an enterprise."

"Keep it for supper," cried the girl gaily. "And tonight I will come back by
the bridge!"

"Tonight? Impossible. The bridge is broken."

Jeanne laughed again, and was off. When the great standard appeared in the
streets, and Jeanne came into view with her company, many of her captains
gladly flocked to her. Dunois, La Hire, d'Illiers, Zaintrailles, Gaucourt, and

many others crossed the river with her; some remained behind to protect the city against attack.

A difficult task lay before the French. First they had to overcome a solid earthwork that rose up in front of Tourelles. The rear of this rampart connected to the main fort by a drawbridge, under which ran a deep, swift strip of the Loire River. The rampart itself was strong, fortified with high walls with a great, dry moat running in front of it. Even if the French succeeded in taking it, the enemy could escape by crossing the drawbridge into the Tourelles, which was considered impregnable.

Six hundred crack English soldiers held the Tourelles, commanded by that fearless and daring knight Sir William Glasdale. The walls were defended by cannon, and the garrison was well supplied with armaments. It would be nearly impossible to drive these English troops from such a heavily fortified position.

But the French were well equipped with swords, arrows and crossbolts, hand-held shields, and large movable wooden shelters to protect them, ladders, beams to span ditches, and all the munitions of war. They also had more men, which was absolutely necessary to overcome the seemingly unconquerable position of the enemy.

In the field, the French army lay in the morning sunlight waiting for Jeanne and the captains. When she appeared, with D'Aulon carrying her standard, the soldiers began bustling. As Jeanne passed through the ranks and took up her position at the edge of the dry moat, her captains assembled the men into companies, each group flying its own standard.

At six o'clock, the French cannon situated behind their lines began to bombard the rampart with stone balls. The army attacked the walls on every side. The noise of attack and repulse was terrific. With their shields slung over their backs, the French ran up their scaling ladders in swarms, attacking the men at the top with such fury that the English cried out in amazement: "Do they think they're immortal?"

Again and again the English flung the ladders down, dashing the attackers into the ditch. With bow shot, gun shot, axes, lances, and leaden maces they beat back the French, killing and wounding many. But every blow seemed to give the French more strength; they returned again and again to the charge.

The air was filled with the shouts of the captains on both sides: "France and Saint Denys!" "Saint George for England!" Their cries whirled amid the singing of arrows, the twang of bowstrings, the clang of axes on armor, and the roar of guns.

Jeanne stood fully exposed to the fray, her clear girlish voice sounding high above the din and confusion of battle: "Courage! The hour is at hand!"

After many hours of desperate fighting, the spirit of the assailants began to flag. Seeing her troops weaken, Jeanne seized a scaling ladder and, placing it against the walls, started to climb up beneath a rain of arrows and stones. As she mounted the wall she cried clearly to her men below, "On, on! They are ours!"

With a great shout the French swarmed across the moat carrying ladders until a whole forest of wooden steps rose up against the walls. Up Jeanne climbed, still crying out encouragement, then, suddenly—a bolt whizzed, and she uttered a sharp cry of pain. Jeanne reeled and fell.

A great "Hurrah!" went up from the English. The witch had fallen, and her mysterious force was gone.

But De Gamache, the captain who had said he would never follow a girl into the fields, lifted her up and carried her to his horse.

"Brave girl," he said, "forgive me."

"Never was a knight so gallant," she said.

The bolt had shot through, its ugly point extending six inches behind her shoulder. Jeanne wept with the pain. Her attendants were afraid to drag the bolt from her shoulder, so Jeanne pulled it out herself, then, as the blood gushed out, she fainted. Father Pasquerel dressed the wound with a compress, and slowly Jeanne came around. She made her confession to the priest, and then lay quietly.

Meanwhile, the battle, which had been raging for thirteen hours, languished. The exhausted French drew back, and Dunois himself thought there was no hope of victory. The day was nearly spent, and the men were worn out. Dunois sounded recall, and gave orders to retreat back across the river. The captains had not expected to take the fort in a single day, in fact not in a single month. The bugle notes sounding retreat were welcome music to both sides.

But not to Jeanne. She was stunned when she heard the bugle. Ignoring her wound, she immediately got to her feet and managed to mount her horse. She rode straight to Dunois. "Doubt not," she said. "They are ours. Rest a little. Eat something. Refresh yourselves, and wait for me."

She rode off into a nearby vineyard, dismounted, and spent the next quarter of an hour in prayer. When she appeared again her eyes were shining, her whole appearance inspired.

"Oh," she cried, "the place is ours." And she spurred her charger back toward the moat.

At the moat's edge Jeanne saw her flag held by a strange Basque soldier she had never seen before. "My standard!" she cried, seizing hold of the floating end. As she and the man struggled for possession, the flag waved wildly like a signal for immediate onset. Her men gathered for the attack.

The Basque tore the standard from her hands and ran across the moat, planting the flag near the rampart.

Jeanne's company stood around her. "Watch," she said to the knight at her side. "Watch till the tail of the flag touches the wall."

A few moments passed. The great standard fluttered in the May breeze. Then the knight cried, "Jeanne, it touches!"

"Then enter," she cried, her voice thrilling through the air. "In God's name, enter! All is yours."

The troops rose as one man, and flung themselves against the walls. The English, flabbergasted at the new onset, defended themselves valiantly, but the French overwhelmed them. As the French swarmed over the top of the earthwork, the defenders panicked at the sight of the white figure standing beneath the standard, the rays of the setting sun striking a dazzling radiance from her shining armor. They had killed the witch, yet there she stood without a sign of injury.

"I see a crowd of butterflies hanging about her," one soldier cried in terror, throwing down his weapon and turning to flee into the Tourelles.

"No, it's a dove," gasped another who followed him.

Arrows flew on every side of Jeanne, but never touched her. The French fought on, incited to superhuman effort by the bell-like voice: "Oh, on! All is yours!"

And the rampart was taken.

Showering down curses upon them, Sir William Glasdale stood on the drawbridge, making a desperate effort to save his men by covering their retreat across the drawbridge into the Tourelles.

Suddenly a foul smoke rolled up from the water beneath the drawbridge, suffocating Glasdale and his men. The citizens of Orléans had loaded a barge with sulfur and other evil-smelling things, and floated it directly under the drawbridge. Tongues of flames shot up from the barge, licking the rafters of the drawbridge, darting through the planks. The cannon from Orléans pounded the roofs and walls of the Tourelles with stone balls. Jeanne's quick eye saw the danger to the withdrawing men. "Classidas!" she cried. "Yield! Surrender to the King of Heaven."

Before the compassionate voice faded away, the drawbridge, under the weight of rushing men in heavy armor, gave way. Glasdale and his companions plunged downward into the great river, and disappeared under the weight of their own armor; the raging fire prevented any rescue attempt. At the sight Jeanne broke down and wept, then kneeling began to pray for their souls.

The greater body of the English troops had succeeded in reaching the Tourelles, but they found the fortress assailed from all sides. The French knights who had remained behind in Orléans now came out for the assault. The struggle was soon over. Of all the stout defenders of the fort, not one escaped. All were slain, drowned, or taken prisoner. The flames of the rampart and drawbridge blazed out the story of a new defeat.

The bells of Orléans pealed forth joyously as Jeanne reentered the town by the captured bridge, as she had said she would do. The streets were so crowded with people that she could barely pass through. They pressed about her, kissing her hand, her armored shoes, patting her charger, and touching the floating folds of her standard. Others went before her, crying: "Make room! Room for the Maid of Orléans!"

Jeanne was no longer the Maid from Vaucouleurs or Domremy, she was their Maid, the deliverer of their city, sent by the King of Heaven. And so she has remained to this very day, the Maid of Orléans.

Through the delirious joy Jeanne rode in a maze of happiness, fatigue, pain, and profound pity for the souls of those who had died. She stopped to give thanks in the Church of St. Paul, and then rode to her lodging and fell into bed.

On Sunday morning, she arose. Still weak from her wound, she put on a coat of armor somewhat lighter than she had worn before. With Dunois and the other captains she marched out of the Regnart gate. The English had emerged from their remaining fortresses and were drawn up outside in full battle array. The confident French soldiers were eager to attack them, but Jeanne was reluctant.

"It's Sunday," she said. "We will not attack. But should they attack you, fight bravely and you will win."

She then sent for an altar and a priest, and asked him to celebrate mass in front of both armies. When one mass was done, she asked him to celebrate another. The French and English soldiers heard both masses with devotion.

"Now look," she said to her captains. "Do you think they are still determined to attack?"

"No," was the answer. "They have turned back."

"In God's name," she said, "let them go. Our Lord does not wish us to fight today."

La Hire took a hundred knights and trailed behind the English just to make sure the retreat was genuine. In their haste to leave, the enemy had collected whatever property they could carry, abandoning their heavy guns and ammunition, their huge shields and provisions. At one deserted fort La Hire found Jeanne's first herald, still bound to a stake, ready for burning.

The French army returned to Orléans, parading through the city in a grand procession. Every year since, on May 8, the citizens of Orléans celebrate their deliverance from the ancient enemy with a great festival in remembrance of this procession.

That which had been declared impossible was done. The siege of Orléans was raised. Jeanne D'Arc had shown her sign.

CHAPTER 21

A WEEK OF WONDERS

After a few days' rest Jeanne set out for Chinon, where the Dauphin was waiting. To lift the siege of Orléans and to lead Charles to his coronation were the two missions she had wished to perform. The first was done and she wished now to accomplish the other as soon as possible. The troops were dispersing rapidly; if Jeanne was to keep the army together, Charles needed to provide supplies and money.

As she came into Tours she was surprised to see the Dauphin, accompanied by some of his courtiers, ride out to meet her. She immediately rode forward and bowed low in her saddle. But Charles put out his hand and lifted her up, then bowed to her as though she were a queen.

"Rise, dear Jeanne," he said, "and receive our welcome and our thanks for what you have done. It was a great deed, gloriously performed. Such performance merits rich reward, so tell me what reward Charles may give you."

Jeanne looked at him eagerly. There was only one desire in her heart.

"Dauphin, the only reward I want is to lead you to your coronation at Reims. I beg you, we should set forth at once."

"At once?" The indolent monarch shrank from the suggestion. La Trémouïlle, the court favorite and Charles's right-hand man, interrupted.

"Impossible. Why, the road is filled with English and Burgundian strongholds. His Majesty should not be exposed to such risks. We need to build an army strong enough to open the way, and that would take at least six weeks."

"But now is the time," cried Jeanne. "We must strike before the Duke of Bedford has time to send reinforcements. If we wait our task will be the harder."

"Patience, Jeanne, patience," said the Dauphin. "We will go, I promise you, but not just now. You have been wounded, too, I hear, and need the rest. So have patience for a little while, please."

So Jeanne was forced to be idle while the Dauphin dawdled away the days. She was right, of course, the time was ripe for action. Charles had only to mount and ride and everything was his. If he had gone straight to Reims after Orléans and then on to Paris, every city would have opened its gates to him.

But through the influence of La Trémouïlle, Regnault de Chartres, the Archbishop of Reims, and Raoul de Gaucourt, the former governor of Orléans, the golden opportunity was lost.

These men did not want the Dauphin to shake off his indolence, and they worked hard to stop the plans that Jeanne had for Charles. It was never the English or Burgundians that Jeanne had to fear most. True, they were her open enemies, but with a good company of soldiers she could overcome them. It was the constant efforts of these "friends" at court that undermined her. The court politicians opposed Jeanne at every step.

Jeanne's true friends were the captains of the army that went with her on the campaigns, and the simple people of France who believed that she had a mission from Heaven. So, although she was longing for the dash of action that would drive the enemy from the land, she was forced to spend time at court instead. Charles spent the next two weeks listening to his councilors debate; then he went on to Loches, thirty miles from Tours, where there was a castle he wished to inhabit.

Since she was part of Charles's household, Jeanne went also. Every place she entered, the people crowded around her horse and tried to kiss her shoes or her hands. Robert le Macon, the abbot who had questioned her at Poictiers, rebuked her sharply for allowing this to happen.

"Truthfully," Jeanne answered, "I don't know how to guard against it, unless God would guard me. They love me because I have never done them any unkindness, but helped them as I could."

Charles gave her rich gifts to distract her, but though Jeanne liked pretty clothes and presents she never lost sight of her mission. And she did not stop entreating the Dauphin to go to Reims.

Now Alençon and Dunois, her good friends, came to the court and added their pleas to her own, but still Charles would not move. One day Jeanne's patience was at an end. Knowing that the Dauphin was again meeting with Sir Christopher d'Harcourt, Gerard Machet, Robert le Macon, and Dunois, she boldly knocked on the door of the council chamber. After being admitted, she went directly to the monarch and threw herself at his feet, clasping his knees.

"Noble Dauphin, you hold so many and such long councils," she cried. "Come instead to Reims and receive your worthy crown."

"Do your advisers tell you to say this?" asked d'Harcourt, the Bishop of Castres.

"Yes," replied Jeanne.

"Will you not tell us the nature of this advice?"

Jeanne hesitated before replying. She did not like to talk about her Voices. Then she said, "I understand what you want to know and I will gladly satisfy you."

"Jeanne," said Charles kindly, "it would be very good if you could tell us, but are you sure that you are willing to speak about it?"

"Yes, Sir," she answered. Then she turned to them and spoke with visible emotion.

"When I am upset that my messages from God are not believed, I go off by myself and pray, complaining and asking God why I am not listened to. And when I have finished my prayer I hear a Voice saying, 'Daughter of God, on, on! I will help you. On!' And when I hear the Voice I feel great joy. I wish I could always feel that way."

Jeanne's face shone as she spoke, so that the men who heard her sat speechless looking on. Then all of a sudden her face changed. Her features became strained and she was overcome by emotion. She turned toward the Dauphin and pleaded: "The time is short. Use it, use it, Sir. I shall last such a little while, only a year and little more. Oh, Sir, it is such a short time to work for France."

Charles was deeply moved. "Dear, Jeanne," he said, "I will go whenever you—"

Robert le Macon interposed softly: "When the roads are clear between here and Reims, Your Majesty. It would not be wise to risk your person on an uncertainty."

"Let me clear the road, Dauphin," Jeanne exclaimed quickly. "I beg you, grant me permission to do it."

"Many strongholds along the Loire will have to be broken up," the Dauphin said dubiously.

"They can be broken up. Then you can travel safely."

"Well, you have permission, Jeanne," said the monarch, half laughing. "Never was there such a soldier!"

"When may I begin, Sir?" Jeanne asked.

"As soon as you please."

Joyously Jeanne left the room and began to gather the army together again. As word spread that the English towns on the Loire would be attacked, a tide of popular enthusiasm rose and men came from all over to join the army, eager to fight, with or without pay. The people were beginning again to hope for their country. Selles, a town about fifteen miles from Loches and fifty miles south of Orléans, was chosen for the recruiting camp.

To this town one day came the two young Counts de Laval, Guy and his brother André, who could not rest until they had seen Jeanne. Their father had been killed at Agincourt and they had been brought up by their mother, who had defended their castles against the English, and by their grandmother, who had once been married to the Bertrand Du Guesclin, a great warrior for France. Full of boyish enthusiasm for Jeanne, they wrote home to their mother and grandmother, describing her:

> She seems wholly divine, to see or hear. Monday she left Selles to go to Romorantin. The Marshal of Boussac and a great many soldiers and common people were with her. I saw her all in white armor with a battle-ax in her hand, getting ready to mount a great black stallion which was very nervous and would not let her on. So she said, "Lead him to the cross," which was in front of the church nearby. There she mounted without his budging, just as if he had been tied. And she turned to the church door and called in her sweet woman's voice: "You priests and churchmen, make processions and prayers to God." She then set out on the road, calling, "Forward! Forward!" with her

battle-ax in her hand, and her banner carried by a page. Her brothers went with her, all clad in white armor.

At Romorantin, Jeanne and Alençon were joined by Dunois and other captains, and together they entered Orléans on the ninth of June. The people received her with joy, and set about providing her impoverished army with supplies and artillery, making their gifts directly to Jeanne, whose courage and wisdom they believed in.

The people of Orléans were grateful for their deliverance, but to make that deliverance secure the Loire had to be cleared of the strongholds that menaced it. The only bridge between Orléans and Gien stood at Jargeau, which lay on the south bank of the Loire, about ten miles above Orléans. Ten miles below Orléans lay Meung, which had a fortified bridge, and six miles below Meung was Beaugency, with another fortified bridge. These places were all held by the English.

The English then could cross the river either above or below Orléans. By bringing large reinforcements into these places, they could easily try to recapture Orléans at any time. So the goal was to drive the English out of these supporting strongholds as soon as possible.

The first point of attack was Jargeau because it was rumored that Sir John Fastolf was headed there with reinforcements. It was a strong place. After the siege of Orléans had been lifted, Dunois had stormed Jargeau unsuccessfully for three hours. Whatever damage he had done had long since been repaired by the Earl of Suffolk.

On the eleventh of June the French began to advance against Jargeau, but on the way some of the commanders hesitated, arguing to get Jeanne to postpone the attack. She refused.

"Success is certain," she said. "If I were not sure I would rather herd sheep than put myself in such great jeopardy."

The men who had fought at Orléans were in the front rank. Encouraged by their earlier success they rushed to the attack without waiting for the men-at-arms or the artillery and tried to storm the place. The garrison easily beat them off and drove them back to the main body. Then Jeanne rode forward, standard in hand, and led the main troops to the rescue. The English were now driven back; the French occupied the area around the walls and passed the night there.

The next morning Jeanne placed the artillery in position and Alençon wondered aloud at her expertise.

"Where did you learn these military matters, Jeanne?" he asked. "Who taught you where to set those guns? You work as though you were a captain with twenty or thirty years' experience."

"My Lord tells me," Jeanne answered. "When I see a place I know at once where the artillery should be."

And the young duke's wonder grew, for he knew that she had never seen weapons and ammunition until Orléans the month before. While the captains were planning the attack, word came that the Earl of Suffolk was parleying with La Hire, offering to surrender in two weeks. No doubt he believed that before his time was up Fastolf would arrive with reinforcements.

"Tell them they may leave now in their tunics, but without their weapons or armor," Jeanne said. "Otherwise we will storm the place at once."

Suffolk refused her terms and immediately French cannons began to fire. One of the towers of the town was destroyed and the French sharpshooters picked off some of the garrison. But the English also used their artillery with telling effect. As Jeanne and Alençon stood watching the bombardment, she cried out to him suddenly, "Change your position. That gun will kill you!" pointing to the gun on the walls. Alençon stepped aside quickly, and a few moments later a soldier was killed on that very spot.

Soon Jeanne urged an assault on the walls. Alençon thought the move was premature, that the artillery should continue to bombard before they attacked. As the trumpets sounded the assault, he did not advance. Jeanne turned to him. "Why do you hesitate?" she asked. "Have no doubt. When it pleases God the hour is at hand. God helps those who help themselves."

Still he hesitated and she added, "Don't be afraid. You know I promised your wife to bring you back safe and sound." And at that they both rushed to the attack.

The English resistance was effective and stubborn and for several hours the struggle went on, with Jeanne in the midst of it. Banner in hand, she started up one of the scaling ladders and tried to mount the wall. One of the garrison soldiers threw down a stone which crashed through the banner, hit the light helmet she wore, and knocked her to the ground. For a moment she lay stunned and then, springing to her feet unhurt, she cried, "Friends, friends, on! On! Our Lord has condemned the English. They are ours! Have courage."

The French knew that cry. They knew that victory awaited them and they swarmed over the wall, sweeping all before them. Suffolk retreated toward the bridge, hoping to escape across it, but the French followed him too closely. One of his brothers and many soldiers were killed and wounded but he and all who were left alive were captured. As the Duke of Suffolk was surrounded, a French knight cried, "Yield, Suffolk! Yield!"

"I will yield to no one but the most valiant woman in the world," answered Suffolk proudly. And he would give his sword only to Jeanne herself.

So Jargeau was taken.

Jeanne could not stop the troops from sacking the town and even the churches. Some of the prisoners had been beaten or killed as their captors quarreled over the right to ransom them, so Jeanne decided to send the other prisoners down to Orléans by boat during the night.

Alençon and Jeanne received a royal welcome when they returned to Orléans. Jeanne was presented with a rich robe in the colors of Orléans: the inner cloak was dark green; the outer robe was crimson lined with white satin and embroidered with a nettle, the symbol of Orléans.

Meung and Beaugency were next, and Jeanne felt they should start a new action right away. Sir John Fastolf was at Janville, and since Jargeau had fallen he would probably move to help the garrison at Meung. So Jeanne allowed the army only one day of rest.

"Now we must go to see the English at Meung," she told Alençon. "We will march tomorrow after dinner."

Meung was downriver about ten miles from Orléans. Its well-fortified bridge was about a mile outside the town. The next afternoon the French attacked and the town fell easily. Placing a French garrison in the bridge towers, Jeanne and her forces camped for the night in the fields; the next morning they pushed on downriver to Beaugency.

These towns with their castles and towers rose conspicuously on the flat plain of the Loire, and troops moving along the plain were easily seen by the watchmen on the walls. As soon as the English saw the French approaching, they fled into the castle, leaving men hidden inside houses and sheds in an attempt to ambush the French. The English had been left under the command of Matthew Gough, a Welshman, while Talbot had ridden on to Janville to speed up Fastolf.

As the French marched into Beaugency, the men hidden in the houses jumped out and attacked them, but they were driven back into the castle. Jeanne placed the guns and battered the castle until evening. That night news came that the Constable of France, Comte de Richemont, was advancing with a force of men to join her.

Richemont was a famous leader, but he was in disfavor with the Dauphin and exiled from the royal court, largely because of a feud with La Trémouïlle. Richemont had wanted to help lift the siege of Orléans but the Dauphin had forbidden it. So his imminent approach made Alençon and Jeanne uneasy.

He was no friend to Jeanne, since he thought it was a disgrace that France's army should be led by a woman. The constable was not alone in this opinion. People who came in personal contact with Jeanne D'Arc believed in her, but those who had never met her thought she was a witch. The captains and soldiers revered her, believing that she was truly sent by God, and the simple people never doubted her.

The French generals were divided over the advisability of receiving the Comte de Richemont. He was Alençon's uncle, and while the young duke had no personal quarrel with him, the Dauphin's command was that Richemont should not be received if he were to come with his troops. Alençon said that he would have to leave if Jeanne accepted the constable's aid. Jeanne was not pleased at Richemont's coming, but she would never turn away any champion of France. She persuaded Alençon that they ought to accept the aid Richemont offered.

"He is French," she said. "And Frenchmen ought to lay aside private quarrels for France. In God's name, then, let us welcome him."

In the end, both Jeanne and Alençon rode out to meet the constable.

"Jeanne," said Richemont, as she jumped from her horse to greet him, "they tell me that you are against me. I don't know if you come from God—or elsewhere. If from God, I don't fear you, for He knows my good will. If you come from the Devil, I fear you even less."

"Brave man," said Jeanne, smiling. "I didn't ask for your help, but since you're here, welcome!"

They rode together back to Beaugency. There was no time for talk, since Talbot and Fastolf had arrived with their forces and were resting nearby— between Meung and Beaugency. Jeanne prepared her men for battle. The French army took up a strong position on a hill in front of Beaugency.

Although night was coming on, the English took their battle stations and waited for the attack to come. From their battle line the French watched, but made no move to fight. The English became impatient and sent two heralds, saying that three English knights would fight anyone who would come down to the plain. Jeanne declined the challenge.

"Rest today," she sent back word. "It's late enough. Tomorrow, if it pleases God and Our Lady, we shall see you at closer quarters."

Later, scouts reported to Jeanne that the English were withdrawing from the plain and were heading north.

"They are going to Meung," cried Jeanne joyfully. "They will occupy the town and try to retake the bridge, thinking they can come back down on the other side of the river and relieve the garrison here at Beaugency. But the commander at Beaugency will think that Talbot has deserted him and he'll surrender immediately."

Which is exactly what happened. When Matthew Gough heard that the English army had left, he felt his case was hopeless. He had seen with his own eyes that the French had been reinforced by Richemont and believed that Talbot had left him to his fate. At midnight, Gough surrendered his troops.

At dawn the French moved back to Meung, where they found Talbot battering the bridge. He had been at it all night long, but the bridge was still in French hands. Hearing that Gough had surrendered, Talbot and Fastolf took off across the wooded plain of Beauce toward Paris, taking all the English forces with them.

The French captains were unsure about what to do next. Their troops had never won an open-field, hand-to-hand battle with the enemy. They would rather avoid such an engagement than risk another disaster. Alençon assembled the captains for a council of war. He turned first to Jeanne.

"What will we do now?" he asked.

"Have good spurs," she told him.

"What?" he cried, astonished. "Are we going to turn our backs?"

"No," she answered, laughing. "The English will run and we'll need good spurs to chase them."

That prophecy put heart into men who had been ready to run themselves. Now they eagerly prepared to follow the retreating English. La Hire and Dunois, with a company of eighty men, mounted their best horses and rode ahead, while the main body of the army came more slowly behind them. Jeanne preferred riding with the leaders, but they were afraid of ambush and wouldn't take the risk. Jeanne was angry, but accepted that it was best for her to remain with the main body, for the men needed her encouragement.

It was a long ride and a dangerous one. The wide plain was covered with a dense growth of underbrush and trees, and any number of the enemy could hide there. The French made their way cautiously and some of the captains began to show signs of uneasiness. Jeanne encouraged them constantly.

The pursuit continued until they neared Patay, a town midway between Meung and Rouvray, where Fastolf had won the Battle of Herrings in February. La Hire and his scouts were scouring the country looking for the English. All at once they surprised a stag and the startled animal bounded away from their horses, and disappeared into the bushes. Instantly a shout of English voices rose up as the deer plunged among them and, since they did not know that the French were so near, the English soldiers began to shoot at it.

La Hire stopped and sent a messenger back to the main army telling them to hurry forward. Then he and his company spurred forward and charged the English before they had time to set up their defenses. The sudden onslaught threw the English archers into confusion and disorder. The French pressed onward. Sir John Fastolf began to gallop back to help the English advance guard, but the guard thought he was fleeing from the enemy. The troops panicked, broke, and fled toward Patay, leaving provisions and guns behind them. Talbot himself fought on desperately, but was finally taken prisoner. Fastolf wanted to turn back to the field, but his escort dragged him off and he finally rode off toward Paris.

The battle of Patay was won. But it had been a terrible fight. Finding a Frenchman cruelly beating a wounded prisoner, she flung herself from her horse, and cradled his head in her lap. She sent for a priest to give him final rites and comforted him until he died. Jeanne wanted the English out of France and she fought them to achieve that end. But pity was always in her heart, and she felt the same toward a wounded enemy as she did toward one of her own countrymen.

So ended a week of great wonders. Between June eleventh and eighteenth Jeanne had taken three strong towns from the English, and routed the enemy in the open field. All the Loire region and the whole river basin was now in the power of France. It was not Alençon nor Dunois nor the French generals who had secured the victories. It was the dauntless girl, the peasant maid who after scarcely one month in the field bore herself like a general—this girl of seventeen was the best soldier of them all.

CHAPTER 22

THE CULMINATION

The next day was Sunday and Jeanne and her men returned to Orléans in triumph. The streets were crowded with people wild with joy at sight of the Maid. Cheering processions of townspeople went to the churches to thank God and the Virgin Mary and all the saints for the mercy and honor shown to them. Without the Maid, they said, such marvels could never have been accomplished.

News of the victory of Patay spread quickly throughout France. In villages loyal to the Dauphin, people celebrated with processions and prayers, bonfires and bell ringings. The very same news alarmed the English and Burgundians. When Sir John Fastolf and other fugitives carried the story of the disaster into Paris, the people rioted, believing that they would be attacked next. The English troops were thoroughly demoralized. The superstitious rank and file were terrified of the Armagnac Witch, and the Duke of Bedford was running out of men and armaments.

Back in Orléans, Jeanne rested while the citizens planned for the arrival of the Dauphin. All the time Jeanne had been fighting his battles, the Dauphin had been frittering away his time at Sully. When he did not appear in Orléans after a few days, Jeanne went to Sully get him. She met him at St. Benoit-sur-Loire on his way to Neufchâteau. Charles showered Jeanne with praise.

139

"You have earned our gratitude, Jeanne," he said. "What can I give you for your amazing labors?"

"Sir, all I desire is for you to leave immediately for Reims to be crowned."

"We promise we will go, dear Maid. But first you must rest. You have endeared yourself to us, and above all we desire your welfare. To please your king, you must rest from your labors."

Now, Jeanne had just cut a great army to pieces and taken three fortified towns. Hearing of her great victory the citizens in smaller towns and fortresses had risen and driven out their English foes. The golden lilies floated over the Loire countryside nearly to Paris. She had done all this so that the Dauphin might safely march to Reims. And now he wanted to delay again. It was too much! Jeanne longed to complete her mission, for she knew that her time was short. She burst into tears.

"Jeanne, my child, what is it?" asked the king.

"Gentle Dauphin," she said brokenly, "you are not king until the sacred oil anoints you. The whole realm shall be yours when you are crowned. Come to Reims!"

"We will go, beloved Maid, and soon. But isn't there some other gift you wish?"

"Sir, I ask that you forgive the Comte de Richemont and receive him again at Court. He helped us at Beaugency and at Patay. For the sake of France, Sir, grant me this favor."

Charles shook his head. Alençon and Dunois added their pleas, but the Dauphin would not relent. Richemont, who had helped strike the great blow to the English, was rejected again. He finally returned home to his own estates and Charles lost a good soldier.

Having cleared the way for the Dauphin's coronation, Jeanne was amazed to still find herself facing obstacles. Charles was plainly reluctant to act; more delays and more discussions held them up.

But all France was aroused now and calling for the king. After all the great deeds she had wrought, people said, the Maid should not be stopped now. La Trémouïlle, in response to the pressure from the citizens, agreed to risk an advance. Jeanne went to Orléans to bring up the remainder of the troops and munitions. When she returned she settled her army in the fields near Gien.

Starting the Dauphin on the road to Reims was easier said than done. Many cities and towns in France were still held by English and Burgundians. Some of the Dauphin's councilors wanted to attack strongholds on the upper Loire; others wanted to attack at Rouen. Jeanne insisted that the Dauphin should march directly to Reims. Her Voices had told her to take him there to be crowned at the great cathedral so the people would recognize him as the true king. Jeanne, sublime in her faith, insisted that was the thing to do. And in a hurry, too, before Bedford could bring over new troops from England.

Worn out by futile arguments and time wasting, Jeanne returned to her encamped army. The soldiers declared that they would go wherever she wished to lead them. Princes, great lords, and knights, and squires of high and low degree pledged their loyalty. Jeanne's exploits had made her famous throughout Europe, and these men had come from all parts of loyal France, bringing their companies with them, eager to serve. Even though there was little or no money to pay the men, they remained willing and enthusiastic.

On Monday, June 27, Jeanne started out across the Loire River with part of the army, and two days later the Dauphin and his councilors reluctantly followed her. The march to Reims had begun at last.

Fifty miles east was the town of Auxerre, which was loyal to Burgundy. If the townspeople opened their gates to the Dauphin, they could expect retaliation from the Burgundians. As the king and his army approached, the citizens closed the gates to the city. Then the townspeople sent food out to the French troops and money to La Trémouïlle. Accepting the bribes, the French passed them by. Other smaller strongholds on the road yielded on command.

Soon the French army approached Troyes, the capital of the Champagne province. The whole province was excited by the advance of the royal forces. Some cities were for France and others for England. The cities were not sure of each other, and none wanted to be the first, or the last, to open its gates to Charles.

Troyes was the place where the treaty giving France to England had been signed; the city where the French princess, Catherine, was married to Henry the Fifth of England; and where the Dauphin had been disinherited. After the treaty had been signed, the townspeople had aligned themselves with the English and the Burgundians. Now they feared Charles's vengeance.

Charles stopped about fifteen miles outside town. He sent a letter into the city saying that if they submitted to his rule now, he would forget the past and hold them in good grace.

Jeanne also sent a letter to the people of Troyes, asking them for their allegiance in the name of the King of Heaven. Charles, she said, was their rightful king, moving toward Paris by way of Reims, with the help of Jesus. Even if they refused to yield, she wrote, Charles would still enter the city.

Both letters were received in Troyes on the morning of July fifth. The people of Troyes sent copies of the letters on to Reims, begging for help. They planned to hold out against Charles until the death.

In the meantime, the French army camped outside the walls of Troyes, hoping the town would surrender. The townspeople held off, expecting the army to pass them by as they had passed by Auxerre. But the Dauphin had to secure Troyes. The city was so strongly fortified and thickly occupied with enemy troops that he would be putting his own army in grave jeopardy if he left Troyes behind him, untouched. Charles called a council to decide on his next move. Jeanne was not invited to attend.

A number of the councilors advised against assaulting the city. Some thought they should retreat; others that it was safe enough to press on to Reims leaving the hostile fortress in their rear. Robert le Macon, who had been chancellor to Charles VI, reminded them that they had started on this venture because Jeanne had told them it was the will of God. He suggested that she be invited to meet with the council. At this very moment, Jeanne knocked at the door. She was admitted at once, and the Archbishop of Reims explained the dilemma.

"If I speak," she said to the Dauphin, "will you believe me?"

"I don't know," he answered. "If you say things that are reasonable and productive, I shall certainly believe you."

"Will you believe me?" she asked again.

"Yes," said the Dauphin, "depending on what you say."

"Attack and, in God's name, I promise that within three days I will bring you into Troyes."

"Jeanne," said Le Macon, "even if you could do it in six days it would be worth it."

"Don't doubt it," Jeanne said, continuing to address the Dauphin. "You shall be master of the place tomorrow."

The council broke up, and Jeanne began immediately to prepare for the assault. During the night the whole army set to work collecting material— timber, logs, even old doors and tables—to shelter the men, mount the guns, and fill up the dry moat that surrounded the walls. Everyone, including the noblemen, the knights, and Jeanne herself, worked hard through the night. Into the wee hours of the morning, the townspeople of Troyes could hear their commotion and flocked to their churches to pray. When the sun rose, the people could see that the French were ready for the assault. When they heard Jeanne's voice call out the command to attack, fear washed over them. The people, led by the town bishop, threw the gates wide open and surrendered without firing a shot. They then sent a committee to Charles, who promised them that if they gave the town up to him, the armed troops could leave peacefully with their property.

Jeanne was suspicious of the enemy's intentions. Even though she had been up all night, she stationed herself at the gate to see the troops march out. Her suspicions were well founded. The English and Burgundian soldiers came marching through the gates with their horses and armor and their "property," which turned out to be a band of French prisoners, being held for ransom. The poor fellows cast appealing, pitiful glances at their victorious fellow countrymen as they passed. Jeanne stopped the march.

"In God's name," she shouted, "they shall not take them."

Her captains explained that under the terms of the surrender the prisoners were property and the soldiers were entitled to take them away.

"They shall not have them," Jeanne repeated. "It's monstrous. I will see the Dauphin."

Jeanne convinced the Dauphin to ransom the prisoners from their captors, paying a reasonable sum for each man.

The people of Troyes feared Jeanne, and she felt their ill will plainly when she entered the town. In all the other French towns, the people enthusiastically thronged around her. Here they sent a Franciscan monk to confront her. Friar Richard had a reputation for preaching emotional sermons warning people of the coming of an Anti-Christ and urging them to repent their sins and prepare for eternity. As he approached Jeanne he crossed himself devoutly and sprinkled holy water before him to exorcise the evil spirit that he believed possessed the girl. Jeanne laughed. She was used to being thought of as a sorceress.

"Approach me boldly," she cried. "I shall not fly away."

The monk fell on his knees in front of her. To show that she was no holier than he, Jeanne also knelt. They spoke quietly together and after that the monk was one of her most devoted followers.

The day after the surrender Charles entered the city in triumphant splendor, going directly to the cathedral where he received the oaths of loyalty from the people. One day later the troops marched on Chalons, but met no resistance there. By now all opposition to the French army had collapsed, and one by one the towns opened their gates to Charles. With his army growing larger and stronger every day, Charles marched in triumph towards Reims.

The people of Reims had no intention of submitting to Charles. They would resist to the death, they said. But when they offered the captain of their garrison fifty men to resist the French he said it would take at least three hundred to hold the city against Jeanne D'Arc. It was finished. When Charles reached Sept-Saulx, a fortress near Reims, representatives came forward to offer full obedience and the keys of the city.

The march to Reims, which has been called the "bloodless march," was ended. The wonderful and victorious campaign had lasted only six weeks, almost every day of which was distinguished by some victory. While the Dauphin and his councilors had been afraid of the result, Jeanne had carried them through in triumph. Every promise she made had been fulfilled. Nothing now stood between the disinherited Charles and his rightful crown.

On Saturday morning, July sixteenth, the archbishop, Regnault de Chartres, who had been forced out of his city by the Burgundians, returned to make preparations to receive the Dauphin. In the afternoon, Charles, with Jeanne riding by his side, and followed by his councilors, princes and nobles, the captains, and a great train of soldiers, entered the city. The streets were thronged with people cheering lustily at the sight of the monarch and the wonderful Maid with her shining armor and fair sweet face.

The royal expedition planned to lodge in the archbishop's palace near the great cathedral. But as they neared the palace Jeanne looked out into the crowd and uttered a cry of joy, for gazing at her from the crowd were her father, Jacques D'Arc, and her uncle, Durand Lassois. The king turned to her: "What is it?"

"My dear father is standing there among the people," she cried, waving at hand. "My uncle, Durand Lassois, is with him; he is the one who took me to Vaucouleurs."

"I remember. We must see them both," said the monarch. "Bring them to us later."

Jeanne waved again at her father and uncle as she passed by. That evening

"Courage! The hour is at hand!"
Page 124

"Forward! They are ours!"
Page 170

Charles was led to a platform that had been erected in front of the cathedral. Amid the red glare of bonfires, flaming torches, the clamoring of bells, and shouts from the crowds, he was presented to the multitudes by the peers of France.

"Here is your king whom we, peers of France, crown as King and Sovereign Lord. If anyone here has an objection, let him speak. With your permission, tomorrow Charles shall be consecrated by the grace of the Holy Spirit."

The people shouted "Noel! Noel! Noel!" in a frenzy of delight. Thus the preliminary ceremony ended in dark night. While the others of the royal party attended a great feast in the palace of the archbishop, Jeanne slipped away to a little inn called the Zebra, where she knew she would find her father and uncle. To her delight, Jeanne found her father standing with an arm around each of her brothers, his face beaming with gladness. He started toward her as she came through the door, then stopped suddenly and gave her a questioning look. But Jeanne flung herself upon him like a child.

"Father!" she cried. "Dear father! Oh, how glad I am to see you."

For a moment Jacques was too overcome to speak, but he held her close as though he would never let her go. When he spoke at last his voice trembled.

"Do you forgive me, my little one? All the harshness and severity I showed you? I didn't know, I didn't understand—"

Jeanne smiled at him through her tears.

"How could you understand, father? For a long time I didn't understand myself. But it's over now. My mission will be over tomorrow when the Dauphin is crowned. Then I am going back home with you. My dear mother, how is she?"

"Well, Jeanne, but she longs for you."

"And I for her," said Jeanne tearfully. "I shall never leave you again, father. I will be happy to be home."

Her Uncle Durand interrupted. "I don't think you'll be content to be at home, Jeanne, after all this. You have done everything you wanted to do. And I was the one who helped you."

"You were, Uncle Durand; and the king wishes to thank you personally."

"You can't mean the king want to see *me*?" exclaimed Durand Lassois, dumbfounded.

"I do," said Jeanne, laughing. "He says that by helping me reach Sir Robert you did more for the country than any other man in France."

Durand could scarcely contain himself at this news. Presently, he said wistfully: "Are you ever afraid in battle, Jeanne? We heard that you were wounded once. Don't you want to run when the guns begin to shoot and the arrows fly?"

"I don't fear wounds or battle," she told him. "I fear only—treachery." A shadow crossed her face as she spoke.

Beyond that it was a happy family party that night at the little inn. Mixed with the wonder and admiration with which her simple peasant family regarded her, there was also great love. The weary girl, longing for home and rest, gave herself up to the blessed comfort of her family. Far into the night she talked, and then just before dawn she returned to the palace.

There was little sleep anywhere in Reims that night. Everything had to be prepared for the coronation: decorations for the cathedral and town, provisions for the ceremonies. The English had carried many treasures from the city, and now the cathedral had to be searched to find proper vessels for the anointing and feast that would follow. The preparations went on all night long. Joyous crowds filled the streets and the great square before the cathedral, where the Dauphin, according to custom, kept vigil the night before his coronation.

At dawn the town began to fill with visitors wishing to attend the rites. All France seemed to pour into the place, for the people were to have their rightful king at last. After this, there would be only one King of France, Charles the Seventh, the only person to be anointed with the sacred oil in the city of Reims, where all the kings of France had been crowned. Although Charles had been crowned after a fashion at Bourges, in the eyes of the nation he was not king until the sacred oil, said to have been brought down from heaven by a dove to Saint Remi, touched his brow. Jeanne understood this better than all the politicians who surrounded Charles, because she was a daughter of the French people and understood their feelings and loyalties. By taking the Dauphin to be crowned, Jeanne had gained a decided advantage over the English claimant to the throne.

The ceremonies were to begin at nine o'clock Sunday morning, July the seventeenth. Long before the hour, the ancient cathedral was filled to overflowing with nobles and knights, dignitaries of the church and the city, all dressed in gorgeous clothing made from gold and silver cloth, brocades of crimson and azure, and silks dyed in all the colors of the rainbow. Their fabulous dress mingled with the sheen from glittering spears and shining armor. Charles waited at the foot of the high altar, garbed in a robe of cerulean blue over which was scattered the golden fleur-de-lis.

Outside the cathedral the streets were thronged with people in holiday attire, wearing leaden medals that bore a likeness of Jeanne. After the coronation the king had thirteen gold medals struck in honor of the Maid, engraved with her emblem—a hand holding a sword—and the inscription Strong in the Counsel of God. He gave these medals and other rich gifts to the city of Reims.

Suddenly there came a blare of trumpets as four peers of France emerged from the palace, followed by a great company of men dressed in shining armor. With flags and banners floating in the air they road to the old Abbey of St. Remi to collect the sacred vial of oil that had been sent from heaven to anoint Clovis in the eleventh century. Before the abbey, the noble messengers knelt and swore an oath never to lose sight of the holy vessel until it was restored to its appointed place.

The Abbot of St. Remi then came out, dressed in his richest robes and surrounded by his monks, bearing the treasure in his hands. Under a splendid canopy, blazing in the sunshine with cloth of gold, they marched toward the cathedral under escort of the noblemen. Their entrance into the cathedral was proclaimed by a mighty choir of voices chanting sacred hymns accompanied by pealing bells and blaring trumpets, until a mighty volume of sound rolled and swelled through the vaulted domes of the ancient building. The abbot handed the treasured vessel to the archbishop.

Now began the long and imposing ceremonies of the coronation. First there were prayers and anthems and sermons. At length an armored knight standing on the altar steps called for the twelve peers of France to come and serve their king.The Dauphin knelt before the archbishop, his arms extended through slits cut in his royal cloak. According to ancient custom, the archbishop raised the holy flask and anointed the Dauphin upon the brow, both shoulders, on the inside of his elbows and the palms of his hands. He then took the crown and held it high above the Dauphin's head; the twelve peers of the realm, coming closer, held the crown securely and then gently lowered it upon the head of the kneeling prince.

"Arise, Charles, King of France," cried the archbishop in a loud voice. Charles seated himself in the throne chair, and as the peers lifted the chair high in the air so that all might see him, the archbishop cried again: "Behold your king!"

A great shout of "Noel! Noel! Noel!" came from the assembly, while the crash of chimes, chanting voices, and trumpets rolled through the arches, until the vaulted chamber echoed with sound.

Throughout the ceremony, Jeanne stood close to Charles on the steps of the altar, her standard in her hand. Afterward, when asked why she held her own flag instead of the French flag, she answered: "It has borne the burden, it should share the glory."

Pale with emotion Jeanne had carefully watched every step of the ceremony. When at last it was ended, she stepped forward and fell at the feet of the newly crowned monarch, embracing his knees, and weeping for joy.

"Gentle King, now is God's pleasure fulfilled. He has shown that you are the true king and the kingdom of France belongs to you alone."

Her soft, broken words pierced all hearts and many wept at the sight of her. The girl was so young, so fair, so slight. Yet she had performed great deeds. In three months she had given France a king, and had given the king a country. In spite of incredible obstacles, she had accomplished her mission. A great soul, wedded to intense purpose, had performed miracles and changed the destiny of a nation.

At the sight of her the king also wept. Perhaps at that moment he felt more gratitude toward Jeanne than ever before or afterward. Lifting her, he said, "You have brought us to our crowning, beloved Maid. Speak, and whatever you ask shall be granted."

Again Jeanne fell to her knees. "Most noble King, I ask you to remit the taxes of my village. Its people are poor, and it is a great hardship for them to pay."

"Is that all, Jeanne?"

"Yes, Sir."

"Then in consideration of the great and profitable services you have rendered us, at your request we decree that Domremy, the native village of Jeanne D'Arc, deliverer of France, is forever excused from taxation."

Again the people shouted fervently. They recognized the justice of the request, and wondered only why she asked for so little.

For many centuries afterward, the special exemption lasted. In the official records, against the names of Domremy and its adjoining village of Greux, the tax collector wrote: "Nothing—for the sake of the Maid."

Jeanne had gained a kingdom, yet all she requested in return was that her poor oppressed village might be spared from taxation. For herself she asked nothing.

CHAPTER 23

THE TURNING OF THE TIDE

Following the coronation, a great feast was held in the archbishop's palace. The tables stretched out into the streets so that all the princes and nobles, as well as all the people of Reims, could be served. Jeanne, who always ate and drank little, soon slipped away from the festivities. She had other work to do.

First she sent a letter to Philip, the Duke of Burgundy, who had aligned himself with the English. Jeanne had written to him before asking him to attend the crowning of the king, but had received no reply. She believed fervently that all Frenchmen should unite against the common enemy, laying aside their private differences to serve France. In her second letter Jeanne asked him to abandon his old feud with his cousin Charles and heal the breach that had divided France.

The letter sent, Jeanne prepared to return home with her father. She took out her old red homespun dress and smoothed its folds tenderly. It was a coarse fabric, unlike the satin and brocade court suit she now wore, but the simple frock meant home and mother to her. One by one the members of the household came to say good-bye. But it was not to be.

The next day Jeanne called on the king and asked for his permission to return to Domremy. Her mission was ended, she told him. She had done the two things that she had been commanded to do: she had raised the siege of

Orléans and she had led him to his coronation. Now she was ready to return home with her father and brothers.

The monarch listened with surprise. "Go back now, Jeanne?" he exclaimed. "That cannot be. We need you."

"But you are crowned and the towns will receive you happily. Whatever fighting there is left to be done the knights can do. You don't need me any longer."

"Dear Maid, what about Paris? Who else can lead the army to storm Paris as well as you? You will inspire the men, give them heart and courage, and frighten the enemy. We cannot do without you yet, Jeanne. We need you; the country needs you. We beg you—no, we command it, Jeanne."

Her king and country needed her. That was enough for the girl whose every heartbeat was for France. Sorrowfully she made her way to the Zebra, the little inn where Jacques and Durand were staying.

"Father," she said sadly, "I cannot go home with you. I must remain with the army. The king commands me."

Jacques's face clouded over. "Your mother thought you would return home after your work was done. She will be so disappointed."

"I am disappointed, too, father, but the king says he needs me and France needs me." As she had done when she was a little child, Jeanne laid her head on her father's shoulder and cried like the homesick girl she was. Her father comforted her tenderly. His own disappointment was great.

"We went to see the king, Jeanne," Durand said suddenly. "He was graciousness itself. I'm not surprised that you help him, he is so sweet and pitiful."

"Oh, he is," agreed Jeanne. "Father, the king has exempted both Domremy and Greux from the taxes."

"Now that is good news to carry home," cried Jacques.

"And the town has given each of us a horse," Durand said proudly. "And we can stay here in Reims as long as we wish without paying. All because we are your kin."

Jeanne smiled. She had also received many gifts which she had intended to carry home herself. Now she gave them to her father to deliver, and then said a fond farewell to them. Her heart was full as she returned to the palace of the archbishop and once again took up her position as a general of the royal army. She never saw either her father or her uncle again.

Jeanne expected the king to march on Paris immediately, but to her surprise Charles dallied at Reims for four days. Finally, on the twenty-first of July, with banners flying, the royal army rode from the gates with glad hearts and high hopes. Jeanne with her standard rode in front of the king. With the Maid leading them, the troops believed themselves invincible. Once Paris was taken, the power of the English in France would be entirely broken. Both Bedford, the English regent, and the Duke of Burgundy knew it, too.

The right move was to advance at once and storm Paris while the troops were filled with confidence. There was no time to waste, for Bedford at this very moment was marching from Calais with fresh troops newly landed from England.

But Charles took his time, stopping here and there to receive acclamations in town after town. The army was still sixty miles from Paris, but, luckily, Bedford had not yet reached the city. One vigorous push and the royal army could take Paris. But instead of going directly into the city, Charles turned about, first going south to Château-Thierry, then southeast to Provins. With all his marching, after ten days he was still only ten miles closer to Paris.

The enthusiasm of the troops was dwindling. Jeanne viewed his vacillating maneuvering with despair. What was the king trying to do? At length Jeanne asked Charles for an explanation. To her surprise she learned that ambassadors from the Duke of Burgundy had come to the king in Reims requesting a truce between Charles and the duke. The envoys were even now traveling with the royal army; they had agreed to deliver Paris to Charles at the end of two weeks.

"In two weeks?" repeated Jeanne in dismay. "In God's name, gentle King, the English Bedford will have time to bring his new troops up from the coast. Burgundy is only trying to gain time for him."

"You question his honor?" demanded Charles. "His intentions are most kind, we assure you, Jeanne. It is our dearest wish to be at peace with him."

"Make peace, Sir, but—"

"But what?"

"Make it at the point of a lance," she cried. "No other peace will last. Advance quickly, Sir, and Paris is ours, and with it all France."

"But this way we can take it without bloodshed," he said. "Your way much blood will be spilled. By this truce with our cousin Philip, the city will be ours peaceably. Isn't that best?"

"It may be," Jeanne said sadly.

With heavy heart she left the king and reported to the captains. Silently they heard her, for none believed that Philip of Burgundy would ever deliver Paris to the king.

So, turning this way and that, stopping here and there for ease and enjoyment, the unworthy king, dragging with him the despairing Maid, headed slowly across the Loire valley. At Bray, where Charles expected to cross the Seine, he found a strong Anglo-Burgundian force in possession. He turned around and headed back toward Paris. Jeanne and her captains rejoiced, for they wanted to remain near the city until the truce was ended.

The erratic marching and indecision of the king and his royal council were ruining the spirit of the men-at-arms. But the country people, who knew nothing about the negotiations with Burgundy, were wild with delight at the coming of Charles. Wherever he went they crowded around him to cheer, and Jeanne was touched by their demonstrations of loyalty.

"Here are good people," she remarked one day to the Archbishop of Reims when the army neared Crépy. "When I die I would be happy to be buried in this country among these folk."

"Jeanne, where do you expect to die?" asked the archbishop, who had never been a supporter of Jeanne's. He expected her to make a prediction that he might use against her to prove her a witch.

"When it shall please God," she answered, "for I know no better than you do the time and place. If it pleased my Creator I would lay down my arms now and return home to my father and mother to help keep the sheep."

There was a note of sadness in her words. Even Jeanne's brave spirit was feeling the strain of the fluctuating, futile marchings.

On August eleventh Charles received a brutally insulting letter from the English regent, Bedford, who by this time had brought his troops near Paris and now waited between that city and the French army. In the message Bedford challenged the king to fight in the open field. Any man with an ounce of red blood in his veins would have accepted the challenge, but Charles merely ignored the letter.

Three days later, the two armies came face to face at Montepilloy. It was near evening, and after a brief skirmish they both encamped for the night.

The next morning the royal army found Bedford entrenched in a strong position. His flanks and front were carefully protected by earthworks and a stockade of stakes. Thrust deep into the ground, the formidable stakes would break any charge of the French cavalry. To the rear the English were protected by a lake and stream, so that they could not be attacked from that direction.

The English position was too strong to permit direct attack. The French divided into four divisions, with Jeanne, Dunois, and La Hire in command of a large body of skirmishers. Several times the French knights rode up to the stockade and taunted the English until some rushed out. But the main body of the enemy stood firm.

When Jeanne saw that they would not come out, she rode, standard in hand, up to the palisade and struck it a ringing blow hoping to excite the enemy into action. The English called, "Witch! Milkmaid! Go home to your cows. If we catch you we'll burn you."

They waved a crude copy of her flag showing a spindle and distaff and bearing the motto "Let the Maid come. We'll give her wool to spin." This mocking defiance enraged the French soldiers. As the English sallied out in answer to the jibes and taunts of the French, no quarter was given. But with all their endeavors the English would not leave their strong position.

The long summer day passed and when it grew too dark to distinguish friend from foe the French retired to their camp and the king retreated to Crépy. Early the next morning the Regent turned the English army toward Paris. The French royal army should have pursued him, but the captains feared pursuit without Charles.

The cities of Compiègne, Senlis, and Beauvais now submitted to the king and the Maid. At Beauvais anyone who refused to recognize Charles as the French king was driven out and his property confiscated by the crown. Among these was Pierre Cauchon, the Bishop of Beauvais. He blamed Jeanne for the loss of his income and his diocese and later took a dire revenge upon her.

Charles dallied at Compiègne, much to the distress of Jeanne. She saw that the troops were losing heart. The fifteen days were ended, and Paris still had not been turned over to Charles. The king was now busy entangling himself with new truces with Burgundy. Jeanne grieved at the monarch's shilly-shallying, and suspected that he was happy with the grace God had given him and didn't want to undertake any further enterprise for the good of his nation.

As time passed without bringing any action of any sort, Jeanne's patience became thoroughly exhausted. She had been told she had only one year to do her work, and Charles was wasting the time that should have been used for France. One day she said to Alençon, "Get the men ready. I wish to see Paris."

Her words struck a responsive chord in Alençon's breast, and the captains gladly prepared for the march. On August twenty-third the troops set forth under Jeanne and Alençon, stopping briefly at Senlis so that Count de Vendome's forces could join them. They hoped that by their example the king would follow them with the main body of the army. After three days' march they rode into the sacred town of St. Denys, only six miles from Paris.

It was the city of the martyred saint whose name was the war cry of France. It was also the city of the tomb; for, as Reims was the place where French kings were crowned, so St. Denys was the town where French kings were buried. From antiquity they had lain here in the great Abbey, where also lay the crown of Charlemagne. Many sacred relics of the saints were also buried here, among them a head said to be that of St. Denys himself.

As the army approached the town, the citizens loyal to the English and Burgundians retreated to Paris. Those who remained were royalists. At the church Jeanne stood godmother for two little babies who had been presented for baptism. She had lately been asked to perform this duty in towns all over France. In was her habit to name boys after the king; girls she called Jeanne.

This was the supreme moment in the affairs of the French nation. Everything the French had gained in the summer would now be entirely lost or fully perfected by the attack on the capital. Courier after courier was sent to the king to urge his coming. Finally Alençon himself rode back to beg the king to come. Reluctantly the monarch advanced as far as Senlis, and there stopped. Jeanne and Alençon didn't know it, but the king's councilors were advising him against further march.

In the meantime, Jeanne used the time to study the city for the best point for attack. Alençon sent personal letters to the town dignitaries asking them to surrender to the king.

The authorities in Paris were not idle. They strengthened their fortifications and spread stories among the people of the dire vengeance that Charles had sworn to wreak on them. He would allow his troops to ransack and plunder the city, they said, raze it to its very foundation so that where Paris had once stood only empty fields would remain. Terrified by these tales, the citizens were afraid to venture out into their vineyards or their gardens.

Finally, two weeks later, Charles arrived at St. Denys. Late as he was, his coming was still hailed with delight. The army was wound up to a high pitch of excitement, eager for assault. Charles himself was not so eager. In truth, the last thing in the world that he desired was this attack.

The day he arrived, Jeanne and the captains started toward the city walls to make the usual demand for surrender. The king rode with them.

The demeanor of the army had changed. At Blois, at Orléans, on the march to Reims, the men were orderly and devout. Action had kept them disciplined and righteous. After the coronation, rogue soldiers and bandits had flocked to join the army, and these newcomers were rude, foul, and disorderly. Idleness had further demoralized the men.

Now, as the king and Jeanne D'Arc rode toward the walls of the city, one of the camp followers thrust herself forward boldly from the crowd of onlookers gathered to watch the troops pass and spat upon the king. Jeanne's youthful purity was roused to a glaze of indignation and she brought up her sword quickly and gave the creature a smart blow with the flat side of the weapon.

"Get you gone," she cried sharply.

Instantly the blade parted in two. One piece fell to the ground and Jeanne gazed silently at what remained in her hand.

"It's the holy sword," exclaimed Charles, aghast. "It's a bad omen."

Jeanne did not reply. News of the incident flew from lip to lip, and soon the story spread through the army. The Maid had broken the miraculous sword. Men shook their heads, saying that it boded ill for the future. The king sent the sword to his own armorers to be mended, but they could not put the pieces together again, which was further proof that the sword was of divine origin.

At a council that night the captains decided to attack Paris the next day. While the king remained at St. Denys, the army withdrew to La Chapelle, a village midway between St. Denys and Paris, and camped for the night.

Jeanne did not like the date chosen for the attack. "It is the Feast of the Nativity of the Blessed Mother," she told Alençon. "It is not proper to fight on such a day."

"We must, Jeanne," he answered. "We have been pushing for the assault and if we decline now La Trémouïlle will persuade the king that we are causing the delay."

"Then if we must, we will do it. After all, it is the duty of Frenchmen to fight the enemy whenever the need arises."

In spite of her words, Jeanne was still reluctant to prepare for the assault. As she rose the next morning, the church bells were ringing to announce the great festival of the church; she could even hear bells faintly tinkling as far away as St. Denys and Paris. All the citizens of Paris would be at church, for no one would expect an attack on such a day.

The troops made a late start. It was eight o'clock before they marched out of La Chapelle and made their way toward Paris. The morning was bright and beautiful, though unusually warm for the season. In the sunshine the towers and battlements of the city gleamed and glistened. It was a great city, far greater than Orléans, and a prize worth fighting for. But their delay in reaching Paris had greatly reduced their chances of taking the city.

The French planned to attack between the gates of St. Honoré and St. Denys. Jeanne was to lead with Rais and Gaucourt, while Alençon, placing his guns in the hog market near the gate, stationed his force behind the Windmill Hill, which sloped above the market. From this position he could defend the rear from possible attack. The main body of the army was posted out of range. The king did not leave St. Denys. Charles was the only prince in Europe who did not lead his own army in the field.

When all was ready, Jeanne learned to her great surprise that no serious attack was intended. It was all a ruse to cause the city to surrender. She was determined to force the fight.

At two o'clock in the afternoon the trumpet sounded the call and the roar and rebound of cannon began, the artillery plying the earthwork that protected the Gate of St. Honoré. The outer palisade weakened and its stakes fell with a crash. The earthen wall was fully exposed. With a shout, the French rushed forward with scaling ladders and began to pour over the walls pell-mell, driving its defenders before them back to the walls of the gate itself.

Suddenly, their furious advance came to a standstill; for before them lay two wide ditches, one dry, the other full of water. The archers and gunners standing on the ramparts of the gate jeered at the halted French and sent a rain of stones and arrows down on them, all the while waving their banners

Jeanne called loudly for beams and logs to bridge the moat, then descended into the dry moat, climbing out on the other side onto the ridge that divided the two trenches. Some of the men ran for bundles of wood to use for a bridge, while the others followed her to the ridge. They looked with dismay at the deep moat that stretched before them full to the brim with water. But Jeanne was not daunted. Handing her standard to a man at her side, she took a lance and tested the depth of the water amid a shower of arrows and stones.

"Surrender!" she called to the men on the walls. "Surrender to the King of France."

"Witch! Evil one!" they shouted back.

By this time her men were building a makeshift bridge across the moat and presently they were able to struggle across. The charge began. At this instant, a great commotion was heard in the city. As planned, people loyal to the king were running through the streets shouting: "All is lost! The enemy has entered." It was hoped that this diversion would demoralize the English. Many of the citizens rushed into their homes and shut the doors behind them, but the English and Burgundian soldiers kept their heads and sent more men to arm the gates and the ramparts.

The firing grew heavier: the artillery bellowed and the guns roared in answer. Through the rattle of guns, the whizzing rush of stones, the sound of axes and swords smashing against wooden barriers, and war cries screaming through the air, the silvery tones of a girl's voice could be heard: "On! On, friends! They are ours."

For hours on end, Jeanne stood on the ridge between the two ditches, her white armor gleaming in the sun and her banner floating over her head. Hour after hour she kept her position, exposed to every shot and missile, shouting directions to her men, urging them on while the battle raged around her. Suddenly, a joyful cheer went up from the enemy on the walls: Jeanne D'Arc had fallen, pierced through the thigh by a bolt from a crossbow.

She tried to struggle to her feet. The officer bearing her standard was struck between the eyes and fell dead at her feet. As he fell, Jeanne caught the standard, then sank to her knees. She refused to be carried out of range of fire, and rallied her men to the charge. Then, slowly and painfully, she crept behind a heap of stones. Even then, the dauntless voice rang out: "Friends! Be of good cheer. On! On!"

Wounded, weak, unable to stand, Jeanne urged the soldiers on. There never was anything like it. "A daughter of God," her Voices called her, and, truly, only such a kinship could have created such indomitable spirit and courage.

The din grew fiercer and the heat more stifling. Hours passed and the day waxed old. Twilight fell, and darkness came. The shots were now fewer and more scattered, and then they stopped completely. The trumpet sounded recall. Jeanne did not heed, but kept crying her men on to the charge. The supporting army was out of range and the men would not go farther without her. Gaucourt ordered his men to bring her out of the fire. Jeanne protested but, weeping, she was carried back to her horse, set in the saddle, and conveyed back to La Chapelle. Over and over she cried: "It could have been taken! It could have been taken!"

Early the next morning, in spite of her wound, Jeanne went to Alençon and begged him to sound the trumpets and mount for the return to Paris.

"I will never leave until the city is taken," she said.

Alençon agreed with her, but some captains thought otherwise. Some troops were reluctant. There were whispers that the Maid had failed, that she had promised to enter the city, and Paris had not been taken. They remembered the omen of the mystic sword and shook their heads.

While the captains debated, a cavalcade of fifty or sixty gentlemen serving the Burgundian nobleman Baron de Montmorency rode up and offered their allegiance to the Maid. It was a joyful moment and so encouraging that an immediate assault was planned. But just as the captains were setting out to ready the troops, a pair of messengers arrived bearing the king's orders that no further attack on Paris should be made. Jeanne and the captains were commanded to return at once to St. Denys.

Such a command could not be ignored, so with heavy hearts the entire force obeyed the summons, leaving the siege material on the field. When the company reached St. Denys, the king offered no explanation. Jeanne and the captains discussed what they might do next.

Alençon had built a bridge across the Seine above Paris so that French troops could make an onset from the south as well as the north. In secret he and Jeanne decided to make a new effort in that direction. Early the next morning they slipped away with a few chosen troops and rode hastily to the bridge. They found it in ruins, destroyed in the night, not by their enemies, but by the *king*. Sadly, the little company rode back to St. Denys, which had become the grave of their hopes.

Jeanne's heart was hot with disappointment. Leaving Alençon she crept painfully to the chapel of the abbey and knelt for a long time before the statue of the Virgin Mary. After a time she rose and slowly, awkwardly, unbuckled her armor and laid it piece by piece on the altar until at last the complete suit lay there. With a gesture of infinite yearning she passed her hands over it.

"To St. Denys," she said with quivering lips. Turning, she slowly left the abbey. Jeanne, the invincible Maid, had met her first defeat at the hands of her king.

CHAPTER 24

JEANNE'S LAST FIELD

No longer buoyed by hope, Jeanne began to feel her wound. As she lay on her bed, nearly fainting with pain, her Saints came to her with words of comfort. They still appeared daily, but since the coronation of Charles they had given her no specific directions. Now they consoled her in her humiliation and sorrow, giving her this message: "Remain at St. Denys, daughter of God. Remain at St. Denys."

Jeanne tried to do this, but Charles decided to return to the Loire and ordered the army to get ready to travel. He had signed a new treaty with Burgundy, agreeing to a truce that would last until Christmas. La Trémouïlle and his party had triumphed in persuading the king to sign the armistice. Charles was not difficult to win over, for he would be left to pursue his pleasures, and La Trémouïlle would be free to misrule France as he liked.

While the truce lasted, Charles could not attack any city north of the Seine from Nogent, sixty miles above Paris, to the sea. Oddly, the treaty allowed him to attack Paris; and Burgundy might help the English regent defend that city against him.

The French promised to give Compiègne to the Duke of Burgundy, hoping to draw him away from the English alliance. Compiègne, however, refused to

161

be given, thereby showing more loyalty to the French cause than did the poor stick of a king.

The Duke of Burgundy had his own reasons for agreeing to the truce. He wished to prevent any more towns from deserting his net. England and France could fight all they wanted, but the French could not attack any of the strongholds held by the Burgundians.

It's hard to see what France hoped to gain by such a treaty. Some of the king's councilors sincerely believed that the treaty might produce a lasting peace with both Burgundy and the English. But Alençon and the captains denounced the truce bitterly.

"If the king had taken Paris, he could have made his own terms with the Duke of Burgundy," Alençon said.

"The noble king is deceived," said Jeanne sorrowfully. "There will be no peace with Burgundy for six years, and the king will not enter his capital for seven years."

"Jeanne, do you really know that?" questioned Alençon.

"I do know. My Voices have told me. Paris would have been ours had we persisted in the attack, and in a few months northern France would have been clear of the English. Now it will take twenty years to drive them out."

"Twenty years," repeated Alençon. "Have your Voices told you that, also?"

"Yes, fair duke. Oh, the pity of it!"

"The pity of it," he echoed. "For now we must start for the Loire, and all the cities and towns that have pledged themselves to Charles must be abandoned to the mercies of the English. They have begged us not to leave them, but the king tells them he doesn't want to strip them of provisions to feed the army. With the English free to invade and rob them, they will be worse off than ever before."

"I shall not go," Jeanne said quietly. "My Voices have told me to remain here and I shall obey."

She reckoned without the king. When Charles was ready to march he commanded her attendance. Jeanne begged him to let her stay, citing the orders of her heavenly guides. Charles ordered that she be brought along. Jeanne's wound was not yet healed and she was scarcely able to walk. So the helpless maiden was forced on the dreary march against her will.

So eager was the king to return to his amusements that the one hundred and fifty miles from St. Denys to Gien was made in eight days. Once there

Charles disbanded the army. Of the great number who had set forth with banners flying three months earlier, all that remained were the king's bodyguards. The departing soldiers were from many lands, although most were French gentlemen who had served without pay for the love of France and the Maid. Jeanne bade them farewell with sadness: the brave Dunois, the bold La Hire, Poton Zaintrailles, Boussac, Culent, and others. The great army was never mustered again.

Normandy, an English possession, was exempt from the truce, so Alençon asked for permission to lead troops against the English strongholds there. He wanted to take Jeanne with him. "Many men will join me for her sake," he said.

But neither the king nor La Trémouïlle would grant permission. They did not wish the ardent young duke to become a leader, and Jeanne D'Arc already had too much power. Firmly and decidedly, the project was dismissed.

In disgust Alençon returned to his estates. He and Jeanne had become great friends. He believed in her implicitly, and she was fond of him because of his loyalty and the nobility of his character. They said good-bye for the last time, and in that farewell her spirit was broken.

In the days that followed, as the court drifted from castle to castle and from town to town in search of amusement, Jeanne pined away. She had her own household filled with women of rank showing that she was honored by the king. Rich apparel in gorgeous coloring was bestowed upon her. The king was not ungrateful. He knew that Europe was filled with wonder at Jeanne's great victories and he received letters from all the royal courts asking for news of her. But he misjudged the girl by trying to pay his debt to her by showering gifts upon her. Pretty clothes and a life of ease might satisfy other girls, but not Jeanne D'Arc, who lived only for the welfare of the country. All she wanted was to fight for France. Had Charles only availed himself of her influence and the confidence she inspired in his soldiers, it is more than likely that the English power would have been broken in France in 1429 as easily as it was twenty years later.

There was one who recognized Jeanne's influence: the English regent, Bedford. Four years later he wrote that the gains France made against England were due mainly to the "panic the Maid caused in the English and the encouragement she gave to the French." Had Bedford been King of France, he would have known how to use such a power to its fullest.

The king's councilors didn't mind if Jeanne worked, but they did not want her to have more individual triumphs. Her great achievements made their weak efforts seem paltry. On the upper Loire were two Burgundian strongholds outside the terms of the truce. The little towns of St. Pierre le Moustier and La Charité were governed by old enemies of La Trémouïlle. He decided that Jeanne could go against these bastions. If she succeeded, it would satisfy his revenge and enrich his pocketbook. If she failed, she would lose more influence. Either way, La Trémouïlle would benefit.

Glad of any sort of confrontation with the enemy, Jeanne went to Bourges to muster the men. The force would be under a man named d'Albret, Trémouïlle's son-in-law. By the end of October the troops were ready. D'Albret decided to go against St. Pierre le Moustier first. It was a strong little town with moats, towers, and high walls, overlooking the fields that lay between its walls and the Allier River some two miles east.

For several days the French plied the town with artillery. After a breach was made, Jeanne ordered an assault, herself leading with standard in hand. The men rushed to the walls but were driven back; the retreat sounded and the troops were retiring from the point of attack when Jean D'Aulon, Jeanne's squire, wounded in the heel and unable to stand, saw the Maid standing almost alone near the walls. He dragged himself up on his horse and galloped up to her, crying, "Why do you stand here alone? You must retreat with the others."

"Alone?" questioned Jeanne, raising the visor of her helmet and gazing at him with glowing eyes. "I am not alone. Fifty thousand of my people surround me. I will not leave until this town is mine."

The squire looked about in bewilderment, for there were no more than five of her own men near her, yet there she stood waving her standard while the arrows and bolts from the town rained and whistled around her.

"You are mistaken, Jeanne," he said. "There is no one. Come away, I beg you. The troops are in full retreat."

"Look after the shields and screens," ordered the Maid. Mystified, D'Aulon did as she ordered, while the clear voice rang out the command: "To the bridge, every man of you."

Back came the men on the run with planks and beams to string across the moat. The troops returned to the assault, and the town was taken. D'Aulon watched the onslaught in wonder.

"The deed is divine," he exclaimed. "Truly the will and guidance of our Lord are with her."

The French soldiers would have pillaged the town, even the churches, but Jeanne forbade it and nothing was stolen.

Jeanne and d'Albret then marched on to Moulins, an important town farther up the river. The army was ill-equipped for the siege, without munitions, food, or warm clothing against the bitter November weather. Jeanne moved her forces into position and waited for supplies. But the king sent neither money nor supplies. The citizens of Bourges voted to send money, but it was never received. Only Orléans, generous as always, sent money, gunners, artillery, and clothing.

The troops pummeled the strong town with what artillery they had, but a siege requires provisions and other supplies. The king left them to get along without any support. The men became discontented. A month was wasted in a display of artillery and one feeble assault that resulted only in loss of men.

In great displeasure Jeanne disbanded the siege. She could inspire men to fight, but she was not a magician. God would give the victory to those who helped themselves. Hungry, cold, disheartened troops could not fight without munitions and provisions. The troops retreated from the town, leaving some of their artillery on the field.

Thus ended the fighting for the year 1429. In spite of huge opposition Jeanne had accomplished incredible deeds since she started out from Vaucouleurs, and would have repeated these marvelous feats if she had not been hampered by the king and his council.

Charles was at his beautiful château at Mehun-sur-Yévrè, where Jeanne joined him. She was downhearted and sad at the failure of the siege of La Charité. The treaty Charles had signed had left northern France open to English invaders and robbers alike, and the English were forcing exile or death on the defenseless people who had been loyal to the king. Many villages were abandoned, their citizens driven into other parts of France. There was sickness and famine everywhere. In Paris wolves prowled openly, and its citizens died by hundreds. Paris, the beautiful city of covered bridges, orchards, vineyards, and towered fortresses, abandoned by the English and Burgundians, had been left to protect itself. The Duke of Burgundy was looking after his personal property, while the English regent, Bedford, swept the adjacent country with fire and sword. Jeanne had been desperately needed in northern France, but she had been sent on an unsuccessful, useless expedition instead. Her heart was heavy with despair.

The king did not suffer. He and Queen Marie showered attentions on Jeanne, holding feasts in her honor and plying her with gifts of fine clothes. In December the king conferred a patent of nobility upon her, sealing it with a great seal of green wax over ribbons of green and crimson, the Orléans colors. In the patent the king changed the spelling of her name to d'Ay.

> In consideration of the praiseworthy and useful services which she has rendered to the realm and which she may still render, and to the end that the divine glory and the memory of such favors may endure and increase to all time, we bestow upon our beloved Jehanne d'Ay the name of Du Lys in acknowledgment of the blows which she had struck for the lilies of France. And all her kith and kin herewith, her father, mother, brothers and their descendants in the male and female line to the farthest generation are also ennobled with her, and shall also bear the name Du Lys, and shall have for their arms a shield azure with a sword supporting the crown and golden fleur-de-lis on either side.

Jeanne would have rather had a company of men to lead into northern France. She cared nothing for either the grant of nobility or the shield and never used them. She preferred to be known simply as Jeanne the Maid. Her brothers, however, were delighted, and ever after bore the name of Du Lys.

The winter passed and Jeanne turned eighteen. The truce with Burgundy was now extended until Easter. Jeanne waited, and in March the king was staying at Sully. Easter was early that year, falling on March twenty-seventh. As soon as it was over Jeanne left the court and rode northward with her company, headed for the town of Melun some twenty-one miles south of Paris. Melun had been in English hands for ten years, and then Bedford had turned the town over to Burgundy. The citizens of the town had rejected the Burgundians and supported France. Now the English were trying to retake it.

Jeanne arrived with her men in time to help the citizens of Melun resist the onslaught. Joyfully they welcomed her, giving over their defense to her command. The first thing she did was survey the walls that protected the town. As she stood on the ramparts ordering some repairs, her Voices came to her: "Daughter of God," they said, "you will be captured before the Feast of St.

Jean. So it must be. Fear not, but accept it with resignation. God will help
you."

Jeanne stood still. The Feast of St. Jean was only two months away. Her face
grew white as the words were repeated, and a great fear fell on her. A prisoner?
Better, far better to die than to be taken prisoner by the English. Memories of
their vicious taunts and threats came rushing back to her. She knew what to
expect. They had threatened her time and again with the stake and the fire.
Terrified, she fell on her knees, uttering a broken cry of appeal: "Not that! Not
that! Out of your grace I beg you that I may die before capture."

"Fear not; so it must be," came the reply. "Be of good courage. God will aid
you."

"Tell me the hour and the day," she pleaded.

"Before the St. Jean. Before the St. Jean," came the reply. That was all.

For a long moment Jeanne knelt, her face bowed in her hands. Then she
bent and kissed the ground before her.

"God's will be done," she said. Rising, she calmly went on with her work, as
though nothing had happened. She knew, but she did not falter. Of all her
brave deeds, this was the bravest. There is an ecstasy in the whirl of battle, a
wild joy in the mad charge of cavalry and the clash of steel on steel. Bravery
and heroic deeds are contagious when bugles call and trumpets blare, banners
wave and captains shout war cries.

But for the prisoner there is no ecstasy, no joy, no valorous contagion
induced by comrades in arms, no inspiration of music, or banners, or war cries.
For the prisoner there is only the chill of the dungeon, the clank of the chain,
the loneliness, and the fear of the awful death that is to come. But knowing
that her capture was certain, this girl of eighteen went her way doing all that
she could to help her country in the little time she had left.

While Charles and his council rested serenely, Jeanne prepared for the
spring campaign. Even as she worked, the English and Burgundians prepared
to move against the town of Compiègne, for whichever side held this prize
would eventually hold Paris. For now the citizens of Compiègne remained
loyal to Charles, declaring that they would rather die than yield to England or
Burgundy. It was crucial for the enemy to put down Compiègne, for the
French were rising, even without their king. All over northern France there was
activity as French troops began to gather to go against the enemy.

Jeanne moved from Melun to nearby Lagny, through a countryside full of enemies. Paris itself became excited when it heard that the Maid had arrived safely in Lagny, fearing that she was ready to renew her attack on the city. The English were also stirred up when they heard that Jeanne had taken to the field. "The witch is out again," their captains declared. Hearing this news English troops preparing to embark for France deserted in crowds.

As the English and French troops maneuvered, bands of pillaging mercenaries roamed northern France, burning and robbing every hamlet and village. Jeanne, with Foucault, Kennedy, and Baretta, decided to go against the raiders. They caught the first band of freebooters as they were laying siege to a castle, already laden with the spoils of a sacked village. The French, although fewer in number, attacked and fought a bloody fight in which all the murdering thieves were captured or slain, and their leader, Franquet d'Arras, was turned over to Jeanne.

She hoped to exchange her prisoner for one of her own chiefs who was being held captive in Paris. But it turned out that her man was already dead. The people of Lagny demanded that Jeanne turn over her prisoner to them for trial by civil law. Jeanne did as they asked. Franquet's trial last two weeks. He confessed to the charges of murder and theft and was executed. The Burgundians, although accustomed to robbery, murder, and treachery, said Jeanne was responsible for his death and later their complaint was used against her.

Another event at Lagny would also work against Jeanne later. A three-day-old infant had died before it could be baptized, which meant that the child could not be properly buried in consecrated ground. According to the custom of the time, the child was placed on the church altar in the hope of a miracle. The parents came to Jeanne and asked her to join with all the maidens of the town to help them pray to God to briefly restore life to the child so that it might be baptized.

Jeanne never professed to work miracles. She did not pretend to heal people by touching them with her ring, nor did people attribute miracles to her. But as asked she joined the other maidens in church and entreated Heaven to restore the infant to life long enough to be baptized. As they knelt and prayed, the little one seemed suddenly to move. It gasped three times and color flooded its cheeks.

The maidens cried: "A miracle! A miracle!" and ran for the priest. When he came to the side of the child, he saw that it was indeed alive and immediately baptized it. As soon as this had been done, the little life that had flared up so suddenly went out again. The child was buried in holy ground. Later, this act was included in the list of charges brought against Jeanne, even though she was only one of several maidens present.

From Lagny Jeanne went to various other places in danger. She made two hurried trips to encourage the citizens of Compiègne who were being threatened by both English and Burgundians. Then she returned to Crépy en Valois.

Then came the news that Compiègne was surrounded on all sides. Jeanne ordered her men to get ready for the march. She had no more than two or three hundred men, and her captains said their force was too small to penetrate the enemy. This sort of warning never had any effect on Jeanne.

"We are enough," she cried. "I will go to see my good friends at Compiègne."

At midnight Jeanne set out from Crépy, and by hard riding arrived at Compiègne in the early dawn, to the great joy and surprise of the governor, Guillaume de Flavy. At the sight of her, the people set the bells ringing and the trumpets sounding a glad welcome. Her men were exhausted with the night's march, but Jeanne, after going to mass, met with the governor to plan their defense.

Like Orléans, Compiègne had one side situated on a river. Across the river a broad meadow extended to the low hills of Picardy. This was low land, subject to floods, so the bridge that crossed the river from Compiègne extended as a raised road or causeway all the way to the foothills, about a mile distant. At the end of the causeway was the tower and village of Margny, where the Burgundians were camped. About a mile and a half to one side of the causeway was the village of Venette, where the English lay encamped; and to the right side stood Clairoix, where the Burgundians had another camp.

The first defense of the city, facing the enemy, was the bridge, which was fortified with a tower and earthworks. Jeanne planned to sally forth in the late afternoon and attack Margny, which lay at the far end of the causeway. Margny taken, she could then turn to the right and strike Clairoix, cutting off the Burgundians from their English allies.

De Flavy proposed to protect the ramparts of the tower and earthworks with men and arms so Jeanne could fall back across the bridge if she needed to. He also stationed a number of small boats filled with archers along the bank of the river to shoot at the enemy if the French were driven back.

By five o'clock everything was ready. The warm May sunshine was cooled by a breeze from the west, sweet with the scent of flowers and growing grass. The walls of the city, the windows and roofs of the houses, the buildings on the bridge, and the streets were lined with people waiting to see Jeanne and her company set forth. Presently Jeanne appeared, standard in hand, mounted on a great gray horse, wearing a rich crimson cloak thrown over her armor. At the sight of her, the people went wild, shouting and cheering, throwing flowers before her. Jeanne turned a happy face toward them, bowing and smiling, as she rode forth to her last field.

With her rode D'Aulon, his brother, Pothon le Bourgnignon, her own brothers, Jean and Pierre, Father Pasquerel, and a company of five hundred men. Across the bridge they clattered, then sped along the causeway to Margny. As they reached the village Jeanne's clear voice rang out: "Forward! They are ours!"

With a shout the troops hurled themselves on the Burgundians, taking the enemy completely by surprise. Chaos broke out. Cries of triumph rose from the French as they chased the Burgundians hither and thither amid the clashing of steel; cries of dismay came from the Burgundians as they scattered through the village. The town was taken just as Jeanne said it would be.

But just then Jean de Luxembourg, commander of the Burgundians at Clairoix, reined up on the cliff above Margny. Seeing the scrimmage below he wheeled, returned to Clairoix, and brought up his troops at a gallop. When Jeanne's men turned toward Clairoix, Luxembourg's men attacked their right flank. The French rolled back, overwhelmed by the unexpected onslaught.

Rallying her men Jeanne charged and swept back the enemy. Again the French were repulsed; again Jeanne drove back the Burgundians. The battle raged on the meadow, first in one direction, then the other. As they surged and retreated, the French were slowly pressed back to the causeway. As more reinforcements arrived for the Burgundians, the French broke and ran for the bridge and the boats. Jeanne tried to rally them to the charge, but for once her men were deaf to her voice.

Trying to protect her army, Jeanne covered the rear, charging the enemy with those men who remained by her side and driving them back half the length of the causeway. Much later a Burgundian reporter named Monstrelet would write that she was "the chief and most valiant of her band, doing deeds beyond the nature of woman."

Suddenly, a loud hurrah sounded from a stand of trees on the far left, and galloping and running across the meadow came the whole English army. Assailed on all sides, the routed French troops turned into a seething mass of struggling fugitives crowding the causeway, running for their lives. The gunners mounted on the ramparts trained their cannons on the mass of men, but the fugitives and enemy were so commingled that friend and foe could not be distinguished. De Flavy did nothing.

D'Aulon begged Jeanne to retreat. "The day is lost," he cried. "All are in retreat. Make for the town." But Jeanne shook her head.

"Never," she cried. "To the charge."

D'Aulon, her brothers, and the remainder of her own little company closed around her, resolved to sacrifice their lives in her defense. D'Aulon and Pierre seized hold of her bridle rein and forcibly turned her horse toward the town, carrying her back in spite of herself. The little company was trapped, fighting, struggling, contesting every inch of ground, beating off the enemy and advancing inch by inch toward the bridge.

"We shall make it, Jeanne," cried Pierre D'Arc, but the words died on his lips. A ringing order came from the gate: "Up drawbridge. Close gates!"

Instantly the drawbridge flew up, and the barrier descended with a clanging thud. Jeanne was shut out.

Pierre groaned, but his sister smiled at him bravely. D'Aulon shouted: "Treachery! In God's name, open for the Maid."

But the gates were closed and the drawbridge remained up. In a split second, as the enemy closed around them in overwhelming numbers, Jeanne and her brothers exchanged a last look of farewell. Man by man the little company was cut down or captured. D'Aulon was seized, then Jean, then Pierre. Jeanne found herself struggling on alone. An enemy soldier grabbed her wrists while an archer tore her from the saddle by the long folds of her crimson cape; in a moment they were all upon her.

"Yield your faith to me," cried the archer who had dragged her down.

"I have given my faith to another, and I will keep my oath," rang out Jeanne's answer.

At this moment the bells from the churches of Compiègne set up a wild clamor in a turbulent call to arms to save the Maid. The urgent pealing sounded too late. Jeanne D'Arc was a prisoner.

CHAPTER 25

IN PRISON CELLS

The enemy shouted in triumph as Jeanne was led back over the causeway to the Margny stronghold. The sun had long since set, and the dusk was dying down into darkness. All along the causeway were broken swords, scraps of armor, and dead soldiers, friend and foe together. Jeanne D'Arc was too great a prize for a mere archer to claim, so Jean de Luxembourg bought her immediately from the man, allowing him to keep her crimson cloak, her saddle cloth, and horse. Then she was transported to Luxembourg's camp.

The Duke of Burgundy arrived from his camp at Coudon, eager to see the girl who had almost uprooted the dominion of the English in France. Other English and Burgundians also assembled from camps far and wide, rejoicing over the taking of the Maid, as if they had won a great victory in the field. The capture of Jeanne D'Arc had broken the spell. They had feared her more than all the French captains put together, and now they were relieved to see that she was human, like other women.

Philip, Duke of Burgundy, found her sitting calmly in the room in which she had been imprisoned. He was stunned at her youth.

"So you are the one?" he cried.

"I am Jeanne the Maid, sir," she answered, regarding him gravely. "And you, no doubt, are that Burgundy who has tricked the king with fair words and false promises?"

"I am Philip, Duke of Burgundy," he replied haughtily. "What I have done I did for our royal master, Henry, King of England and France."

"Ay! And for your country's wreck and woe."

"Those are bold words," the duke said, flushing. "Take care what you say. Neither man nor witch may speak to me that way."

"My lord duke, if my words are not true, then I beg your pardon. If they are not true, then why do you besiege the good city of Compiègne, bringing suffering on your own people? They are French, just as you are."

"The city was promised to me," he said angrily. "Charles the Dauphin gave it to me. It was in the truce. He broke his word when he tried to get it back."

"And how did you keep your word?" Jeanne asked. "I think you promised Paris to Charles."

Without reply, Philip turned on his heel and left the room.

He sent letters to Bedford, the English regent, and his other allies announcing that the witch of the Armagnacs was his prisoner.

The tidings spread across France. From lip to lip the news flew that the Maid was taken. Paris rejoiced, its citizens showing their delight by building bonfires and singing joyful hymns in the Cathedral of Notre Dame. But in the loyal cities and in the hearts of the peasantry there was mourning. At Tours the entire population appeared in the streets with bare feet, singing the Miserere in penance. Orléans and Blois made public prayers for her safety.

In Reims, the Archbishop Regnault de Chartres, always an enemy to Jeanne, said, "She never took advice. She did everything according to her own will. That is why she was captured."

But another archbishop, Jacques Gélu of Embrun, addressed bold words to the king on her behalf: "Spare neither means nor money, however great the price, to recover this girl. Otherwise you will incur indelible shame."

But the king preferred the "indelible shame," for he made no effort to ransom or rescue Jeanne. He had been a poor discredited Dauphin with only tenuous claims to the throne when Jeanne came to him at Chinon. She had restored the realm and made him king, yet he preferred to keep his money for his pleasures than to pay ransom for the maiden who had done so much for him. Charles the Seventh has been called Charles the Well-Served and he is rightly so called; for others always did his work for him and won his victories.

But Charles the Dastard is a better name for him. The ingratitude of royal princes is well known, but the heart sickens and the mind revolts from the thought that anyone could be as callous as the King of France.

Not everyone was as indifferent to Jeanne's value as Charles. Her enemies began to argue with each other, trying to secure the prisoner for their own ends. The University of Paris, which wanted her to appear before the Council of Holy Inquisition, worried that it would lose jurisdiction over her. In fact, no effort was ever made to rescue the girl whose only crime was to have defended, with matchless heroism, her country and her king.

The English were also eager to get possession of her, and were willing to pay huge rewards for her delivery into their hands. Most Englishmen believed that Jeanne was really a witch, for at this time no one believed that she could accomplish her deeds without supernatural aid. Since they did not wish to think that God was against them, they said her inspiration had to come from the devil. They had always threatened to burn her if they caught her. If Jeanne could be condemned and executed as a witch, then Charles would be dishonored. Henry of England could regain his position as true sovereign of France.

Bedford sent Pierre Cauchon, the Bishop of Beauvais, to Luxembourg to purchase the Maid. Cauchon had a personal grudge against Jeanne because she had run him out of his diocese. He was just the man to send for dickering in such a trade. Jean de Luxembourg was needy and already in debt to the English. He sent Jeanne north to his stronghold in Beaulieu while the negotiations went on.

D'Aulon was sent with her, and during this period of imprisonment Jeanne was treated honorably. One day D'Aulon said to her, "That poor town of Compiègne will now be in the hands of the enemies of France."

"It shall not," cried Jeanne in a flash of inspiration. "No place which the King of Heaven has put in the hands of King Charles with my help shall be retaken."

In spite of her brave words, the fate of Compiègne worried her. Her guards told tales of how the people were suffering under siege. Jeanne watched eagerly for a chance to escape and go to their aid.

On one side of her room was a window with narrow planks nailed across it; there was just enough space between the planks for a very slender person to slip through. Jeanne decided to risk it.

She slipped through the planks and found herself in a dark, musty corridor.

Along the corridor a closed door gave entry to the room where her guards stood watch. There was a huge key in the lock. Jeanne turned it quietly, locking the guards inside, then darted away through the dim passage. Alas! A porter, who normally would never be in that part of the castle, suddenly came out of another room opening upon the corridor and ran straight into her. Without a word, Jeanne was marched back to her chamber, like a naughty child. That night, the guards were doubled.

"It did not please God that I should escape this time," she told D'Aulon later.

Jean de Luxembourg was alarmed when he heard of the escape attempt. Jeanne D'Arc was too rich a prize to lose carelessly, so he sent her farther north to his stronghold of Beaurevoir, where his wife, aunt, and stepdaughter lived.

There Jeanne was shut up at the top of a sixty-foot tower. The ladies of the household visited her every day and became very fond of her. They brought her a frock and asked her to change from her masculine clothing. But Jeanne politely refused, saying: "When among men it is better to wear the garb of a soldier. But if it were time for me to change my dress I would do it for you two ladies who have been so kind to me."

Many people visited her while she was held prisoner at this castle, and their news about Compiègne made her fretful and anxious. D'Aulon was no longer with her, and for the first time Jeanne was entirely alone. There was no word that her king or her friends were doing anything to help her. All she heard was talk of how the English wished to buy her. Visitors and guards told her of the besieged Compiègne and that the citizens were being driven to desperation. Their fate preyed on Jeanne's mind and she lost confidence and hope, becoming very despondent.

"When Compiègne is taken everyone over the age of seven is to be killed," one visitor told her.

"I would rather die than live to see such destruction," she said. "I would also rather die than be in the hands of my enemies of England." After the visitor left, Jeanne paced the floor in great agitation.

"How can God leave those good people to perish?" she cried.

Again she thought of escape. She must go to the rescue of Compiègne. Jeanne was so young that she could not fully realize that her allotted time was over. All at once, in her desperation, she chose to leap from the tower.

"Do not leap," admonished her Voices. "Be patient. God will help you, and also Compiègne."

"I want to be with them," Jeanne said.

"You must bear these things gladly," Saint Catherine told her. "You will see the King of England."

"I don't want to see him," cried Jeanne, like the young girl she was. "I would rather die than be in English hands."

"Do not leap," Saint Catherine repeated. "Be patient. All will be well."

But Jeanne was too upset to hear. For the first time since her saints had come to her, she deliberately disobeyed their advice. Climbing to the top of the tower she commended herself to God and leaped.

Some hours later, the guards found her lying unconscious at the foot of the tower. The Luxembourg ladies feared that she was dead, but eventually she regained consciousness. For three days she could neither eat nor drink, although no bones were broken and she was not seriously injured.

"I have sinned," the girl confessed humbly to her Saints the next time they visited her. She asked God's pardon for her impatience and disobedience. She was forgiven and comforted.

"Do not fear," Saint Catherine said. "The people of Compiègne shall be saved before St. Martin's day."

After she was forgiven, Jeanne began to eat again and soon she was fully recovered. In two weeks, Compiègne was rescued by citizens led by Vendome and Zaintrailles. The enemy was completely routed, leaving their artillery and supplies in the field. Many other strong towns nearby soon proclaimed their loyalty to the king, but it was the courage of Compiègne that really shattered the English and Burgundian campaign of 1430.

In the meantime, Jeanne's price had been settled at ten thousand pounds in gold, the ransom of a prince. Jeanne was a peasant maid, but the English knew her worth. Jean de Luxembourg's wife begged him not to sell Jeanne to the English. She knew what fate lay in store for the girl and she tearfully pleaded with her husband not to take blood money. But de Luxembourg, pleading poverty, would not listen. The sale was made.

The money changed hands in Arras, where Philip, Duke of Burgundy, held court. The English immediately moved Jeanne to their strong fortress of Crotoy, a castle by the sea. Now that they had her they rejoiced as if they had received fabulous wealth. They treated her honorably, however, like any prisoner of war.

Some ladies of Abbeyville came down the Somme River by boat to visit her. They wept when they left, kissing her affectionately and wishing her good favor from Heaven. Jeanne thanked them warmly for their visit and asked them to pray for her. A priest who was also being held prisoner was allowed to visit her daily to say mass and give her holy communion. The month that she spent at Crotoy calmed her mind and gave her strength for what lay ahead.

The University of Paris was impatient for its prey. The English hesitated about taking Jeanne D'Arc to Paris for trial. The northern country seemed to be turning again toward Charles, and Jeanne might be recaptured by the French before they could reach Paris. But they didn't want to take her all the way to England. For these reasons they decided to hold the trial in Rouen in Normandy, where the English were strongest, under the zealous eye of Pierre Cauchon and an officer of the Holy Inquisition.

The English now moved Jeanne to Rouen, traveling slowly along the coast through Eu and Dieppe in order to avoid any risk of rescue. They arrived at Rouen in the beginning of the year 1431. Jeanne was immediately taken to the castle and lodged in its great tower. It was a gloomy edifice, and the room to which she was confined was in the first story, up eight steps from the gate, where light and air struggled feebly through a narrow slit in the thick wall.

Jeanne was to be tried by the church, yet instead of being placed in an ecclesiastical prison where she might be guarded by women, she was placed in a military prison and guarded by soldiers. The severities inflicted upon her here were terrible. For the first time she was heavily bound. Her hands, feet, and throat were bound to a pillar, and she was kept in an iron cage; even at night leg irons gripped her ankles and were fastened to a chain that passed under her bed and locked onto a heavy beam. Five crude English soldiers guarded her around the clock, and it was their policy to degrade and humiliate this modest young girl at every opportunity.

Where were La Hire, Dunois, Alençon, and other captains that no sword was drawn for Jeanne? This was the age of chivalry, when women were supposed to be the objects of a kind of worship, and every knight swore to help them in times of need and trouble. Shame to England that so used her! And ten times shame to France who deserted her!

Jeanne had only one comfort: many times a day her saints came to her whispering word of consolation.

"But I do not always understand them," Jeanne later told her judges, "because the guards make so much noise."

And thus, in chains, in an iron cage, Jeanne D'Arc spent her nineteenth birthday.

CHAPTER 26

ON TRIAL

Great in everything as she was, we here see her at her greatest.
The Maid of France
Andrew Lang

The days passed drearily in her prison cell, but Jeanne endured all of it rather than give her word not to try to escape. The monotony was varied by visitors who came to stare at her.

In the castle where she was confined there were Bedford, the English regent; the Cardinal of Winchester; the child king Henry of England; the Earl of Warwick; and the chief officers of both the royal and vice royal court, along with a number of guards and men-at-arms. One visitor was Pierre Manuel, advocate of the King of England. Questioning her he said, "You would not have come here if you had not been brought. Did you know before you were taken that you would be captured?"

"I feared it," Jeanne answered.

"If you feared it, why weren't you on your guard?"

"I did not know the day or hour," she answered.

The Earl of Warwick brought the Earl of Stafford and Jean de Luxembourg to see her. Luxembourg was the one who had sold her to the English.

"Jeanne, I have come to ransom you," said Luxembourg, laughing as the girl rose to a sitting posture from the bed where she was chained. "That is, if you swear not to fight against us."

"You mock me," she said. "I know the English mean to kill me. They believe after I am dead they will be able to win the kingdom of France. But if there were a hundred thousand more English than there are, they will never win France."

Lord Stafford became enraged and half drew his dagger, but Warwick said that killing Jeanne outright was too merciful a death, and it was the English policy to have her executed ignominiously as a witch.

After long days of waiting, Jeanne was told that she was going to be tried for heresy. She asked that some of her own people be among the judges, but this request was refused. The charge of heresy against a young woman to whom the church was the breath of life seems strange. She lived in an ecstasy of religious fervor and spent her time in prayer and religious exercise. She confessed regularly and heard mass and took communion whenever she could. Yet here she was accused by the church of being a heretic. Her crime in the eyes of the clergy was saying that she obeyed voices that came from God.

In her cell Jeanne did not know about the arrangements being made for her trial. They were on a large scale and commanded the attention of most of Europe. No homage she ever received conveys such a sense of her importance as this trial which was intended to neutralize her influence.

Since she had been captured in the diocese belonging to the Bishop of Beauvais, Pierre Cauchon, he claimed jurisdiction over her. Cauchon had been a sympathizer of the English. With Jeanne's triumphs he had been driven out of his city and had fled to England. He had returned with the Cardinal of Winchester, eager for reward and revenge. He was an ambitious and educated man, and he delighted in the opportunity he now had to please his English patrons and avenge his private grudge.

As Cauchon was the presiding officer, the trial should have been held in his diocese, but it seemed expedient to hold it in Rouen, because of the disturbances that had broken out near Paris. Bishops, abbots, priors, representatives of the University of Paris, learned doctors, and noted priests, sixty of the greatest intellectuals of the church—all of them French, but sympathetic to the English faction—gathered together to put to death a young peasant girl.

It took time to arrange all the preliminaries for the opening of the trial, and it was the end of February before everything was ready. According to French law, such cases are always preceded by an inquiry into the former life of the accused, as had been done at Poictiers. A new investigation was carried out, but the investigators could not find any evidence to justify or strengthen the accusations. All the examiners could discover was that Jeanne D'Arc was a good, honest person who had left a spotless reputation behind her in her native village. One commissioner reported that he had learned nothing that he would not willingly know of his own sister, although he had made inquiries in five or six parishes. Cauchon called the man a traitor and refused to pay him for his work.

Since the preliminary investigation uncovered nothing that could be used against her, the prosecutors made an effort to trap Jeanne into incriminating herself. One morning a man entered her cell and said he was a shoemaker from Lorraine. He was a prisoner also, he said, but had received permission to visit her. Jeanne was happy to see anyone from the valley of the Meuse, and the two fell into conversation. During the talk he said in a low voice: "Jeanne, I am a priest. I have come to help you."

Jeanne's face grew radiant. "A priest?" she said. "Then you can hear my confession?"

"Gladly, my child." And the girl innocently opened up her heart to him.

The man was a priest, Nicholas Loyseleur, a representative of the University of Paris, but he was full of treachery and hypocrisy. He served Cauchon well, for Jeanne trusted him completely and did not dream that every word she said was overheard and recorded by a secret listener, for there were hidden openings in the walls from which everything that took place in the room could be spied upon and every word heard. But nothing Jeanne said to the priest was any different from what she proclaimed in public.

Finally, on Wednesday, February twenty-first, the great trial began at eight o'clock in the morning in the royal chapel of the castle.

Jeanne sighed with relief as the officer of the court who was sent to bring her to the chapel took off her chains.

"You are summoned to appear before the court, Jeanne D'Arc," he explained.

"May I hear mass before I go to court?" she asked.

"No, it is not permitted. Come!"

So, surrounded by a strong guard, Jeanne was led through the corridors to the royal chapel. In that short walk she drew in the first breath of fresh air that she had had in almost two months.

The chapel was a large room but not large enough to accommodate all those who sought admission. Rouen was full of people who supported England and Burgundy. Present were soldiers, citizens, priests, and lawyers, for the great trial had attracted a variety of churchmen, all with an attendant train of clerics and secretaries.

Forty-four of the assessors, as the assistants of Cauchon were called, were present, sitting in a semicircle around the presiding bishop. Doctors of theology, doctors of canonical and civil law, abbots and canons were assembled in all of the solemnity of their priestly and professional robes. There were clerks, ready with their pens to record the proceedings, lords and notables of every degree of rank, all gathered to see how easily the witch would be condemned.

Jeanne did not pay attention to any of these as she was led to a solitary bench that stood on one side of the room, near the bishop's stand. But raising her large, grave eyes, she gazed at the judge, Pierre Cauchon, Bishop of Beauvais. His was a cold, cruel face, and an intellectual face on which ambition was marked. Involuntarily Jeanne shuddered as she looked at him.

After she was seated Cauchon addressed her, summarizing the accusations against her, and all the public reports and suspicions upon which the trial was based. Then he required her to take the oath upon the Bible to speak the truth, and to answer all questions addressed to her.

"I know not what things I may be asked," Jeanne said clearly. "Perhaps you may ask me questions which I cannot answer."

As the sweet voice rose in answer to the bishop's command, there was a stir in the assembly and every eye turned to the young woman in the prisoner's seat. They saw a slender girl, just past nineteen, dressed in a page's suit of black, her dark hair cut short, intensifying the pallor of her face and the melancholy of her large eyes. She looked very young as she sat there, thin and pale from her imprisonment.

"Swear to tell the truth upon whatever you may be asked concerning the faith and facts within your knowledge," replied the bishop.

"As to my father and mother," said Jeanne, "and what I did after setting out for France, I will swear willingly. But the revelations which have come to me from God I will reveal to no man except Charles, my king. I shall not reveal them to you because I received them by vision and by secret communication and am forbidden." After a moment's reflection she added: "Before eight days I shall know if I may tell you of them."

The bishop urged her to take the oath without conditions. She refused, and finally they were obliged to offer her a limited oath. Then, kneeling, Jeanne crossed her hands on the Bible and swore to answer truthfully whatever they asked, so far as she could, concerning the common faith of Christians, but no more. Then she was asked about her name and early life.

"In my own village I was called Jeannette, but I have also been called Jeanne. My surname is D'Arc or Romée, since where I come from girls take the name of their mother."

Then she told the names of her father and mother, her godfather and godmothers, the priest who had baptized her, the place where she was born, her age, concluding with: "From my mother I learned the Our Father, the Hail Mary, and the Credo. From my mother I learned all that I believe."

"Say your Our Father," commanded the bishop abruptly; for it was believed that no witch could repeat the Lord's Prayer except backward.

"Hear me in confession, and I will say it for you willingly."

Several times she was asked to say the Our Father, but her reply was always the same: "No, I will not say it for you unless you hear me in confession."

"We will willingly give you one or two worthy men who speak French. Will you say the Our Father to them?"

"I shall not say it except in confession" was her answer, which was a protest to these priests who had refused her all the sacraments of the church.

Cauchon ignored the appeal and, as the session was about to close, forbade her from trying to escape from the prison that had been assigned to her in the castle. If she did so, she would be immediately pronounced guilty of heresy.

"I do not accept such an ultimatum. If I escape, no one shall be able to reproach me with having broken my faith, as I have not given my word to anyone."

"You tried several times to escape from prison," Cauchon said, "and to be sure you would not succeed we had to put you in irons."

"It is true that I wished to get away," Jeanne said, "and I still wish it. Is that wish not shared by every prisoner?"

Then Cauchon called in John Grey, the English general who had charge of the prison, and he told him to guard Jeanne securely and not to permit her to talk with anyone without permission from the court. Jeanne was then led back to her cell and again put in irons.

The assessors were not all agreed about the legality of the trial, but they were afraid of what might happen to them if they opposed Cauchon. Nicolas de Houppeville of Rouen had spoken his mind freely at the preliminary consultation and had gotten into a lot of trouble for it. He had said, "I don't see how we can bring a case against the prisoner, since we who are prosecuting her are acting as the judges. Also, she has already been examined by the clergy of Poictiers under the Archbishop of Reims and they found her guiltless."

De Houppeville had stated the case clearly: the church, which had acquitted her in Poictiers, was now trying Jeanne for the same offense. But Cauchon reprimanded the priest sharply. When de Houppeville went to take his seat among the assistant judges, the bishop had him arrested and thrown into prison. After that Cauchon heard no more complaints from any of his other assistants.

The next morning the trial resumed in a room at the end of the great hall of the castle. Jeanne was unchained and brought before the prosecutors without counsel, advocate, or attorney. The day before she had been interrupted at almost every word, and secretaries recorded her replies as they pleased, distorting her answers as they saw fit. Guillaume Manchon, the chief clerk, threatened to quit if this were permitted, wanting the records to be kept correctly. Again the bishop asked Jeanne to take the oath without conditions. To which she replied, "I swore yesterday. That ought to suffice."

"Every person who is asked to swear in any matter relating to the faith cannot refuse," the bishop said, "even if he is a prince."

"I took the oath yesterday," Jeanne said again. "That ought to be sufficient. You ask too much of me."

The contest ended in the same way as the day before, with Jeanne taking a limited oath. Then Jean Beaupère, a professor of theology, resumed the examination. Throughout this trial Jeanne was the only witness examined.

Beaupère asked her about her early life, her visions, coming to the king, the sign she had shown the king, and wearing men's clothing. They asked her about carrying a poisonous plant called a mandrake, about the fairies of the Fairy Tree, and the healing properties of Gooseberry Spring. The questions were purposely mixed and confused to try to trap her into contradictions. Over and over he returned to the subject of the sign she had shown the king, and out of loyalty Jeanne would not reveal it. If anyone ever knew that Charles doubted his own right to the throne, he himself could be condemned for seeking assurance from a witch.

The sign and the wearing of men's clothing were referred to time and again. The whole process was intended to catch an unsuspecting victim and was a violation of justice and a citizen's rights. Day after day they continued and Jeanne showed as much courage in facing the doctors and priests as she had ever shown in battle. The readiness and beauty of her answers often astonished the assembly. They asked her one day: "Do you know that you are in the grace of God?"

This was a trick question. If Jeanne replied "yes," she was presumptuous. If she replied "no," she condemned herself. One of the assessors, Jean Lefèvre, spoke up quickly: "That is an unsuitable question for such a girl."

"Hold your peace," cried Cauchon angrily. "It will be better for you." And Lefèvre was silent.

"Answer," commanded the bishop, turning sternly to Jeanne.

The assembly awaited the reply so quietly one could have heard a pin drop.

"If I am not in grace, may God bring me to Him; if I am, may God keep me there."

The reply was sublime. The doctors were amazed and talked among themselves. "Jeanne, you speak well," several said. Cauchon was clearly upset.

Another time she was asked if she had ever been present when English blood was shed.

"In God's name, yes. How mildly you talk! Why didn't they leave France and go back to their own country?"

Hearing this, an English lord cried out, "She is a brave girl! If only she were English!"

The public hearings lasted six days through long weary hours filled with tiresome repetitions and hidden stratagems to catch her unawares. But little progress was made, so Cauchon brought the hearings to an abrupt close. As at Poictiers, Jeanne's personality was beginning to make itself felt. There was a visible softening toward her, and one or two of the judges tried to give her warnings or aid her by whispering suggestions.

In the streets people were whispering that the judges were "persecuting her out of perverse vengeance, that they kept her in a secular prison for fear of displeasing the English, and that the English believed they could have neither glory nor success while she lived."

Jean de Lohier, who was passing through Rouen, declared boldly that the trial was not legal. He said that it was held in a castle, where men were not free to give their honest opinions. Also that the King of France was a party in the suit, yet he did not appear nor did he send a representative. And that Jeanne was a simple girl being tried on profound matters of faith without the help of counsel. To Manchon, the chief clerk, de Lohier said: "You see how they are going on! They try to catch her in her words. She says straight out, 'I know for certain I touched the apparitions.' If she would only say instead, 'It seemed to me that I touched them,' no one could condemn her."

Cauchon was furious when he heard this, thinking that de Lohier's advice might somehow reach Jeanne. He made sure de Lohier left the country. Cauchon then decided to make the trial private, with only himself and a few trusted henchmen in attendance. He told the others that they could study the evidence at their leisure, and expressly forbade them to leave Rouen before the end of the trial.

The private examinations were chiefly the same as the public ones, with Cauchon and his favorite assessors freer to interpret Jeanne's answers as they wished.

One day they asked her what she meant when she said that Bishop Cauchon put himself in danger by bringing her to trial. She answered: "This is what I told him: You say you are my judge. I know not whether you are, but take care that you judge well, or you will put yourself in great danger. If our Lord should chastise you for it, I have done my duty in warning you."

"What is the danger that may befall him?" the assessor asked.

"I don't know. My Voices have told me that I shall be delivered by a great victory."

Jeanne's thin face suddenly filled with radiance. She went on: "Perhaps Bishop Cauchon will be judged then. My Voices also said, 'Be resigned, have no care for your martyrdom. In the end you will come to the Kingdom of Paradise.' They have told me this simply, absolutely, and without fail. I don't know if I will have to bear more suffering; for that I refer myself to God."

It was plain that Jeanne expected to be rescued. Her Voices told her she would be "delivered by a great victory." To one so young that meant rescue, and she waited like someone who is waiting for some great good to happen.

But as the time passed without bringing either rescue or help of any sort from her friends, Jeanne did not discredit or reproach them. She remained completely loyal to her king. Brother Isambard gave her some advice one day about submitting to the General Council of Basle, which included men of all political parties. Jeanne was glad to hear of it.

"If there are any on our side, I am quite willing to submit to the Council of Basle," she cried.

"Hold your tongue," shouted Cauchon to Isambard. Turning to Manchon, the clerk, he continued angrily: "Make no note of that answer." But Jeanne protested: "You write what is against me, but not what is in my favor."

Manchon had already written, "And she appeals—" He dared write no more.

In the afternoon Brother Isambard, Brother Guillaume Duval, and Jean de la Fontaine, three men who honestly wished to help Jeanne, went to the prison to give her advice. They were intercepted by the Earl of Warwick.

"If any of you advise her for her good, I will have you thrown into the Seine," he told them.

After that, Isambard kept silent, fearing for his life, while Brother Duval fled to his convent of St. Jacques and never came back. The private examinations ended the day before Passion Sunday. Cauchon called a meeting of the assessors to consider the evidence and decide further action. D'Estivet, his secretary, was told to make a digest of the proceedings in the form of an action of accusation to be submitted to all forty-four assessors. In the meantime the bishop visited Jeanne, presenting her with an ultimatum: If she consented to wear woman's dress, she might hear mass whenever she wished, but not otherwise. To which Jeanne sorrowfully replied that she would have done so before now if she could, but that it was not in her power to do so. Surrounded by men, guarded by crude and vicious soldiers, for the sake of her womanhood she had continued to wear masculine clothing.

During Holy Week her troubles began again. Early Tuesday morning she was taken to the room at the end of the great hall where the court was held before. All the assessors were present. Cauchon made a speech in which he said that her judges had no wish to punish, but sought to instruct and lead her in the right way. Now, after the case was over, he offered her the privilege of having as counsel one of the learned doctors present.

Jeanne answered him courteously: "In the first place, concerning my good and our faith, I thank you and all the company. As for the councilor you offer me, I thank you also, but I have no need for any councilor other than Our Lord."

Thomas de Courcells read the seventy charges against her. They were mostly frivolous and some were unjust. It was charged that she had received no religious training, that she dressed in man's attire, that she had bewitched her banner and her ring (the poor little ring which her father and mother had given her so long before), that she believed her apparitions were saints and angels, that she had blasphemed, and other charges to the number of seventy. After each one the reader paused to ask, "What do you have to say to this article?"

And Jeanne would reply as she could, referring all her acts to the judgment of God. It did not matter how she replied, for these men had already decided she was doomed. Jeanne D'Arc was guilty of one thing: she had wounded the English pride. That was her crime. She had frightened them, had driven them half the length of France, beaten them in their fortresses and conquered them in the field. That was her crime and it was intolerable. Nothing but burning her alive could satisfy the mortified pride of the English.

After all the charges were read out loud, Jeanne was sent back to her cell to wait. Cauchon and his few chosen men took their time distilling the seventy charges and her replies to twelve articles, which they sent to the University of Paris for review. During this time Jeanne was admonished "gently and charitably" in her cell, tormented by priests who said they were trying to lead her back into the way of truth. Under the strain she fell ill with fever and nausea. Warwick sent immediately for several medical men who were among the judges.

"Do you best for her," he urged. "My king wishes that on no account should she die a natural death. She was expensive to buy, she is expensive to keep, and she shall die in the way he wishes—at the stake."

The doctors felt her pulse and found fever. They reported to Warwick that she should be bled, a common treatment at that time.

"Get away with your bleeding," he cried. "She might kill herself."

Nevertheless, the doctors bled her and she grew better. As soon as she was somewhat recovered, Cauchon came around with more "charitable admonitions."

"We have come to console you in your suffering," he said. "Wise and learned men have read and examined your answers concerning the faith. You are only a poor, illiterate woman, and we come to offer you instruction. Listen to our words, because if you are obstinate we must abandon you. You see to what peril you expose yourself, and it is this we would avoid for you with all the power of our affection."

"I thank you for what you say to me for my good," answered Jeanne wearily. "It seems to me, seeing how ill I am, that I am in danger of death. If God calls me to Him, I ask that I may make my confession and that I may be buried in holy ground."

"If you desire the rites and sacraments of the church," said Cauchon, "you must do as good Catholics do and submit to the Holy Church."

"I am a good Christian," she told them. "I have been baptized. I shall die a good Christian. I love God and I serve Him. I wish to help and sustain the church with all my power."

Jeanne would say nothing further, and Cauchon and his priests left her for the time being. On May second the trial resumed with all the assessors in attendance. Cauchon summed up everything that had gone before, saying that in spite of their diligence and gentleness nothing had been decided. He suggested that Jeanne be admonished before them all. Jean Chatillon was invited to make a speech in which he should try to convince Jeanne D'Arc to tell the truth.

Jeanne listened dutifully to his long address and finally asked her admonisher to come to the point. The trial turned upon whether Jeanne was willing to submit her words and deeds to the judgment of the church.

"I love the church," she said, "and desire to sustain it with my whole power. It is not I who should be kept from going to church and hearing mass."

As to what she had done for her king and her country, she submitted it all to God, who had sent her. "I refer myself to God, my master in all things. I love Him with all my heart."

The question of submission to the church was again asked, and she replied again that she submitted all to God, Our Lady, and the saints.

"And my opinion is," she added, "that God and the church are one."

To the specific questions about her dress, her visions, and revelations, she gave her old answers.

"I will say no more," she answered briefly, with some impatience, when they urged her further and threatened her with the sentence of fire. "And if I saw the fire, I should say all that I am saying to you, and nothing else."

A week later she was led from her cell again, but this time she was taken to the torture chamber, where she found nine of her judges waiting. She was once more asked to speak the truth, with the threat of torture if she remained stubborn. But with the rack and screws before her and the executioner ready for his work, she said: "If you were to tear me limb from limb and separate soul from body, I could tell you nothing more. And if I were to say anything else, I should always say that you had compelled me to do it by force."

She told them that she had asked her Voices if, hard-pressed as she was, she should submit to the church.

"If you would have God come to your aid, wait for Him," was their answer.

"Shall I burn?" she had asked them.

"Wait for Our Lord. He will help you."

Torture was spared that day, "considering the hardness of heart," and Jeanne was returned to her cell. Cauchon later put the question of torture to fourteen of his assessors. Two voted for it: Courcells and the spy, Loyseleur, who thought that it might be "a good medicine for her soul." The majority, however, were in favor of mercy, saying they had enough to condemn her without it.

A few days later the decision of the University of Paris arrived. After an explanation of the consideration given to each of the twelve articles, they gave their verdict on each indictment, ending with: "If this woman, charitably examined by competent judges, does not return spontaneously to the Catholic faith, publicly confess her mistakes, and give full satisfaction to her judges, she will be given up to the secular judge to receive the punishment her deeds require."

Jeanne listened as one of the assessors read out the judgment. When he had finished, she responded, "What I have always said in the trial, I wish still to say and maintain. If I were condemned, if I saw the torch lighted, the woodpile prepared, and the executioner ready to kindle the fire, and if I myself were in the fire, I would not say otherwise, and would maintain to the death all that I have said."

Manchon, the clerk, was so struck by this reply that he wrote on the margin of his paper: *"Responsio Johannae Superba."*

"Have you nothing further to say?" Cauchon asked.

"No," was the reply, and he declared the trial concluded.

"We summon you tomorrow to hear the law which will be laid down by us, to be carried out afterward and proceeded with according to law and right."

Jeanne was taken back to her prison and the company of John Grey's men. It was the twenty-third of May, and she had been a prisoner for a year; for nearly five months of that time she had been chained like a wild beast. She had been tortured, badgered, and bullied through the most cruel and unjust trial the world has ever known. And she had faced this daily torment with high spirit and undaunted demeanor. But now she was weary and despondent.

Her Voices had promised "deliverance by a great victory," and deliverance had not come. The next day there would be the sentence and then death by fire. All night Jeanne lay in her chains trying to commune with her saintly visitors, but her guards were noisy and she could not hear much of what her Voices were saying: "Answer boldly all that is said to you," they told her. "God will help you. Don't be afraid."

The morning came, and she was listless, sad, and inexpressibly weary. The traitor Loyseleur was on hand early, urging her to submit to the church.

"Do what you are told, and you may be saved," he said. "Accept the woman's dress, and do as I tell you; then you will given over to the church. Otherwise you will die."

Jean Beaupère, one of the assessors, also came to see her.

"You will soon be led to the scaffold to be preached to," he said. "If you are a good Christian, put your faith in our Holy Mother Church and the ecclesiastical judges."

So they talked to her. Soon the cart came that was to carry her to the cemetery of St. Ouen, the place where she would be sentenced. Loyseleur, Massieu, the usher of the court, and a number of the priests rode with her, pleading with her to submit. They drove through the marketplace so she would see the preparations that had been made for the death sentence. A lofty scaffold with a stake upon it, the logs all arranged around it, ready for lighting, stood in the marketplace waiting for its victim.

It was a beautiful day in May. The blue sky was cloudless. The streets were filled with crowds of excited people who pushed and struggled behind the rows of English soldiers guarding the passage of the cart. The whole scene spoke of life and liberty. And beside her Loyseleur was whispering, "Submit! Submit!"

In front of the Church of St. Ouen was an open space with room for a large group of people. Here were two platforms, one facing the other. On one of these, in the midst of prelates and nobles, Cardinal Winchester sat with Bishop Cauchon and the Earl of Warwick. On the other platform was the preacher Guillaume Erad. It was usual to preach to a witch before burning her. Jeanne stood here, too, and the priests who had accompanied her. Below and all around a crowd of English soldiers gathered.

When all were in their places the preacher rose and began his sermon: "A branch cannot bear fruit unless it stays on the vine." The speech was long and eloquent. When it was half over he suddenly began to speak about France and her king: "Ah, France, you are much abused. Charles, who calls himself your king and governor, is a heretic who has joined himself to the words and deeds of a worthless woman, defamed and full of dishonor."

Then pointing at Jeanne he cried: "It is to you, Jeanne, that I speak. I tell you that your king is a heretic."

Jeanne could bear a great deal, but she could not stand to listen to an assault on the king. Her voice rang out clearly: "I swear on my life that my king is the most noble Christian of all Christians, that he is not what you say."

So she spoke, defending the coward who had made no effort in her behalf. There was a sensation among the people as she spoke, as though they were moved in spite of themselves, and voices began to murmur excitedly. At this the English soldiers who surrounded the two platforms drew closer and made threatening gestures toward the crowd. The preacher resumed his sermon and concluded with a last solemn exhortation to the prisoner to submit to the church.

As her Voices had told her, Jeanne replied boldly to the preacher's words: "I have told you doctors that all my deeds and words should be sent to Rome to our Holy Father, the Pope, to whom I appeal. As for my deeds, I burden no one with them, neither my king nor anyone else. If there is fault it is my own and no one else's."

Three times she was asked if she was willing to renounce her acts and words which the court condemned. To which she replied: "I appeal to God, and to our Holy Father, the Pope."

The bishop said that the Pope was too far away and that he and the others were the officers of the church, each in his own diocese, and that it was necessary that she admit that they had the right to decide her case. Then

Bishop Cauchon began to read her sentence. He had prepared two sentences: one to be carried out if she recanted and the other, death by fire. It was this second one that he began to pronounce. And all around Jeanne there was a tumult of voices urging her to submit. Some among the crowd called to her entreatingly: "Submit, Jeanne, submit. Save yourself."

Distracted, the girl folded her hands and raised her eyes. "Saint Michael, help me," she called pleadingly. Her Voices were speaking, but in the confusion she could not hear. And all around her she heard those others: "Submit! Submit! Why will you burn?"

There is a limit to human endurance. And in spite of her belief in her mission, her faith in her Voices, and her duty to her king, the indomitable spirit broke under the strain. She could bear no more.

"I submit," she cried in anguish. "I am willing to hold all that the church ordains, all that you judges shall say and pronounce. I will obey your orders in everything. Since the men of the church decide that my apparitions and revelations are neither sustainable nor credible, I do not wish to believe or to sustain them. I yield in everything to you, and to our Holy Mother Church."

"Then sign," cried a churchman, thrusting forward a paper. "Sign, and so renounce and repudiate."

Jeanne looked at him, bewildered and confused by the commotion around her.

"Renounce?" she said. "What must I renounce?"

Massieu, who was among those who brought her there, now shouted: "Sign. Sign."

"Sign," cried Erad the preacher. "Sign, and you will be put in charge of the church."

Jeanne could not write, but she mechanically made her mark, putting it where they told her. Then one of them guided her hand and traced the name *Jehanne* at the bottom of the page. Jeanne gave one last cry as she permitted it: "All that I did was done for good, and it was good to do it."

Manchon, the clerk, wrote on the margin of his record: "And Jeanne in fear of the fire said that she would obey the church."

So Cauchon substituted the other sentence: "Seeing that you have returned to the bosom of the church by the grace of God, and have revoked and denied all your errors, we commit you to perpetual prison with the bread of sorrow and water of anguish, to purge your soul by solitary penitence."

A tumult arose in the square at this, and people crying with disappointment and rage began throwing stones at the platform. The English didn't want to be cheated of their prey, and many were angry that there was to be no burning. In the midst of it, Jeanne called feverishly to the priests around her: "Now, you people of the church, lead me to your prison; take me out of the hands of the English."

One of the priests left her side and ran over to Cauchon to ask where she was to be taken.

"Back to where she came from," said Cauchon grimly.

Dismayed and miserable, Jeanne was taken back to the torment of her cell.

CHAPTER 27

FOR HER COUNTRY

That afternoon the Duchess of Bedford, wife of the English regent, sent a tailor to Jeanne with a woman's dress. Jeanne put it on without a word, and allowed her hair to be dressed in feminine fashion and covered by a close-fitting cap. Several priests visited her, telling her of the great pity and mercy the clergy had shown her, and warning her that if she returned to her old ways the church would abandon her. At last they left her.

Left alone at last Jeanne's conscience began to trouble her. In the moment she had recanted she had been false to her highest instinct: the voice of God speaking in her heart.

"I have sinned," she cried in anguish. "I have sinned grievously." She begged her saints to come to her.

Life in the cell was a horror. Jeanne was now supposed to be under the gentler ministrations of the church, but she was still a captive as before: degraded, hopeless, weighed down by heavy chains. Even at night when she lay on her cot, her feet were in leg irons fastened to a heavy chain.

After the spontaneous demonstration in the square, Cauchon understood that the English would never be satisfied with Jeanne's imprisonment, no matter how harsh. The girl must burn. But he had boxed himself into a corner.

She could not be sentenced to death now unless she relapsed. Relapse she must, he thought, willingly or unwillingly. He spread the word to her jailers.

Three days later, on Sunday morning, Jeanne awoke to find that her dress had been taken from her while she slept. On her bed lay the old page's black suit.

She called the guards. "Sirs," she said in her gentle voice, "I am forbidden to wear men's clothing. Give me the woman's dress, I pray you."

The guards refused, laughing. Jeanne knew now that they had gone back on her sentence. She accepted her fate calmly. By Monday morning news had spread that by wearing men's clothing again Jeanne D'Arc had revoked the terms of her sentence. Cauchon and his acolytes flocked to the castle. They found Jeanne overcome with grief, her face stained with tears. Some of them were moved to compassion.

"Why have you done this?" demanded Cauchon.

Jeanne assumed the blame for the whole matter. "It is more suitable for me to wear men's clothing when I live among men," she said. "I resumed it because you have not kept your promise. You said I would be able to go to mass every day and receive communion and that I should be taken out of irons."

"You promised not to resume the dress of a man."

"I am not aware that I took such an oath. I would rather die than be in iron. If you will release me from these chains, and let me go to mass, and keep me in a kinder place than this, then I will do as the church desires."

"Have you heard your Voices since the sentencing?" Cauchon asked.

"Yes." Jeanne's sad face brightened when she spoke of her Voices.

"What did they say?"

"Saint Catherine and Saint Margaret told me that God had great pity for me. I have condemned myself that my life might be saved. Before the sentencing my Voices told me to answer that preacher boldly; they said he was a false preacher. He accused me of many things that I never did. If I said that God did not send me, I condemn myself, for God did send me. My Voices have told me that I committed a sin by declaring that what I did was wrong. Everything I said, I said because I was afraid of the fire."

Manchon, the clerk, wrote on his record: *Responsio mortifera*—"The answer that caused her death."

"Do you believe that your Voices are Saint Margaret and Saint Catherine?"

"Yes, I do believe it," she cried gladly. "And I believe that they come from God. I would rather do penance once—that is to say, I would rather die—than endure any longer the misery of a prison. I have done nothing against God and the faith, in spite of what you have made me say. I did not understand what was in the recantation. I did not intend to revoke anything, except according to our Lord's pleasure. I am willing to resume woman's dress. But for the rest, I can do or say no more."

It was enough. She had relapsed, and the will of her enemies could now be accomplished. The next day Cauchon assembled his assessors in the chapel of his house. They all agreed that Jeanne must be handed over to the secular arm of the church, and they would pray that it "might deal gently with her." If she showed signs of sincere penitence, she would be allowed to make her confession.

Jeanne D'Arc was to be brought to the old marketplace at eight o'clock the next morning, where she would be declared "relapsed, excommunicate, and heretic, and that it may be done to her as is customary in such cases."

At dawn on the thirtieth of May, a Wednesday morning, Brother Martin Ladvenu went to Jeanne's cell to tell her of her approaching death and to hear her confession. Terrified and trembling, Jeanne heard the news.

"Alas!" she cried. "will they treat me so horribly and cruelly, and must my body, which has never been corrupted, be burned to ashes today? I would far rather be beheaded seven times than burned. Had I been in the church prison and been guarded by church people, and not by my enemies, this would never have befallen me. Oh, I appeal before God, the great Judge, against these wrongs that they do me."

In the midst of this outburst, Cauchon entered the cell. Jeanne turned upon him quickly.

"Bishop, I die through you."

"Jeanne, be patient. You die because you have not kept your promise, but have returned to your errors."

"If you had put me in the church prison and given me women for guards, this would not have happened. For this crime against me, I summon you before God."

"Didn't your Voices promise you deliverance?"

"Yes," Jeanne admitted.

"Then you must agree that the Voices are evil and never came from God. Otherwise they would never have deceived you."

Her Voices had said, "Take all things peacefully. Heed not this martyrdom. You shall come at last into the Kingdom of Paradise." The voices had spoken of deliverance by a great victory, but Jeanne misunderstood the message. Now she said, "I see that I have been deceived. But," she added, "whether they are good spirits or bad spirits, they really appeared to me."

Having recanted again, Jeanne was allowed to receive communion. The sacrament was brought into the cell without stole or candles. Ladvenu was indignant and refused to administer a diminished rite. At his request the communion Host was sent with a train of priests chanting litanies as they passed through the streets with torches burning.

Outside in the prison courtyard, and throughout the streets of the city, people gathered to pray for her. Their hearts were touched with pity at her sad fate.

Jeanne received communion with tears and devotion. The churchmen expounded their views all the time that the sacrament was being administered. Afterward, Pierre Maurice spoke kindly to her.

"Brother Pierre," Jeanne said, "where shall I be tonight?"

"Haven't you good faith in the Lord?" he asked.

"Yes," she answered. "With God's help I shall be in Paradise."

Jeanne was dressed in a long black robe and a tall headdress bearing the awful inscription "Heretic, Relapsed, Apostate, Idolator." For the last time she was led out through the corridor and down the steps to the waiting cart, which would carry her to her doom. Brothers Isambard and Massieu, both her friends now, accompanied her. The cart was escorted by one hundred and twenty English men-at-arms. As the train started up, a man pushed his way through and flung himself weeping at Jeanne's feet. It was Loyseleur, the spy, who now implored her pardon. Jeanne forgave him. The guards drove him away.

The streets, windows, and balconies of the houses, every place where a foothold could be had, were crowded with people trying to get a good view of the Maid on her last journey. Many secretly sympathized with her, but dared not show it for fear of their English masters.

Three scaffolds had been erected in the old marketplace: one for the high churchmen and the English lords and one for the accused and her preacher. Jeanne would not be allowed to die without enduring yet another sermon. The third platform stood in the middle of the square. It was a wooden platform set in a mass of plaster with a great beam rising from it. At the foot of the beam, bundles of wood logs were piled. A placard was stuck into the mass of plaster and logs with the words, "Jeanne, self-styled the Maid, liar, mischief-maker, abuser of the people, diviner, superstitious, blasphemer of God, presumptuous, false to the faith of Christ, boaster, idolater, cruel, dissolute, an invoker of devils, apostate, schismatic, heretic."

A large number of soldiers held back the turbulent crowd. These soldiers openly rejoiced as the cart containing the Warrior Maid was driven into the square. The witch who had humbled England was on her way to death. The victor of Orléans and Patay was taking her last ride. France would soon be on her knees before mighty England.

Jeanne looked out at the sea of faces, some sympathetic, others openly exultant.

"Rouen!" she cried. "Am I to die here?"

A silence fell on the multitude as the Maid took her place on the platform and the preacher, Nicholas Midi, began his sermon. "If any of the members suffer," he began, "all the other members suffer with it."

Jeanne sat quietly through the sermon, her hands folded in her lap, praying silently. Finishing his sermon with a flood of invective, the preacher said, "Go in peace."

As his words ended, Bishop Cauchon rose, and once more heaped a shower of abuse on her helpless head. Then he turned her over to the executioners.

"We give you over to the secular power, entreating it to moderate its sentence and spare you pain of death and mutilation."

A great hush fell on the crowd. Presently a sweet, girlish voice, broken by sobs, was heard as Jeanne knelt on the platform and offered up her last prayer.

She invoked the blessed Trinity, the blessed Virgin Mary, and all the saints of Paradise. She called pleadingly on her own Saint Michael for help to aid her "in devotion, lamentation, and true confession of faith." Humbly she begged forgiveness of all men. She asked the priests present to say a mass for her soul, and she asked all whom she might have offended to forgive her. She declared that for whatever she had done, good or bad, she alone was to answer.

As she knelt praying, the crowd, touched to the heart, broke into a burst of weeping and lamentation. Winchester wept and the judges wept. Even Pierre

Cauchon was overwhelmed with emotion. Here and there an English soldier laughed and suddenly a hoarse voice shouted out: "You priests, are you going to keep us here all day?"

Without making any formal sentence, the bailiff of Rouen waved his hand, saying, "Away with her."

Jeanne was roughly seized by the soldiers and dragged to the steps of the stake. She asked to be given a cross. One of the English soldiers took a staff and broke it across his knee in unequal parts. Hurriedly tying the pieces together he handed the makeshift cross to her. She thanked him, took it, and kissing it pressed it against her bosom. She asked Brother Massieu to bring a cross from the church and hold it up so that she could look at it through the smoke.

Massieu brought a tall cross from the Church of Saint Savior and Brother Isambard held it before her to the end. Jeanne said, "Hold it high before me until the moment of death, that the cross on which God is hanging may be continually before my eyes."

Jeanne climbed the steps of the scaffold as bravely as she had climbed the scaling ladders at Orléans. Isambard accompanied her, consoling her. As she was being bound to the stake, she looked out on the towers and hills of the beautiful city for the last time and a cry escaped her lips: "Ah, Rouen! I fear that you shall suffer for my death."

Cauchon, hoping that now she would utter some word denouncing King Charles, came close to the foot of the scaffold. Once again Jeanne cried out to him: "Bishop, I die through you."

Only once did her spirit falter. When the executioner applied the torch to the wood, and a dense volume of smoke rolled up, she gasped, "Water, holy water!"

Brother Isambard still remained with her, though the pitiless flames had already began to climb up. She told him to go down before the fire caught his robes. And at last she was alone.

The red flames leaped up from the dense, suffocating smoke. The air quivered and whirled with red, stifling heat. Suddenly, from out of that fiery, awful furnace, came the clarion tones of the Maid, clear as on the battlefield, exultant with the triumph of a great victory: "My Voices were from God! They have not deceived me! Jesus! Jesus!"

And so died the Maid. She was a martyr not for religion, but for her country. She died, but the lesson of her life lives on: faith and work. For by these two, marvels may be wrought and the destiny of nations changed.

"The men-at-arms will fight; God will give the victory."

CHAPTER 28

AT DOMREMY

After Jeanne's death many told of signs and wonders. It was said that a dove flew up toward heaven at the moment that her spirit took flight. There was a tale that the executioner went weeping to Brother Isambard, confessing that he was lost, for he had burned a saint. Another said that an English soldier trying to throw a burning log on the pyre had fainted. That her heart, that great heart that beat for France, was not consumed by the flame. These and many other stories were told. The truth was that even her enemies were uneasy about her death. There was a strong suspicion that what she said was true—that Jeanne D'Arc was sent from God.

News of her death swept across France, bringing grief to those who loved her and satisfaction to those who feared her. One lovely afternoon in June, two weeks after the tragedy at Rouen, two young women were coming through the forest down the hill path beyond Greux from the Chapel of Our Lady of Belmont. It was Saturday, the Holy Virgin's day, and the two had been to the shrine. The Valley of Colors had never seemed so lovely, so flowery, so fragrant as on this golden afternoon as the two women walked in silence through the tangle of vines and grasses that grew along the path.

"It is more than two years since Jeanne went away," the younger one said, speaking the name that was in both their hearts. "Oh, Mengette, it makes me

202

sad to think of her shut up in a gloomy dungeon when she loved the fields so much."

"Yes, Hauviette. And how strange it is that Jeanne, who was always so good and pious, is charged with heresy. The very idea of such a thing! To think of it, when she loves the church so. I think those who try her are the heretics."

"Mengette, if anyone should hear you!" Hauviette looked fearfully around her. "It would go hard on you."

"I don't care who hears me," declared Mengette. "We have told all those investigators who came to Domremy about her goodness and purity. Even if they were Burgundians or English we told them the truth although they would have preferred to hear lies."

"I wish that we knew how she was. It is a long trial."

"Yes." The two women sighed and silence fell between them.

Down the hill path, through Greux, and on through the oak wood the two friends walked until they came into the clearing where the Fairy Tree stood in its solitary grandeur. They paused under its spreading branches.

"The investigators from Rouen were so curious about the tree," Mengette said. "They asked many questions about it and the Gooseberry Spring. Hauviette, did Isabeau tell you that they wanted to know whether Jeanne ever carried a mandrake?"

"Yes, she told me, as if Jeanne would ever handle an awful plant like that. Look, Mengette!" She broke off suddenly, looking down toward the village. "Something has happened, people are running all through the streets."

"They're running toward the D'Arc house," Mengette cried out. "There must be news of Jeanne. Hurry."

Jeanne's two friends ran into the village and entered the front yard of the cottage. Colin de Greux left the crowd of villagers and came to meet them.

"There is news," he said. "It is all over. Poor Jeanne!" He covered his face with his hands.

"What do you mean, Colin?" Mengette said.

Hauviette grew white. "Is she—is she dead?"

Colin nodded. "Burned," he said. "As a heretic and a sorceress. The priest has just received word."

"Oh," Mengette gasped. "It can't be true. It can't be."

Hauviette could not speak.

"Yes, it's true," Colin said. "And to think that I teased her so. And made her go to Toul, and, and—" His voice broke.

Hauviette recovered herself a little and laid her hand softly on his arm.

"She forgave that, Colin, I know," she said. "Jeanne never thought badly of you."

"I know," he said. "When she left Domremy for Vaucouleurs she stopped as she passed through Greux and said: 'I am going to Vaucouleurs, Colin. God give you good fortune.' And he has, for I have prospered more than any other young man in the village. It is as though her wish made it happen."

"Perhaps it did," said Hauviette gently, finding comfort in her own grief by consoling him. "But look, Mengette is going in to Jacques and Isabeau. Let us go, too, to try to comfort them. Jeanne would like us to do that."

"You are like her," he said, looking at her and taking the hand that lay lightly on his sleeve. "You think of others before yourself. Yes, let's go to them."

Hand in hand they made their way through the sorrowing people into the cottage. Jacques D'Arc lay grieving on the cupboard bed and Isabeau bent over him, ministering to him with a sadness too deep for tears. Beside them stood Father Frontey, tears flowing down his cheeks.

"Don't be sad," he said. "I believe she went straight to Paradise. I heard her confessions too often not to know that she was pure as a lily. In Paradise she dwells beyond all trouble. We who are left behind must not grieve. You have other children. Jean and Pierre will soon return."

And so he tried to comfort them, but for some grief there is no consolation. For Jacques D'Arc's grief there was no cure. His heart broke under the weight of the anguish, and a few days later he died.

Sometime later Pierre and Jean returned to their mother and took her with them to Orléans, where she lived the rest of her long life and received many honors from the city that did not forget her daughter. Twenty years later the long-dormant manhood of Charles the Seventh was finally stirred to action and he decided to make amends to the memory of the girl who had done so much for him. At his request, Isabeau carried her daughter's appeal to Rome.

On the platform at St. Ouen, Jeanne had said: "I have told your doctors that all my deeds and words should be sent to Rome, to our Holy Father the Pope, to whom, and to God first, I appeal."

She had been told then that the Pope was too far off to hear her appeal.

Now Isabeau carried that appeal to him, asking for justice to be done to her daughter's memory.

The case of Jeanne D'Arc was reopened, witnesses were examined, and even some of the same assessors who had sat in judgment with Cauchon testified in her favor. The church cleared Jeanne's name of every charge against her. Thankful that her child could rest in the approval of the church she loved so well, Isabeau returned to Orléans where she spent the rest of her days in peace.

In peace, for at last the English were gone from most of France and Charles lived in Paris. All of Jeanne's prophecies had come to pass.

Jean D'Arc was made captain of Vaucouleurs when old Robert de Baudricourt died. Pierre married and lived with his wife and mother at Orléans. Both brothers took the name of Du Lys, which the king had conferred upon them through Jeanne, and they were ranked among the nobility, honored and revered for the sake of one who had sought no honor but that of serving her country—plain Jeanne D'Arc.

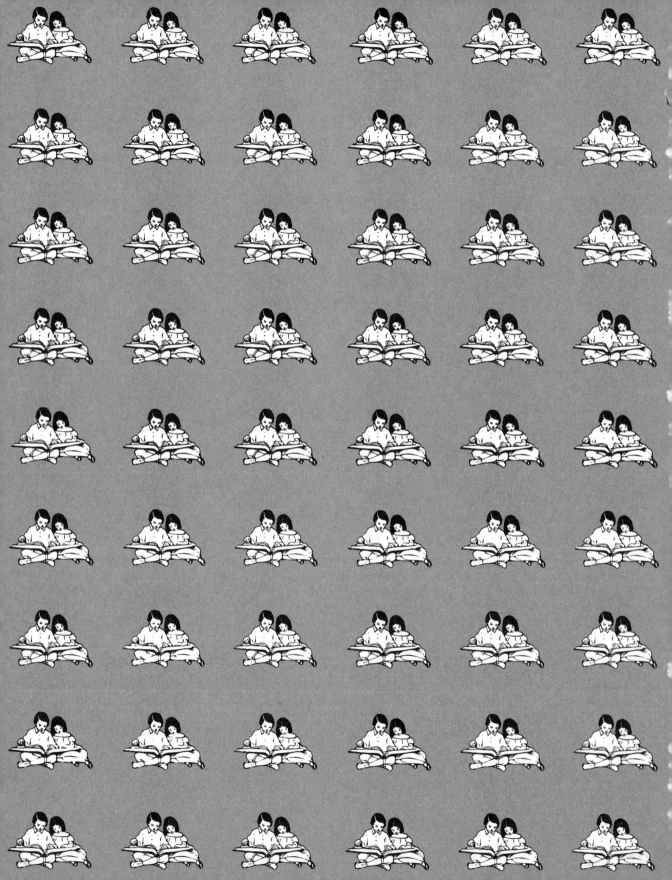